She shook he
girls' night out after all.

"Girls' night out plus two guys. Sorry about intruding."

"I don't believe that for a minute. You were standing right there when my friends and I talked about coming here tonight, so I know this wasn't a coincidence."

Malcolm shrugged. "There aren't a whole lot of places to hang out in Aspen Creek that aren't overrun with tourists."

"Clearly outsiders aren't a problem for you. After all, you brought one with you."

"Guilty as charged. But in my defense, he took one look at Marissa and that was all she wrote. He wanted the opportunity to see her again. And who am I to stand in the way of true love?"

"You don't expect me to believe you've turned into a romantic," Veronica said with a skeptical laugh.

"I believe in love," he said, slightly offended, although he had no idea why. He'd just had a similar thought. "I just don't know if the whole living happily ever after is for me."

"I don't understand how you can feel that way. Not with your parents."

"Do you feel differently? Are you seeing someone? Are you planning to settle down?" The words pierced his heart and he forced the reaction away.

Dear Reader,

Welcome back to Aspen Creek, Colorado, where love is in the air yet again. This time it finds Veronica Kendrick, the children's librarian, and her former best friend, Malcolm Wilson. The two were once inseparable and Veronica believed Malcolm would always be there for her. And he had been. Until the lowest point in her life, when he was missing in action.

Malcolm has missed Veronica. He knows he messed up years ago and has regretted his behavior for years. Now he's back in Aspen Creek and is determined to rebuild their friendship. Malcolm knows how stubborn Veronica can be and expects winning her forgiveness to be difficult. He's never walked away from a challenge and doesn't plan to start now.

Malcolm and Veronica had never been more than friends, so they are surprised when romantic feelings start to develop. Becoming friends again is hard enough. Will they risk that fragile relationship on the chance that they could become something more to each other?

I hope you enjoy reading *The Cowboy Who Came Home* as much as I enjoyed writing it.

I love hearing from my readers, so feel free to visit my website, kathydouglassbooks.com, and drop me a line.

Happy reading!

Kathy

THE COWBOY
WHO CAME HOME

KATHY DOUGLASS

Harlequin

SPECIAL EDITION

Harlequin®
SPECIAL EDITION™

Recycling programs
for this product may
not exist in your area.

ISBN-13: 978-1-335-40225-7

The Cowboy Who Came Home

Harlequin Enterprises ULC
22 Adelaide St. West, 41st Floor
Toronto, Ontario M5H 4E3, Canada
www.Harlequin.com

Printed in U.S.A.

Kathy Douglass is a lawyer turned author of sweet small-town contemporary romances. She is married to her very own hero and mother to two sons, who cheer her on as she tries to get her stubborn hero and heroine to realize they are meant to be together. She loves hearing from readers that something in her books made them laugh or cry. You can learn more about Kathy or contact her at kathydouglassbooks.com.

Books by Kathy Douglass

Montana Mavericks: The Trail to Tenacity

That Maverick of Mine

Montana Mavericks: The Anniversary Gift

Starting Over with the Maverick

Harlequin Special Edition

Montana Mavericks: Lassoing Love

Falling for Dr. Maverick

Aspen Creek Bachelors

Valentines for the Rancher
The Rancher's Baby
Wrangling a Family
The Cowboy Who Came Home

Montana Mavericks: Brothers & Broncos

In the Ring with the Maverick

Visit the Author Profile page
at Harlequin.com for more titles.

This book is dedicated with love and appreciation to my husband and my sons. Thank you for always encouraging me to follow my dreams. It is my sincerest hope that you do the same.

Chapter One

Veronica Kendrick squatted as she returned the picture book to the bottom shelf. She often thought, not without amusement, that reshelving books provided her with a good workout. Certainly the amount of squats she had to do to reach those lower shelves in the children's section made her backside and legs look great in her skirts and pants if she said so herself. So she never complained about the task. Not that she would. She loved being Aspen Creek, Colorado's children's librarian.

She'd gotten the job straight out of college when the previous librarian—and her mentor—took over as the head librarian. Helen Watson had been Veronica's guardian angel for a good deal of her life, supporting her through the rough patches in her childhood. The library had been a happy place, filled with people who loved her. The books Helen recommended for Veronica had transported her from Aspen Creek to places all over the world, to times past and in the future. Now Veronica provided a listening ear to those who needed one. She also did her best to create groundbreaking programming for Aspen Creek's children.

She spotted a mother and two little ones at the desk and hurried over. "Thanks for coming today."

"Are you kidding?" Emily, the mother of three-year-old twins, said. "Coming to the library is their favorite thing to do."

"Is that right?" Veronica asked, stooping down so that she was eye level with Deena and Gina.

"Yes." They held up the oversize books they'd chosen on their own after the children's program ended twenty minutes ago.

"Let's check out these books, then," Veronica said, standing to her full height.

She signed out the books and handed them back to the children. "I'll see you all next week."

As she watched the small family leave the library, a feeling of contentment swept through her at the children's library joy.

"This came for you," Hailey, the research librarian, said, coming over and handing her an envelope.

"Really?" Veronica asked, taking it. It was unusual for her to get personal mail at work. In fact, it never happened. Of course, she didn't receive a lot of mail at home either. She paid her bills online and didn't subscribe to many magazines. She saw her friends in person, and other than Christmas cards, or a birthday card sent from her mother and stepfather, her mail was generally limited to junk mail, which she immediately recycled.

"Yes." Hailey grinned mischievously. "Maybe it's from a secret admirer."

"If I have an admirer, it's the best-kept secret in town. Even I don't know about it."

"Maybe he's revealing himself now," Hailey joked as she walked away.

Veronica glanced at the envelope. The penmanship was curly as if written by a teenage girl. She didn't recognize the Denver return address. Curious. She shoved it into her cluttered purse beside her makeup, wallet, and random stuff she needed to clear out. She'd read it later. Right now she was meeting her friends for lunch.

Draping her purse strap over her shoulder, she hurried from the library. The early summer day was hot and sunny, perfect weather for a lunch with good friends.

The restaurant was a half mile from the library and she set off down the road at a brisk walk. From the time she was a young girl, Veronica had been an athlete. She'd played on her middle school's girls' basketball team and had run cross country in high school. Her college athletics had been limited to intramurals. Even now, years after graduation, she enjoyed a good run. She wasn't a fan of slipping on snow and ice, so in the winter months, she was more inclined to use her treadmill, but now that it was June, she ran along the trails outside of Aspen Creek. This short walk provided a pleasant break from her hours inside the library.

She didn't see her friends at any of the outside tables, so she went inside. Her friends Alexandra, Kristy, and Marissa were sitting at a booth at the far side of the diner, sipping their beverages.

"We ordered you an iced tea," Marissa said.

"Thanks." Veronica sat down. She grabbed her glass, took a long sip, and then leaned back and turned to Alexandra. "I missed you and Chloe today."

"Blame Nathan's parents," Alexandra said, referring

to her fiancé's parents. "They took all of the grandkids to Disneyland this week."

"Lucky you," Marissa said. "That gives you time alone with your fiancé."

Veronica smiled as she perused the menu, debating internally over whether she would have the tuna salad sandwich or the chicken salad. Either would be a good choice and go well with the chocolate brownie and vanilla ice cream she intended to have for dessert.

"You will not believe who is coming back for the goodbye party for Mr. Watson," Marissa said.

"Who?" Veronica asked, glancing over the top of her menu. She would go with the chicken salad.

"Malcolm Wilson."

Veronica's heart lurched and she barely managed to keep from yelping. When had he decided that? She'd been involved with the planning and the last she knew, he hadn't bothered to RSVP. She hadn't seen him since the inaugural Aspen Creek Bachelor Auction two years ago. To say their conversation had been unpleasant would be an understatement. Despite telling herself that she didn't care a whit about him, her heart still skipped a beat as she recalled how attractive he'd looked in his perfectly tailored black tuxedo. His crisp white shirt had contrasted nicely with his rich brown skin. She and Malcolm had never been more than good friends until that friendship had imploded, so her physical reaction had been a shock to her system. Even now, she felt her pulse race at the memory.

Anger and disgust—both at herself and him—replaced the sensation.

"Really?" Kristy said, turning to look at Veronica. "Did you know he was coming back?"

Veronica shook her head and somehow managed to keep her expression neutral. At least she hoped she looked bland. She'd never had much of a poker face. "This is the first I've heard of it."

"I'm surprised. You were both so close in high school."

"That was a long time ago," Veronica said. *A lifetime.* "Things change."

"I know. I was hoping that when the two of you talked after the bachelor auction that you would find a way to become good friends again."

Veronica had been the auctioneer at the charity auction so she'd known in advance that Malcolm would be participating. That had given her plenty of time to steel herself for seeing him and rein in her emotions. Now she had been caught totally unaware and her feelings were all over the place.

"Nope. The status quo works for me." Veronica hoped her tone would put a period on the conversation. The last thing she wanted to do was talk about Malcolm. It was true that they'd once been great friends. All through school, they'd been there for each other in times of need. She'd always known she could rely on him. That had all changed at one of the lowest points in her life. Then he'd shown her just how little she'd actually meant to him. Although they'd been in college at the time, they'd been adults. Old enough to make sacrifices—or not—for each other.

Two years ago at the bachelor auction, he'd approached her in an effort to try to rekindle their friendship. She'd done her best to listen with an open mind—or as much of one as she could muster—as he'd tried to explain why he'd behaved as he had. Incredibly just talking about the past had made her heart ache. Though time had passed, the pain had still been fresh. Too fresh for her to forgive him.

She would be polite if she happened to run into him in town, but there would be no spontaneous lunches or impromptu games of darts. Their friendship was a thing of the past and she wasn't willing to try to rebuild it. She had new friends in her life who she could depend on. New people who she could call on in her time of need, who wouldn't give her some lame excuse and then return to their frat brothers, leaving her broken and feeling even more alone.

"That makes me so sad," Kristy said.

"Why?" Alexandra asked.

"You didn't grow up here, so you don't know how close Malcolm and Veronica were. It was like one of those sitcoms that you used to see on TV."

"Really?" Alexandra asked, laughing softly.

"Yes," Kristy replied. "I hung out with them too, but I was more like a costar instead of one of the leads."

Despite how ludicrous it sounded, Veronica couldn't hold back her smile. The times that she'd spent with them had been the bright spot in her otherwise gloomy life. If it hadn't been for Malcolm, Kristy, and a few other special people of Aspen Creek, she wasn't sure if she would have made it. When she'd been nine, her father had left her mother for a woman he'd been having an affair with. The moment the ink had dried on the divorce papers, he'd remarried the other woman and started a new family, forgetting about the old one. Forgetting about *her*.

Although she'd only been a child, divorce hadn't been a foreign concept to her. She'd known that mothers and fathers often didn't get along and sometimes decided to live in two different houses with the kids shuttling between the two. What she hadn't known—hadn't expected—was that some fathers turned their backs on their children completely. Walter Kendrick had been one of those.

At first he'd made promises to come see her. Promises that he hadn't kept. She'd been caught entirely off guard when days and then weeks had gone by without any contact from her father, who she'd adored.

And the neglect wasn't just emotional. Though he was a successful architect and had inherited family money, he'd made only the minimum in child support payments—and that sporadically. Hard times had come for Leslie and Veronica. They'd lost the five-bedroom home and for a very brief—very terrifying period of time—they'd been homeless. If not for the kindness of their neighbors, they might not have survived.

Leslie, who had been a stay-at-home wife, had had to find a full-time job while going to school to finish her accounting degree, leaving Veronica on her own for hours on end. The librarians and her friends' parents had stood in the gap, making sure that she had adult supervision and companionship, but they couldn't soften the blow of knowing her father had done this to them. It was a lesson she'd never forgotten—one her mother had been sure to emphasize.

Throughout their hard times, Leslie had repeatedly told Veronica to never become dependent on anyone else.

They both knew what could happen if a woman wasn't financially independent. They'd lived it.

"I wouldn't say we were a sitcom," Veronica countered, pushing the thoughts of the past behind her. "We were three friends who hung out together. And your friendship was just as valuable to me as Malcolm's. We were the Three Musketeers."

"You have to say that," Kristy said with a laugh.

"It sounds like the three of you had a good time," Alexandra said.

"The best," Veronica admitted. "But times change. Malcolm and I went our separate ways when we went away to college. Just like a lot of people, we grew apart and lost touch."

"*We're* still friends," Kristy pointed out.

"True. But you and I came back to Aspen Creek after college. Malcolm moved to Chicago."

"I'm not as close to Malcolm as I once was, but I know he'd be there if I needed him," Kristy said.

Veronica didn't agree, but she kept that comment to herself.

"I always send him and his parents a Christmas card," Marissa said. "And after he came back a couple of years ago for the bachelor auction, we reconnected. We've kept in touch ever since then."

Veronica managed to suppress the wave of jealousy that washed over her. She knew she shouldn't be jealous of Marissa for maintaining a relationship with Malcolm. After all, he'd wanted to rekindle his friendship with her. Veronica had been the one to reject his overture. She couldn't have it both ways. Even so, she was surprised to discover that she wasn't as over the demise of their friendship as she'd believed.

"Well, who knows," Kristy said, "maybe the two of you can work things out and become friends again. It's hard to make good friends at our age."

"Hey, now. I'm new to the group and I like to think that I'm a good friend," Alexandra said.

"You are. And we're so glad that you moved to Aspen Creek," Veronica said, as happy to be able to change the subject from Malcolm as she was to assure her friend that she was a welcome member of the group.

"We all are," Kristy added.

"How are wedding plans coming along?" Marissa asked.

"Good," Alexandra said, before launching into a detailed description of the trials and tribulations of finding the perfect wedding dress.

"Why don't you have one designed?" Marissa asked.

Alexandra only shook her head. "You sound like my mother. I'm trying to keep things simple, but she's got all of these grandiose ideas. Believe it or not, so does Nathan."

"That's a surprise," Veronica said. "Nathan doesn't strike me as the type to want a big spectacle. He seems more like the type to want to go to the justice of the peace."

"No one is more surprised than I am," Alexandra admitted. "After all, Nathan was all business, talking about his five-year business plan. That's why he wanted me to pretend to be in a relationship with him."

"Oh yeah. I haven't decided whether or not I forgive you for deceiving us that way," Marissa said with a laugh. "You aren't supposed to keep secrets from your best friends."

Alexandra shrugged her shoulders. "It wasn't my secret to tell. Besides, we'd planned to break up when the time was right and nobody would be the wiser."

"It's funny how life works out," Marissa said. "Your phony relationship turned into the real deal. Is there anything better than falling in love?"

Veronica could think of a hundred things without breaking a sweat. Not that she would tell her friends that. They were enjoying themselves and she would never want to bring them down. Nobody liked a wet blanket.

The waitress took their orders and before long she returned with their meals. As they ate, they talked about the wedding and whatever else came to mind. Ordinarily Veronica would have enjoyed herself immensely, but all that talk about Malcolm had shaken her. Every time the bell over the diner's front door chimed, signaling the entrance of another person, her stomach clenched. She didn't know why she was so jittery. The reunion/farewell party wasn't until next week, so there was no reason to think he would be in town so early. Even if he was already in Aspen Creek, he was probably spending the day with his parents on their ranch, which was outside of town. He certainly wouldn't make the trip to the diner in the middle of the day. The food was good, but it wasn't *that* good.

Veronica was just starting her dessert when the bell chimed again. Though she didn't peek in the mirror to get a glimpse of the person entering the dining room, the shiver that raced down her spine was all that she needed to let her know that not only was Malcolm in town, he had just entered the diner. *Great.*

Malcolm walked into the Aspen Creek diner and glanced around. It looked the same as he remembered. Red vinyl booths lined the walls and chairs pushed up to Formica tables filled the space in the middle of the room. The aroma of grilling burgers and frying potatoes floated on the air.

A waitress carrying a tray with two plates of the meatloaf special smiled at him. "Take a seat anywhere and someone will be with you shortly."

Malcolm smiled back and nodded. Although he always visited his parents on their ranch over the Christmas holidays and popped in occasionally throughout the year when his schedule allowed, it had been a couple of years since he'd come into town. He generally went straight to the ranch when he came to the area, but today he'd decided to stop in at the diner first. He'd been feeling nostalgic, remembering all the times he'd come here during his high school years—and the person who'd always been by his side back then. The last time he'd been in Aspen Creek, he'd hoped to reconnect with Veronica and finally put the anger of their past behind them. He'd even entered the bachelor auction when he'd learned that she would be the auctioneer.

He could have saved his time. Oh, they'd talked. He just hadn't liked what she'd had to say.

It had been hard to accept at first, but he'd finally realized that their friendship was over. He could have tried harder to get through to her, but he'd decided against it. He didn't want to be a nuisance, pestering her and refusing to take no for an answer. Besides, he had his pride. He wouldn't beg her to be friends. But seeing her and knowing their friendship was over hurt. It was one of the reasons he'd mostly stayed away from Aspen Creek in the past two years.

But he'd found himself missing home more and more. After college, he moved to Chicago where he'd gotten a job as an investment banker. He'd always had a nose for business and over time he'd proven his worth and skill, becoming the youngest vice president in the history of the firm. He had a good life in Chicago—but he wouldn't call it home. There was nothing like the ranch where he'd grown up. It had been in his family for three generations. As his father liked to say, every inch of every acre had been paid for with the blood and sweat of his ancestors. His parents had worked it, taking over from Malcolm's grandparents, who'd taken over from his great-grandparents when they were too old to work any longer. His grandparents had lived out their final years in the small house they'd built many years ago, sitting on carved rocking chairs on their porch, relaxing as the days faded into night.

His parents had surprised Malcolm over the past year. His father had always claimed that every day spent on the ranch was like a vacation to him, yet recently his mother and father had begun to spend time away—something they never used to do. Over the past nine months, they'd gone on two extended vacations, leaving the ranch in the hands of their employees. Now they were talking about traveling around the world on a five-month cruise and seeing the places his mother had always dreamed about visiting. Apparently now that they'd gotten a taste of travel, they were hooked. After all the years they'd worked without taking a day off, Malcolm didn't begrudge them their happiness. Even so, he had a sneaking suspicion that there was more to the story than he'd been told. A man didn't go from living for the ranch to becoming a wanderer overnight. Hopefully he would be able to ferret it out of them in the next four weeks.

Unlike their parents before them, Malcolm's parents didn't expect him to take over the ranch when they were no longer able to run it. He was grateful for that understanding on their part. Over the years it had become clear to them that although he'd been raised on a ranch, ranching wasn't in his heart. He'd gone away to college with the intent of majoring in ranch management, but after taking an elective in finance, he'd felt an excitement that he hadn't felt in his other classes. It soon became clear that his path didn't include running the ranch. Initially his parents had been disappointed, but to their credit, they hadn't tried to change his mind.

Female laughter drew his attention and he followed the sound. His eyes landed on Veronica, who was seated with three other women. Despite the fact that their last conversation hadn't gone well, he couldn't help but smile at the sight of his old friend who was clearly enjoying herself. It was quite a contrast from the last time they'd spoken.

It hadn't gone well at all. Veronica had been furious with him. Although she had kept her voice low and maintained an air of calm—they'd been surrounded by bachelors and many of Aspen Creek's citizens at the time—she had nonetheless managed to blast him. He knew he had disappointed her when they'd been in college. Even now, he felt shame just thinking about how badly he'd behaved back then. Over the years he'd considered reaching out to Veronica and apologizing, but he'd always come up with one reason or another to put it off. A part of him had hoped her hurt and anger would mellow with time, but now he realized that delaying his apology had been the coward's way out.

As he looked at her, he resolved that he would not allow that same cowardice to control him a second time. He intended to make things right with Veronica. Though he hadn't come home with that intent, he now believed that it was important to both of them. She might not need him now, but she deserved to know how truly sorry he was. Looking back, Malcolm realized that he hadn't deserved her. He'd failed her.

He wasn't going to let their latest dustup keep him from trying to earn back her friendship. He hadn't realized how much he'd missed until he'd seen her again. He'd gotten good at ignoring his loneliness, shoving back the urge to contact her whenever something good or noteworthy occurred in his life, but seeing her now made it all come flooding back. Her friendship was important to him. Vital even. He didn't think they would be the same now as when they'd been teens—they were both thirty-four and had lived full lives—but they still could have a good friendship now.

So after placing his to-go order, he crossed the crowded dining room and walked over to her table. It was clear that she was aware of his presence. Her back was ramrod straight and her lip twitched at the corner. She was staring intently at Kristy, their old classmate, appearing determined not to look in his direction. Even after all this time, he knew her mannerisms so well. The thought made him unreasonably happy. The fact that she was putting so much effort into ignoring him let him know that on some level she was still attuned to him. They were still connected whether she wanted to admit it or not.

"Hello, ladies," he said when he reached them.

"Malcolm," Kristy said, her voice filled with pleasure as she jumped up and gave him a hug. "It's so good to see you. I heard you were coming to town."

"It's good to see you, too. Hi, Marissa," he said. He glanced down at Veronica, who didn't bother to acknowledge him. He turned from her to the other woman at the table. "I don't believe we've met. I'm Malcolm Wilson."

"Let me introduce our friend," Kristy said, shooting Veronica a glance before she turned to the other woman sitting at that table. "This is Alexandra Jamison. She and her daughter moved to town about two years ago. Do you remember Nathan Montgomery? She's his fiancée."

"Really? Congratulations. Nathan is a good man." He made a mental note to contact Nathan and congratulate him on his good luck.

Malcolm turned to Veronica. "It's good to see you, Veronica. How are you?"

She turned to look at him. The familiar sparkle was missing from her eyes and he sighed. It was going to take a lot of effort to regain her friendship. Veronica could hold on to a grudge like it had been cemented to her hands, so he knew it would take some effort to get on her good side again. But he did like a challenge. Especially when the prize was this great. "I'm fine," she finally answered.

"Hey, I thought I saw you guys," a woman said, coming up to the table, holding a to-go bag. "I just wanted to make sure that we're all still on for Girls' Night Out tonight."

"Seven o'clock at Grady's," Marissa said, glancing at Malcolm, a sly smile on her face. "We'll be there, Savannah."

Malcolm noticed Veronica's slight grimace and fought back a smile. Clearly she hadn't wanted him to know her plans for the night. Not that it was all that hard to predict. Aspen Creek was a resort town that catered to the wealthy. There were numerous clubs and hotspots that were popular to vacationers, but the citizens preferred going to places that weren't swarming with tourists. There were only a couple that fit that description. Grady's had usually been the preferred destination on Friday nights for people their age.

"See you then," the woman said before walking away.

The bell over the door jangled and Malcolm automatically looked over. He did a double take and shook his head. It was Glenn Kirkland, one of his firm's clients. Malcolm was always bragging about Aspen Creek, touting it as one of the best places to visit. With its views of the Rockies, rolling green hills and fields, and clean, fresh air, you couldn't beat it. Looked like Glenn had taken his advice. "Excuse me. I see someone that I know. Enjoy the rest of the day."

Although his back was to Veronica, he could feel her eyes on him as he walked away from the table and he smiled. The connection between them was still there.

He quickly crossed the diner and held out his hand. "Glenn. What are you doing here?"

"You're always talking about how great this town is. I had a few days free, so I decided to visit. I wanted to see for myself what the fuss was all about."

"I got my food to go, but if you don't mind the company, I'll eat here and join you."

"I don't mind at all."

The waitress came over to take Glenn's order and Malcolm changed his order from to-go to eat-in.

"Everything smells so good," Glenn said. "I'm glad that I decided to come here."

Malcolm smiled. "Trust me. Nothing tastes as good as the burgers and milkshakes they serve here."

Glenn looked over at the table where Veronica and her friends had been sitting. Malcolm followed the other man's gaze. The women were standing, laughing as they hugged each other.

"Those are some good-looking women," Glenn said, appreciation in his voice. "I saw you talking to them when I came in. Which one of them is your girlfriend?"

"What? None of them. But I feel like I should let you know that the one wearing the green blouse and blue jeans is engaged."

"That leaves three."

Malcolm frowned. "I thought you were in town to take a look around, not pick up women."

Glenn grinned. "I'm here to have fun and relax. What could be more fun and relaxing than taking out a beautiful woman? It's not like I know anyone here—except for you, apparently."

Malcolm shrugged. He didn't have an answer for that. "So what are you really planning to do here? I know you well enough to know this isn't strictly a vacation."

"I'm looking for a place to build a new factory."

"In Aspen Creek?"

"It's one place I've been looking at. There's lots of land here. Who knows? A rancher might be interested in selling to me. Maybe even you."

Malcolm laughed. "Sure. Let me think about that."

Someone bumped into his arm as they passed by and Malcolm looked up into the eyes of Evelyn Parks. She owned one of the most popular B & B's in town as well as an agency that coordinated adventures for tourists. Evelyn was one of the people responsible for turning Aspen Creek into a tourist destination. She was also the biggest gossip in town. And she never got her facts straight. Malcolm nodded, but the woman was already rushing out the door.

"Seriously, I need some land, and on paper, this place seemed like a good fit."

"Although I don't live in town permanently anymore, I still care about the people who live here. I don't want to do anything that would harm the town or the property values. The character of Aspen Creek matters."

"Now that I've seen how beautiful the area is, I agree. It's not what I'm looking for. Some areas are just too pristine to touch and this is one of them."

"I knew there was a reason I liked you. You recognize beauty when you see it."

"Speaking of beauty," Glenn said. "Wow."

Malcolm followed Glenn's gaze to the front of the diner. Veronica and her friends were exiting. "What?"

Glenn chuckled, a devilish twinkle in his eyes. "They're all pretty but she is absolutely gorgeous."

Was Glenn attracted to Veronica? Ridiculously, Mal-

colm felt a twinge of jealousy. The idea of the other
man spending time with Veronica when she wouldn't
give him the time of day grated. Malcolm pictured the
strained expression on her face as she'd looked at him
earlier and then imagined her smiling up at Glenn. The
thought had him gritting his teeth, and he inhaled deeply
and slowly blew out the breath in an effort to force himself to relax. He didn't have any rights when it came to
Veronica. To call their relationship a friendship at this
point was a stretch. Besides, they'd never had a romantic relationship. She'd never hinted at wanting one. Nor
had he. Sure, he'd always been aware that she was gorgeous, but she'd been his friend. Crossing that line had
been out of the question. Risking their friendship on the
slim possibility that they might become more had never
seemed worth it to him.

Even so, he recalled the way his heart had leaped in
his chest two years ago when he'd seen her for the first
time in years. She'd grown into an even more beautiful
woman. If they'd been on better terms, he would have
asked her out. As things stood now, even being friends
again might be a pipe dream.

He realized Glenn was waiting for a reply. "Veronica?
Yes, she is gorgeous."

"Is that her name? Red is definitely her color."

"Red?" Veronica wasn't wearing red. That was Marissa. Malcolm supposed she was pretty, but to him, she
was nowhere near as beautiful as Veronica. No one was.

"Yeah." Glenn gave him a look that saw too much.
"Who did you think I was talking about?"

"I just assumed you were talking about Veronica," Malcolm said sheepishly. "The one in the skirt."

"Because you have something going on with her?"

"No. We're just friends. Or rather we were." Malcolm wished he could call back those last words. He didn't want to have that conversation. Especially not with someone he had a professional relationship with. While Malcolm worked hard to have a congenial relationship with his clients, he was a firm believer in keeping his personal issues out of the equation.

Glenn seemed to understand that because he didn't press the matter. Instead he turned the conversation back to Marissa. "Do you know the woman in red personally?"

"I know her. But remember, I haven't lived in Aspen Creek for a while so my information might be dated."

"I'll risk it." Glenn took a swallow of his soft drink. "Is she married? Seeing anyone?"

"No. I know that for sure." Malcolm's and Marissa's mothers were friends. Malcolm's mother had recently told him that Marissa's mother was lamenting her lack of a serious boyfriend. Thank goodness his mother wasn't like that.

"But I'll tell you what. I'm actually thinking about going to Grady's tonight. Lots of locals tend to meet up there on weekends. They have a DJ and if memory serves me right they have a great house band. Some of my friends might be there. Maybe Marissa will be with them. And even if she's not, it's still a chance to meet people, get a taste of the local culture that tourists don't usually see. If you want we can meet up."

If he met up with Glenn, it wouldn't look as if he was

trying to spoil Veronica's night out with her friends. He would just be showing an acquaintance around.

"Well, then, I guess I have my plans for the night."

Malcolm laughed. "Let me get this straight. You're going to go there just to see her? The two of you might not hit it off."

"I'm an optimist. I believe in taking risks and hoping the best will happen."

They finished their lunches and then shook hands. Malcolm told Glenn how to find Grady's and then they set a time to meet up later that night.

Once Malcolm was in his pickup and on the road home, he thought about what Glenn had said about taking risks. The other man was absolutely right. Malcolm generally went after what he wanted. At least when it came to business. He had never applied that same mentality to his personal life. That reticence might explain why he didn't date much and why he hadn't had many serious romantic relationships in his life.

Of course, in high school when most of the kids were pairing off, he'd been short and skinny, two qualities that didn't necessarily appeal to girls. But Malcolm and Veronica had been good friends, spending most of their time together so he hadn't minded not having a girlfriend. In college he'd grown a foot and put on fifty pounds of muscle and the women had come around. He'd dated a lot, but like now, no one had piqued his interest. There was only one relationship he was interested in pursuing. He wanted to become friends with Veronica again.

Truth be told, he had wanted to restore that relationship for quite some time. His efforts in the past hadn't been successful, but he wasn't going to give up. He was going to get Veronica back in his life no matter what it took.

Chapter Two

Malcolm turned onto the gravel road leading to his family's ranch. After he'd finished his lunch, he'd walked around town for a while, getting reacquainted with Aspen Creek, but now he was eager to be home. There was still about a quarter mile to drive before he reached the rambling white clapboard house where he'd been raised. When his great-grandfather had created the road, he hadn't wanted to cut down any more trees than necessary, so the road wound around them. Though it had been a while since he'd been home, Malcolm knew every twist and turn, rise and fall by heart.

He drove past the house until he reached the garage. He climbed out of the truck and then headed for the stables. As expected, his father was inside, brushing one of the horses, singing along to a song that was playing on the small radio that was as much a part of the stable as the stall.

As a kid, Malcolm had spent lots of time here with his father and grandfather. From the time he'd been able to walk, he'd followed his father around the ranch like a shadow, asking an endless stream of questions. Roy had patiently answered every one, teaching him everything that he knew about ranching. As a result, Malcolm could ride with the best of them and he knew how to raise organic beef. The ranch wasn't the biggest in the area, but every generation had added to it. More importantly, they had built a good reputation.

"Hey, Dad."

His father spun around, a wide smile on his face. "Malcolm. I wasn't expecting you until next week."

"I decided to come early. I hope that's okay," Malcolm said, walking straight into his father's outstretched arms.

"You know better than to ask silly questions. We're always glad to have you home. Have you been inside yet?"

"No. I figured we could go in together and surprise Mom."

"Well we can do the first thing anyway. I'm not so sure about the second. I've been trying to surprise your mother for years and haven't succeeded more than once or twice. She has a sixth sense about these things."

Malcolm could only nod in agreement. His mother did seem to know everything before everyone else. He'd been a good kid, but every once in a while, he'd gotten up to mischief with his friends. Nothing serious and definitely nothing worth calling his parents about. Yet somehow, his mother had always known he'd been up to no good. "It's a gift, I suppose."

Roy stepped out of the stall, closed the gate, and then he and Malcolm headed for the house. Over the years, they had worn a path in the grass from the stables to the back door. Initially his mother had fussed that they only had to take a few steps to get onto the gravel, but after a while, she admitted defeat and gave up the fight. Before long, she herself was using the makeshift path. One day, Malcolm and his father had placed stepping stones in the grass, making it easier, and cleaner on wet days, to get from the stables to the house. And he had to admit that it was a lot more attractive.

They stepped into the mudroom and Malcolm waited while his father swapped out his boots for slippers before they went into the kitchen. Cheryl was setting a bowl of salad onto the table. There were three place settings. So much for surprising her. No doubt someone had seen him in town and had called her with the news. Gossip was an Olympic sport in Aspen Creek.

"Hey, Mom."

She smiled at him. "Welcome home. You're just in time for dinner."

"It smells good. Let me put my bag in my room and wash up." He kissed his mother's cheek and jogged up the stairs and into his childhood room. The house had four bedrooms and two bathrooms. His parents had wanted to have a big family, but things hadn't panned out that way. It was only after years of trying that Malcolm had come along. Cheryl had nearly died in childbirth and she'd been advised not to have any other children. Having only one child meant that it had been unnecessary for his parents to convert his bedroom into a sewing or craft room when he'd gone away to college, and it was basically the way he'd left it.

After washing his face and hands, he quickly unpacked and went back downstairs. His mother was setting a serving bowl on the table. Growing up, she'd always had a big meal on the table promptly at six o'clock. Though the ranch was busy, Malcolm and his father had known to be in the kitchen at that time if they wanted to eat while the food was hot.

"This smells delicious."

"Baked salmon, mixed vegetables, pasta and salad," she replied. "I decided to try something new."

His father had always been a beef and potatoes person and most meals had included some type of red meat. Malcolm had expected his father to kick up some sort of fuss, but he'd simply added tomatoes and lettuce into a bowl, drizzling on vinegar and olive oil dressing.

"There's nothing wrong with that. Variety is the spice of life." Malcolm liked all kinds of foods, especially those he didn't have to cook.

While they ate, Malcolm caught them up on the goings-on at his job and they caught him up on the news in Aspen Creek and on the ranch. After they finished their main course, Cheryl pulled a fruit salad from the refrigerator. His mother had always baked the best cakes and pies, so this dessert was a surprise.

"So what are you going to do tonight?" Cheryl asked, spooning fruit into a small glass bowl and passing it to Roy.

"I was thinking about hanging out at Grady's for a while."

"Are you meeting up with anyone in particular? Maybe old friends from school?" Her eyes sparkled and Malcolm knew that she was talking about Veronica.

"There actually is someone I'm meeting—a client who I ran into in town."

"Really?"

"Yes. I talk about Aspen Creek a lot and he decided to drop in and see if it lives up to all my bragging. Of course he was impressed. Anyway, I invited him to join me tonight." He didn't tell her that he knew Veronica would be there too. Although Cheryl had never pressured him to get serious about a woman, he didn't want to give her ideas. "Besides, I'm going to see everyone at the class reunion and goodbye party for Mr. Watson next week."

Barry Watson, the principal of Aspen Creek High School for the past twenty-seven years, was retiring and he and his wife were moving to Arizona at the end of the summer. During his tenure, he had become beloved by students and parents alike.

"That's true."

Malcolm was looking forward to getting together with his old classmates. Although he had made friends in Chicago, he didn't want to lose the connections to people he had grown up with.

Grady's didn't have a dress code and people generally wore whatever they felt comfortable in. That meant that most men dressed in jeans, cotton shirts, and cowboy boots, though others wore dress shirts and casual slacks. Generally the women dressed a little fancier than the men, in short skirts or tight pants. Since Veronica would be there tonight, he put on a button-down shirt and navy slacks, then dug his dress boots out of the closet.

Once he was dressed, he headed back to town. The streets were a little more crowded than they'd been earlier, so he ended up parking a couple of blocks away from the club. It was amazing how much the town had changed in his absence. When he'd been a kid, Aspen Creek had been struggling to stay afloat. During his high school years, the mayor and town council had made wide investments and Aspen Creek became a vacation destination for the rich and famous. Soon, travel magazines were "discovering" what the citizens of Aspen Creek had known all along. The mountains were great for skiing and snowboarding and other cold weather sports in the winter months, and hiking and fishing in the warmer months. As more vacationers arrived, more businesses began to spring up, creating jobs and increasing the tax base.

Even though he passed a number of unfamiliar faces on the streets, Aspen Creek still managed to maintain the friendly, family feeling that had been a hallmark of his youth. It was a true community where people cared about each other and would be there to help out without expecting to be repaid.

He reached Grady's and stepped inside. Immediately he felt a sense of familiarity. Memories of time spent with his friends bombarded him. After graduation from college, he'd come home for a month before starting his new job. He and his friends had come to Grady's just about every night. He'd seen Veronica here a few times, although she hadn't spoken to him. After a week or so, she no longer came. She'd been avoiding him. That had hurt. Back then he'd been unwilling to acknowledge his part in the end of their relationship and had become angry at her. He'd carried that anger with him for a long time, pulling it out whenever he needed to resist the urge to reach out to her and risk facing her rejection again. But with time, the anger had been replaced with sadness. Now, seeing the past with the wisdom that came with age, he accepted how badly he'd messed up. He knew he would have to take the first and possibly second and third steps to restore their friendship.

It was a few minutes to seven, and he looked around. Malcolm didn't see Veronica, but it was still early. He did see Alexandra and Savannah, the woman who'd mentioned the meetup tonight, so he knew they hadn't changed their plans. He was on his way over to their table when he heard Glenn calling his name. The other man had gotten a table not too far from Veronica's friends. Malcolm would be able to catch glimpses of Veronica throughout the night. Not that he was going to sit on the sidelines and just look at her. He was going to make an effort to have a conversation with her. Somehow or another he was going to get her to listen to him. He was willing to hear what she had to say as well. Hopefully when the evening was done, the past would be behind them.

"I got here early in case the place filled up," Glenn said.

Malcolm nodded. "Good thinking. Grady's is a popular place."

"I'm flattered that you'd let me in on such a local secret. I like the idea of getting to know the people around here as a friend of a friend and not as the outsider. Who knows, I might become a part of the community one day."

Malcolm laughed at the image. "Do you really think that could happen?"

"You never know. Life has a way of setting possibilities in front of you. I like to be ready to jump at all times."

"I suppose you're right," Malcolm agreed.

A waitress approached them and took their drink orders and then promised to return with their bottles of beer before she walked off.

"One thing I can say about your town. The women here sure are gorgeous." Glenn waved his hand, encompassing the room. It had begun to fill and there were an equal number of men and women present. Some were obviously couples, while others projected a "single and willing to mingle" air.

"So, now you're interested in the waitress?" Malcolm asked.

"No. I saw the woman I hope to spend my time with while I'm in town. I'm just waiting for her to arrive so I can make my move."

"And what do you plan to do when you leave? You don't have a wife and family somewhere, do you? Because I don't take kindly to working with men who cheat. If you'd cheat on someone who loves you, you'd cheat in business."

"No. I'm single. No wife or girlfriend." His eyes narrowed and his voice grew cold. "I've gotten an up close and personal view of the damage unfaithfulness causes. I lived it. My father cheated on my mother with a string of women. I'm not sure whether or not they knew he was married, but he sure didn't give a second thought to his wife and children."

Glenn took a long pull on his beer as if trying to rid his mouth of a bad taste. Malcolm had an idea of the bitterness the other man felt. Even though Walter Kendrick had not been his father, Malcolm had been disappointed and angry by his behavior. Before he'd left his wife and daughter, Malcolm had admired the man with his fancy

car and expensive suits. The outward trappings of wealth
had appealed to a younger Malcolm, whose father wore
old jeans and drove a beat-up truck. After he'd witnessed
the devastation the other man caused, his admiration
vanished and was replaced by disgust. If it was up to
him, Veronica's father would never know a peaceful day.
Of course that wasn't the way things worked out. From
everything Malcolm was able to glean from his parents,
the older man was living a happy life in Denver. From
all appearances he and his wife were thriving. But the
world was round and the evil you did came back to find
you when you least expected it. Eventually Walter would
get everything that he had coming. Malcolm just hoped
that he would be around to see it.

"If you don't mind," Glenn continued, "I'd rather talk
about something else."

Malcolm raised his bottle and took a long pull of his
beer. "I can get with that."

Glenn didn't seem to hear him. He sat up straighter
in his chair and smoothed the collar on his gray shirt.
Malcolm turned and glanced over his shoulder although
that was totally unnecessary. From the awestruck expression on Glenn's face, Malcolm knew that Marissa had
arrived. He was about to turn back around and make a
wisecrack about being overeager when Veronica stepped
inside behind her friend. She looked so beautiful that
the breath momentarily stalled in his chest and his pulse
began to race. Once more he was shocked by his very
visceral—very new—reaction to her.

Malcolm wasn't looking for a romantic relationship.
Even if he wasn't planning on leaving Aspen Creek after
his visit, he didn't see how the two of them could work as

a couple. They knew too much about each other. He believed that mystery was a very important part of building a relationship. That mystery was missing with Veronica. They'd grown up together, sharing their formative years and important events. Very little had happened in their lives that the other hadn't been a part of.

She'd been a part of his life when he'd been short and skinny. She'd listened when he'd complained about being the very last person picked to be on teams in gym class. The last person that any girl wanted to date. Worse, she'd actually seen him cry. No matter how much they had changed over the years, their memories hadn't vanished and never would. A part of him would always be that boy who'd depended on her for emotional security. No woman could ever find that attractive in a man.

Besides, he wanted to become friends again, which, given their past, was going to be hard enough. He didn't want to muddy the waters by trying for something more that would only make things complicated. Not only that, he lived in Chicago and she lived in Aspen Creek. Long-distance relationships were a headache to maintain. And if neither of them intended to move, then what was the point? Eventually they would break up, possibly ruining their friendship forever.

Veronica was fully grounded in Aspen Creek. Her mother lived here. Her friends were here. She had a job and home. Even in his wildest imaginings he couldn't picture her giving up all of this and moving to Chicago.

It wasn't a wild guess on his part. They'd talked about it when they'd been choosing colleges to attend. She'd lamented the fact that there wasn't a university in Aspen Creek. He'd been looking for new adventures and she'd been trying to keep her life the same. He'd understood it. She'd endured enough upheaval in her life to last a lifetime. The familiar town and people were comforting to her.

But he wanted more than to live out his life in this small town.

"So, are you going to introduce me?" Glenn asked, breaking into Malcolm's thoughts.

"I think we should let them sit down and get comfortable first. Once they have their drinks we'll let them talk for a while." Malcolm wanted Veronica to be in a good mood when he approached her. Pouncing on her the second she sat down was a good way to guarantee the opposite.

"What if some other guy goes over before then?"

"Are you normally this desperate or is this a new thing?"

Glenn laughed. "It is a totally new thing. Do me a favor?"

"What?"

"Don't tell her my last name."

"Really? Why?"

"You have no idea what it's like to be the child of a wealthy and powerful man. Let me tell you. It sucks never knowing who likes you for you and who is hoping to get their hands into your wallet."

Malcolm didn't think deception was the way to start a relationship, but it wasn't his place to interfere. "Okay. You're just Glenn. A friend from work in town for a taste of small-town life."

"Thanks."

Malcolm and Glenn discussed other things for a few

minutes, but neither of them could keep their eyes from drifting over to the table where Veronica and her friends were sitting. Shaking his head, Malcolm stood. "Come on. I'll introduce you to everyone."

"It's about time," Glenn said, jumping to his feet, a wide smile on his face.

As they walked over to the women, Malcolm's heart began to beat faster. He realized that his physical attraction wasn't something he could control. It was only natural for his body to react to Veronica's beauty. In fact, he would be worried if he didn't react. But he'd already resolved not to act on it. Friendship—that was his goal. Nothing more, nothing less.

"Hello, ladies," Malcolm said as he came to stand beside their table. "Fancy meeting you here tonight."

Marissa laughed. "As if we would be anywhere else on a Friday night."

Glenn cleared his throat and Malcolm bit back a smile. Talk about impatient. But then, maybe he wasn't the type to play it cool. "This is my friend Glenn. I've bragged on Aspen Creek so often that he decided to pay me a visit and check it out for himself."

Malcolm introduced each of the women, taking note of the way Marissa smiled up at Glenn. Perhaps the attraction was mutual. The thought made Malcolm smile.

"Would you like to join us?" Marissa asked.

"If it's okay? We don't want to intrude on your girls' night out," Malcolm said even as Glenn started to grab a chair from a nearby table.

"It's no problem," Savannah said. Malcolm couldn't help but notice that Veronica hadn't said a word.

"Thanks," Glenn said.

Malcolm and Glenn pulled over empty chairs. The women scooted closer to each other, making room for Glenn and Malcolm. Glenn slid his chair beside Marissa, who smiled in response.

"Sit here, Malcolm," Kristy said, a devilish smile on her face, sliding her chair to make space between her and Veronica.

"Thanks," Malcolm said, taking the indicated spot. He inhaled and got a whiff of Veronica's sweet scent. A woman who smelled good was his kryptonite. Though he couldn't name her perfume, it was rapidly becoming his favorite. But just inhaling her scent wasn't enough. He needed to connect with her.

"How was the rest of your day?" he asked and then immediately wanted to kick himself. She wouldn't want to discuss work with him. People went to clubs in order to get away from the grind.

Kristy jumped in to help him. "You had the elementary schoolers for story time this afternoon, right? That must have been fun."

Veronica's eyes lit up and she smiled, in spite of herself. "It was wonderful."

"Tell me more," Malcolm urged.

"It started as a program for the preschoolers in the mornings where they play for a while and then I read to them," she explained. "Our elementary school kids told me how much they missed it, so I added a group for them in the afternoon. I read a book to them today and we all read another one together. Then we had cookies. It was a blast."

"Really? That sounds like reading class in school."

"That's what I thought at first. But it's really popular." Her soft alto voice was soothing and he could listen to her talk all night. He sent a mental thank-you to Kristy for getting her started on a topic she obviously enjoyed talking about.

"How do you choose the books?" he asked, wanting to prolong the conversation.

"I chose the last two. I asked for suggestions, but nobody raised their hand."

"Perhaps they're a bit shy, or they're afraid their choices will be mocked. Maybe you should create a suggestion box so they can recommend books anonymously."

Veronica's eyes widened and she shook her head. "That is such a simple solution. I don't know why I didn't think of it."

"You probably would have. Tell me more about the programs that you've instituted."

She shook her head, looking as if she'd just remembered that she didn't want to talk to him. "Maybe later. It is girls' night out after all."

"Girls' night out plus two guys. Sorry about intruding."

She gave him a wry look that he remembered from when they were kids. She never let him get away with anything back then either. "I don't believe that for a minute. You were standing right there when my friends and I talked about coming here tonight so I know you coming here tonight wasn't a coincidence."

He shrugged. "There aren't a whole lot of places to hang out in Aspen Creek that aren't overrun with tourists."

"Clearly outsiders aren't a problem for you. After all, you brought one with you."

"Guilty as charged. But in my defense, he took one look at Marissa and that was all she wrote. He wanted the opportunity to see her again. And who am I to stand in the way of true love?"

"You don't expect me to believe you've turned into a romantic," Veronica said with a skeptical laugh.

"I believe in love," he said. "I just don't know the whole living happily ever after is for me, personally."

"I don't understand how you can feel that way. Not with your parents."

"Do you feel differently? Are you seeing someone? Are you planning to settle down?" The words pierced his heart and he forced the reaction away. Even though he didn't want a romantic relationship, surely he wasn't so selfish that he would want to deprive Veronica of true love. If anyone deserved to be happy, it was her.

"No. And I'm not looking for my Prince Charming or Mr. Right or whatever you want to call him. I'm happy with my life just the way it is. I have wonderful friends and a job that I love. I have a comfortable home. I have everything that I need."

Though he felt the same way, the words sounded lonely coming from her. He was happy with his solitary life but he wanted more than that for her. She deserved more—a man who adored her, children who loved her. The whole nine yards. But starting an argument wouldn't do him any favors with her, so he held up his beer in salute. "I'll drink to that."

Veronica hesitated. Did she really resent him so much that simply talking to him was a problem? That hurt. He knew it wasn't going to be easy to restore their friendship; knew that there would be ups and downs, but he hadn't expected his heart to ache quite so much in the face of her ongoing rejection.

He was about to set down his bottle when she lifted her glass of white wine. They drank together and he hoped that the tense moment had passed.

"Excuse me. I need to go to the ladies' room," Alexandra said.

"I'll go with you," the other women chimed in. Seemingly as one, Veronica and her friends rose and excused themselves for the moment.

Malcolm's eyes followed Veronica as she wove her way around the tables and chairs. She looked incredibly sexy in her sparkly silver top that clung to her firm breasts and emphasized her slender waist, and her short black skirt that stopped in the middle of her thighs, showing off her shapely legs. The tight skirt cupped her toned bottom which swayed sexily with each step she took. When she disappeared from his view, he sighed. Glenn chuckled, bringing Malcolm's attention away from Veronica.

"I take it things are working out between you and Marissa," Malcolm said.

Glenn nodded. "So far. She's really nice."

"Good luck."

"I don't need luck. I have charm and charisma." He winked.

Malcolm threw back his head and laughed. "Says you. But remember, I saw you stumbling over your feet in your haste to get over here."

Glenn ignored that comment and took a swig of his beer before staring at Malcolm. "I thought you said you weren't dating Veronica."

"There's nothing going on between us."

"It's clear you want something. So what are you waiting for?"

"It's complicated," Malcolm said.

"Isn't everything?"

"That Glenn is one good-looking man, Marissa," Kristy said. "And it seems like the two of you are hitting it off."

Marissa smiled and tossed her hair over her shoulders. "I know we've just met, but I really feel a connection to him."

"Wow. That's the first time you've ever said anything like that about a man," Veronica said as she dug through her purse in search of her lipstick. She rummaged around until she found it. "What brought about this change of heart?"

"Hold on. I'm not talking about my heart here. I just said I felt connected to him. That doesn't need to lead to love and romance. I'm not in the market for either. But I wouldn't be opposed to a hot fling. A *short* one."

"You are so bad," Alexandra said.

Marissa shrugged. "Whatever. I'm just not willing to risk getting my heart broken again. I gave love not one but two tries. It didn't work either time. I've decided it's not for me. But just because I don't want a relationship doesn't mean I'm not interested in having a man around. I still have needs."

They all laughed. Kristy stepped away from the mirror over the sink and Veronica took her place. She leaned closer and inspected her appearance before touching up her lipstick. She ran a comb through her hair then brushed a few stray locks behind her ears. Her silver-and-gold earrings dangled from her ears, glistening in the light. Her makeup was fine. She'd had a feeling that Malcolm would show up tonight, so she'd spent extra time on her appearance.

"Your face is facing," Kristy said with a laugh, "so there is no need for you to fix anything, Veronica."

"Speaking of men," Savannah said, "what's going on between you and Malcolm?"

"Nothing," Veronica said quickly, hoping to avoid a conversation.

"It looked like the two of you buried the hatchet," Kristy said.

"I wouldn't go that far," she said.

"You were talking."

"I couldn't very well ignore him. He was sitting right beside me."

"Are you sure that's all there is to it?"

"Positive," Veronica said definitively, although she was feeling anything but certain.

"Okay, then. Are you guys ready to head back?" Marissa asked.

Veronica nodded. "Yes."

As they walked back through the club, Veronica thought about how good Malcolm looked in his white shirt and navy pants and her heart skipped a beat. She told herself to remember that it was the man inside that mattered and not the body, but she couldn't quite convince herself to stop drooling over him. No matter how many times she reminded herself of his flaws, she couldn't ignore her attraction. And a voice inside told her that there might be more to Malcolm than she remembered. After all, he was older and wiser now. She wasn't the same person that she'd been at eighteen. It would be foolish of her to think that he hadn't grown and changed also.

But who knew whether those changes had been for the better or for the worse? Her father had changed for the worse. He'd gone from being a loving husband and devoted dad to a deceitful louse and absent father. Not that she wanted to judge Malcolm by the same measuring stick, but it was a good reminder that she should be wary. Besides, he didn't plan to stay in Aspen Creek. He'd made a life for himself in Chicago.

When she reached the table, Malcolm stood to let her return to her seat. Her eyes were immediately drawn to his muscular body. His chest looked hard and his stomach was flat. Though he no longer worked out on the ranch, he clearly hadn't let himself go to seed as the old men liked to say. As she passed in front of him, his enticing masculine scent wrapped around her. Distracted, she stumbled.

Malcolm jumped up and grabbed her arm, saving her from an incredibly embarrassing flop onto the floor. Veronica suddenly felt an intense temptation to lean her head against his chest. The ridiculous idea was so shocking that she jerked away from him. He inhaled loudly and she looked at his face. His eyes were filled with pain and she knew that he'd been hurt by her reaction. No doubt he thought she was repulsed by his touch. The opposite was true. Her skin had burned at the contact and chills raced down her spine. Though he had released her, she still tingled and she longed for him to touch her again. She nearly laughed out loud at that foolishness.

It was incredible to think that she could be attracted to Malcolm of all people. They'd never been more than friends. Besides, she wasn't even sure she liked him now.

Perhaps she should take a page out of Marissa's book and find a man to satisfy her basic needs without becoming emotionally involved. The minute that thought occurred to her she shoved it aside. Casual relationships weren't her style. She couldn't keep her feelings from getting involved no matter how hard she tried. There was no sense setting herself up for pain when she could avoid it.

"I was only trying to help," Malcolm said, stepping back. "But given the way you reacted, I guess my help was unwelcome."

Before she could correct him, he'd turned away from her, toward the stage. The DJ had finished spinning records and was now introducing the band. Although she wanted to clear up Malcolm's misconception, Veronica hesitated. Perhaps it was better to leave things the way they were. If he was angry with her, he would stay away from her. Then it wouldn't hurt so much when he left, which she knew he would.

Distance was what she wanted. Wasn't it?

Chapter Three

Malcolm tried not to feel disappointed by Veronica's reaction to his touch, but he couldn't quite pull it off. He hadn't expected their relationship to be restored with one conversation, but he'd thought that the two of them had been getting along so well…right up until they'd touched. That fleeting contact had erected a tall and wide wall between them and there was nothing he could do to penetrate it. Not tonight anyway. Given the way his body had reacted to simply holding her arm, he couldn't risk it. Even now, his hand still burned and his body was throbbing with intense and unwanted desire.

His reaction to her was just as confusing now as his sudden appreciation for her body had been. It was as if his emotions were confusing his desire to become friends again with lust. It was a complication he neither wanted nor needed. His life ran smoothly and he liked it that way.

The only way to keep things simple was to keep some distance between them.

Feigning a yawn, he stood up and pushed his chair up to the table. "It's been a busy week for me and I guess everything is hitting me now. I'm going to head out. I'll see you all later."

"You're leaving now?" Marissa asked.

"At least stay until the band finishes this set," Kristy said. A moment later, she jumped as if she'd just been kicked. Malcolm followed Kristy's gaze over to Veronica, who was suddenly extraordinarily interested in her empty wineglass.

"No. I really need to hit the road. But we'll see each other at Mr. Watson's goodbye party next week," Malcolm promised.

"I'll hold you to that," Marissa replied, coming to her feet and giving him a hug. Before she let him go, she whispered, "Don't let her attitude fool you. Veronica is glad you're here."

Malcolm could only nod. He hoped that nobody else recognized his disappointment at how the night had turned out. He glanced around the table, noting absently that Glenn was staying, and letting his eyes linger for a moment on Veronica. "Have a good night, everyone."

Before leaving, Malcolm stopped at the bar and paid for another round of drinks for the table. It had been twilight when he'd arrived, but now the moon and stars were shining in the dark night sky. He inhaled a breath of clear mountain air. Though he didn't come home often, the cool crisp air filling his lungs was as familiar as ever. Life came with trade-offs and for the most part he was happy with the ones he'd made. He'd traded the quiet solitude and fresh air of Aspen Creek for the fun and activity of city life. When things got too hectic and he needed to unwind, he was secure in the knowledge that he had a refuge waiting for him here in Colorado.

He hopped into his truck and drove over the lonesome highway back to the ranch. At this time of night there wasn't much other traffic and he made it home in under an hour. Not that there was a reason to hurry. Life moved at a slower pace in Aspen Creek.

After he parked his truck, he headed for the stables, unlocked the door, and stepped inside. Immediately the scent of hay filled his nostrils and his shoulders relaxed. Things might be tense between him and Veronica but none of that mattered right now.

The stables had always been a place of calm for him. Being around the horses always made him feel at peace. They neither judged him nor had expectations of him. Instead, they just accepted him and all of his faults. It helped that he always carried treats for them in his pockets. At this time of night the horses were sleeping and he didn't want to disturb them by turning on a light. He didn't need one. He could walk around this building blindfolded and not bump into a thing.

Malcolm went to the small office and took a seat at the scarred oak desk and booted up the computer. Although he wasn't involved in the ranch's day-to-day operations, he liked to keep up-to-date on what was going on. He always made sure that the business was doing well financially. He was ready to make a cash infusion if it was necessary to keep the operation running, but it never had been. And sure enough, from the numbers he saw, everything was going well. He checked the vaccination records of each of the livestock, impressed as always by the perfect recordkeeping. Roy had always kept records in a paper file because he'd wanted to be able to pull out individual paperwork if necessary. It had taken a while, but Malcolm had convinced him to keep an electronic record as well, and by this point, it looked like his father had finally gotten rid of paper copies. Roy had usually been resistant to change, but perhaps he was mellowing. After all, he'd gone on several vacations this past year and had even allowed Cheryl to make changes in his diet. Perhaps you could teach an old dog new tricks.

After he finished reviewing the records, Malcolm went into the house. His parents were early to bed, early risers, so as expected they were already in their room. He grabbed a snack and then went into the living room and turned on his laptop. Even though he was technically on vacation, he wouldn't be able to rest without knowing what was going on in his absence. He liked to keep his finger on the pulse of business. Finance was fluid and anything could happen in a moment's time. It would be malpractice to not keep abreast of all opportunities for his clients even when he was on vacation.

Of course, Malcolm enjoyed his job. Some people worked strictly for the paycheck, and there was nothing wrong with that, but that life was not for him. He loved the rush that he felt when he did well for his clients. He studied each prospective before he recommended an investment to his clients. But he didn't do it just for the money although he made a lot of it. There was satisfaction in knowing that because of him, people like his parents who had made wise investments, had enough money to retire comfortably and make the most of their golden years.

Malcolm dashed off a few emails to his secretary before shutting down his computer. He had never been much for TV and he didn't feel like reading. He yawned for real this time and decided to go to sleep so he could get up early and work with his father. In the past, his father had shared lots of interesting tidbits about the land as well as given him advice that was still serving him well today. Roy might have words of wisdom that would help Malcolm reach Veronica.

He could already imagine what his father would likely say. *Apologize, Malcolm. As many times as you need to. Is your happiness and hers worth sacrificing on the altar of your pride?* The answer was an easy no. He would give anything in order to get back the friendship they'd had before, at any cost to his pride. But it wasn't up to him alone. Veronica had an equal—heck, maybe even a greater—say in how things went between them. Right now, he would bet that she was in the "not going to be friends again" camp and he had no idea what he was going to do to convince her to change her mind.

Deciding that he'd brooded enough over a past that couldn't be changed, he headed upstairs to his room and forced himself to go to bed.

The heavenly smell of coffee brewing woke him minutes before his alarm went off. He took a quick shower, dressed, then jogged down the stairs. Over the years, he'd gotten used to the early ranch hours and had even kept them while working in finance. He'd complained loudly about the schedule as a kid but now he appreciated the discipline that had given him a leg up in his career.

"Good morning," his mother said, looking over her shoulder as she stirred a pot.

Malcolm kissed his mother's cheek and looked into the pot. Oatmeal? What happened to the bacon, eggs, and buttered grits he'd grown up on? The pancakes, sausages, and fluffy biscuits? His father had insisted that he needed a hearty breakfast to fuel him for a day of hard work. Things really were changing around here if this was what passed for filling these days. Malcolm poured himself a cup of coffee. "Where's Dad? I expected him to be up by now."

"Oh, your father's moving a little more slowly these days."

"Really?" Malcolm had never known his father to slow down for anything. Something was going on. "How much more slowly?"

"Not enough to put that panic in your voice," Roy said, coming into the room. He crossed over to the coffeepot and poured a cup, adding a dab of nondairy creamer—another new addition to the kitchen—and a teaspoon of sugar.

"I'm not panicking," Malcolm said. He forced mirth into his voice, hoping to cover the concern. "If anything, I was just trying to figure out if I would have to move the cattle on my own today."

"That's not going to happen." Roy leaned against the counter and took a long sip of his coffee. His lips turned down but that was his only reaction. "I'll be ready to go once I get this inside me."

Cheryl ladled oatmeal into bowls and set them onto the table. "You mean after you eat your breakfast."

"I mean after I eat my breakfast," Roy echoed with a laugh.

"Sit down, you two," Cheryl said, setting plates of hard-boiled egg whites, toast with grape jelly, and bowls of mixed fruit beside the oatmeal.

Malcolm joined his parents at the table and studied them while he added walnuts to his oatmeal. Roy and

Cheryl had always been affectionate with each other.
It wasn't uncommon for his mother to rub his father's
shoulders or for Roy to brush a kiss against Cheryl's
cheek. The affection was still evident in Cheryl's eyes,
but there was also something else there. Concern. Worry.
Fear. What in the world was going on? Malcolm didn't
know, but he intended to find out the first chance he had
his mother alone.

"This is really good, Mom," Malcolm said, after swal-
lowing a spoonful of oatmeal and nuts. "Nobody in the
world cooks as well as you do."

Roy frowned at his egg whites before he ate them.

"You're just saying that because you're tired of cooking for yourself."

"I *am* tired of cooking for myself," Malcolm admitted with a laugh. "Have been for years. That's why I eat
out a lot. But that doesn't change the fact that you are a
fabulous cook."

"You should have had some of the food we ate on
vacation," Cheryl said. "Everything on the cruise was
delicious. And French cuisine? I have never enjoyed my
meals that much."

"I still can't believe you guys went on two vacations
in under a year. Dad, you always said that it would take
a cannon to blow you off of this land. I can't tell you the
number of times you reminded me that ranching was a
three-hundred-sixty-five-day-a-year job."

"It's still true. But your mother deserved that cruise
and European vacation she's dreamed about," Roy said.
He lifted Cheryl's hand and kissed it.

"You'll get no argument from me," Malcolm added.
"Now that you know the ranch didn't fall apart while

you were gone, maybe you'll go on more vacations in the future."

Roy only nodded slowly. "We'll see, son. We'll see."

Malcolm glanced at his mother, who was blinking furiously. Something was definitely off. Forget about waiting for a perfect time. He needed to know what was going on now. He set his spoon on his half-eaten bowl of food. "Okay. What's going on?"

"What makes you ask something like that?" Roy asked, digging into his oatmeal.

"Answering my question with another question? Come on, Dad. You know I know that tactic. You called me on it often enough when I was a kid."

His parents exchanged a quick glance and Malcolm knew that they'd just shared an entire conversation. Being married for decades made communication that much easier. But being on the outside, Malcolm had no clue what they had said. He blew out an exasperated breath. "What? What is it that you aren't telling me? Come on. I'm grown. I can handle it."

"It's nothing really," Roy said. "Hardly worth mentioning."

"How about you mention it anyway?"

Roy sighed. "I had a bit of a medical incident last year."

Malcolm's heart sank with fear and his imagination began to run wild as he pictured the worst-case scenario. Telling himself to get a grip, he forced himself to speak calmly, drawing on all of the control he'd learned in his years in the financial industry. Nobody followed a leader who panicked. He inhaled and slowly blew out the breath before speaking. Even so, his voice quavered.

He couldn't be dispassionate about his father. "What kind of incident?"

"Minor. The doctor said it was no big deal. I just need to slow down a bit and make a few lifestyle changes."

Malcolm looked from his father to his mother. Cheryl had never been as good at masking her feelings as Roy. She seemed a little misty-eyed, but she had always been emotional. She cried when she was happy or sad, so these could be tears of sorrow or relief. "Is that all?"

"You know what they say," Roy said, before Cheryl could answer. "Father Time is undefeated."

"Are the two of you at war?" Malcolm asked.

"No," Roy said with a crooked grin that faded away as quickly as it appeared. "But age does eventually catch up with all of us. I'm not as young as I used to be."

"You aren't sick, are you?" Somehow Malcolm managed to keep the dread from his voice.

"No. Nothing like that. I just had a scare. My cholesterol was too high and I had a mild heart attack."

"*You had a heart attack?* And nobody told me?" Malcolm looked from his father to his mother and then back again.

"A *mild* one. I didn't even know I'd had one until after the fact. Then it seemed pointless to mention it. I'm taking my medicine and following doctor's orders. I'm fine. But that incident changed my perspective and made me realize that life is short. Your mother deserves to have her dreams come true. So we went on those trips. We'll be going on another one or two this year. And every year in the future." He picked up his fork and dug into his bowl of mixed fruit, an unmistakable signal that he'd said all he intended to say.

Realizing that he had gotten all of the information he would be getting, Malcolm resumed eating too. If he intended to do his share of work, and pick up any slack if required, he needed to have sufficient fuel in his body.

"So how did things go with Veronica last night?" his mother asked.

"What makes you think that I saw Veronica last night?" Malcolm countered.

"Now who's answering a question with a question?" Cheryl raised an eyebrow.

Malcolm laughed, knowing that he'd been caught. His parents might be dealing with his father's health concerns, but they were as sharp as ever. "It was a mixed bag, which is as good as I expected. She and her friends were having a girls' night out, but they invited me and Glenn to join them. Veronica and I had a good conversation and for a while everything was fine. Then she must have remembered that she's angry at me, because she pulled back. Rather than make things uncomfortable for everyone, I left."

Dad shook his head. "That little girl always had a stubborn streak a mile wide. She could teach a mule a thing or two."

"She's not a little girl anymore," Malcolm pointed out. She was a woman. A beautiful woman whose touch ignited something in him that he couldn't explain. A woman whose appeal he had to resist at all costs.

"I always hoped the two of you would get together one day," Cheryl said softly.

"You did?" Malcolm and his father said at the same time. Clearly the idea was just as shocking to Roy as it was to Malcolm.

"Why?" Malcolm added. "We were only friends."

"So you always said. But when the two of you were together, you both seemed so happy. So content. As if all was well in your worlds. After you stopped being friends, neither of you seemed complete. Whenever I see Veronica in town, she looks happy enough on the outside, but that special spark that the two of you brought out in each other is missing. I never asked what happened to end your friendship, but I always hoped you would work it out."

"I think you're imagining things," Malcolm said. "Veronica seemed just like her old self to me."

"Think what you want. I'm a woman. I know these things. And you were happier with her in your life."

"I'm happy now."

"Then why don't you have a serious girlfriend?"

"How did a conversation about Dad's health turn into criticism of my romantic life?"

Cheryl grinned. "I'm clever that way."

Malcolm shook his head and laughed, accepting defeat.

Once they were finished with breakfast, Malcolm stacked the dishes and placed the silverware on top of the pile despite his mother's protests. In under two minutes, the table was cleared and the dishes were in the dishwasher.

"I see those few weeks of working at the diner are still paying off," Roy said with a laugh.

"Yep." When he'd been sixteen, Malcolm had insisted on getting a job away from the ranch. He wanted something that would allow him to sleep late, so he'd gotten a job at the Aspen Creek Diner. He'd been shocked and disappointed to discover that his hours as a busboy started at seven o'clock in the morning. He'd had to get up thirty minutes earlier than he'd been used to in order to make it to work on time. His tenure with the diner only lasted five weeks, but it was five educational weeks.

"If you would have stayed long enough, you might have gotten the opportunity to work the register," Roy joked.

"If I'd stayed longer, I might have begun to hallucinate from the lack of sleep. But I did learn that all kinds of work takes skill and that most jobs are harder than they look."

"Then it was five weeks well spent," Cheryl said.

The trio walked to the back door and his mother handed each of them a sack lunch, as always watching as they crossed the yard and went into the stable before going back inside. The sun had started to rise and a gentle breeze blew. The morning held hints of the beautiful afternoon that was on the horizon. Spending time with his father could only make the day better.

When Malcolm had been a kid, Roy had employed several ranch hands. Many of them had lived on the ranch though some of them had lived in a rooming house in Aspen Creek. "Is it just us?"

Dad nodded. "Why? Don't you think you can handle it?"

"Of course, but what happened to the hands?"

"There's only two now and they live in town. They'll be here in any minute."

"Only two? What happened to the rest? There were four only a few months ago."

"The same thing that is happening on ranches all

around the state. Workers are scarce. They're moving to the big cities for better jobs and more active social lives. It takes a special breed of man to live and work in ranch country. It's even harder if you don't have a special woman beside you."

"But Aspen Creek is thriving and it's not that far away."

"You're right. The town is bursting with visitors all year round. And that's a good thing. New businesses are opening and existing ones are expanding. There are more places in town for people to go at the end of a workday."

"So what's the problem?"

"All of that success doesn't necessarily translate to more employees for ranchers. Good help is still hard to find. People looking for work in the area tend to stick to Aspen Creek, where there's more to do in your off-hours and where there are plenty of options for different kinds of jobs. It will get even harder to hire hands if Marty Adams builds his factory."

Although his family owned a popular resort, Marty was a renowned chef. "What factory?"

"You know that he manufactures his barbecue sauce. He's thinking of expanding the business and rumor has it that he's looking for a place to build a factory. Maybe I'll sell him a few acres of the ranch."

"Don't even kid about that, Dad."

"Who's kidding?"

Malcolm had been putting his saddle on his horse's back. Now he paused and looked over at his father, who'd swung up into his saddle and was holding the reins.

"How much land are you talking about?"

"He would only need about four or five acres. We've got eight hundred and seventy-five." Roy gestured at him. "Come on, mount up."

Malcolm adjusted the straps on the stirrups and then mounted. "Are you talking about the five acres you worked so hard to buy? Why would you give those up?"

"I didn't say I would sell them for sure. It's just something I'm tossing around."

"I don't get it. All of my life you instilled in me just how important the land was. Three generations of our family worked this land, sweating and saving to buy even more, one precious acre at a time. And now you're thinking about selling off a piece of it so someone can build a factory on it?"

"What else am I supposed to do? It's too big to be a one- or two-man operation. And hands come and go as fast as I train them. Over the years I've had employees who wanted to work in the summer to earn money for school. One guy was really good and it was obvious he'd worked on a ranch before. But it was also clear he was running from something. Maybe the law or more likely himself. Who knows? One day he was gone. He just up and left. No notice. Nothing."

"That's rough."

Roy sighed. "It finally occurred to me that there was no reason for me to keep holding on to the land. Who am I going to pass it to? You?"

Malcolm winced.

Roy blew out a breath. "That didn't come out right. Your mother and I are very proud of the man you've become and the career you have. We like knowing that you're living the life that you want to live right where you want to live it. We couldn't be happier for you."

"But that leaves you without anyone to take over the ranch."

"In a nutshell."

"It's not as if I don't like ranch life," Malcolm said, trying to explain. "Or as if I don't appreciate what you and your parents and grandparents sacrificed in order to build it."

"I know that, Malcolm. It was my choice to take over the ranch from my father. I love this life and wouldn't change a thing. But I know you have a career that you love in Chicago."

"But I love being here on the ranch too. It's home."

"Don't go getting all sappy and sentimental on me. It's not as if we're packing up and leaving today. I haven't even decided whether or not to sell any part of the ranch."

"But you're considering it." Just saying the words made his heart ache.

"I'm considering a lot of things."

"But you want to do more traveling."

"Like I said, that doctor visit opened my eyes. Hearing that I had a heart attack and was in danger of having another one?" Roy shook his head. "I'll admit, I was really scared there for a while. It helped me put things in perspective. Your mother matters more to me than anything in the world. Including the ranch. She deserves to see all the places she wants to see and to do all of the things she wants to do."

"Does she know that you're thinking about selling some of the ranch to Marty?"

"We've talked about the possibility—but that's all it

is. Just a possibility. I'm not sure if that is something that I'm going to do. I'm just spitballing options here. When it becomes a serious consideration, we'll sit down as a family and talk it out. I won't do anything unless we're all in agreement."

Malcolm nodded and then they began to ride across the range. The ranch's quiet beauty usually soothed his soul but today the wide, clear blue sky did nothing to calm his worries. With all of the emotions battling inside him, he felt himself unable to relax.

He inhaled deeply and tried to focus on the sound of the hooves pounding on the grass. Although he loved his life in the city, he had always known that the ranch was here waiting for him whenever he chose to return. He hadn't given much thought to what would happen to the ranch when his parents retired. Honestly, he just thought they would always be here. Now, he had to face the fact that things could be different very soon.

Had he really expected everything in his life to remain the same even as he himself changed? In a word— *yes*. Well it looked as if he was going to have to adjust his thinking. Or his behavior. Because there was a distinct possibility that his last tangible link to Aspen Creek might not be in the family for much longer.

Chapter Four

Veronica squeezed her eyes shut against the light streaming through the curtains in a vain attempt to fall back asleep. After five minutes, she forced herself to admit that she wouldn't be getting any more sleep today. Though she and her friends had stayed out until the wee hours of the morning, and despite the fact that today was her Saturday off, she wouldn't be lingering in bed this morning. Sighing, she got up, pulled up the sheets and blankets in a reasonable facsimile of a made bed, shoved her feet into her house shoes, and trudged down the stairs and to the kitchen. She pressed the button on her coffee maker and then opened the blinds. The glare of the sunlight had her wishing she hadn't done so.

"It's too late now," she muttered to herself.

Veronica had never been a morning person and she'd lived for the blissful weekends when she could sleep late. Though she'd known better, on school days, she'd hit the snooze button, lying in bed five—or ten—more minutes which frequently ended up with her racing around frantically in order to be on time for the school bus. There had been many days when she'd had to run for it while pulling on her coat, reaching the door mere seconds before the driver pulled away from the curb. Even as an adult with grown-up responsibilities, she still found it hard to force herself to get out of her comfortable bed one second before absolutely necessary. That was why her inability to sleep was even more frustrating this morning.

Especially since she knew there was a six-foot-one, two-hundred-pound, brown-skinned, dimpled reason why she couldn't sleep. Maybe it was unreasonable to blame her problem on Malcolm, but she couldn't help herself. From her perspective, it seemed like every problem in the world could be laid at his feet. At least until she'd had her coffee. Then maybe she would be in a more rational state of mind.

The aroma of her brewing coffee began filling the air and she reached inside a box on the table and pulled out a glazed doughnut. Her mother had forbidden her to eat doughnuts and other sweets as a child. According to Leslie, they would rot her teeth and they didn't have money to pay for a dentist. Now Veronica had dental insurance and she indulged in sweets whenever the spirit hit her. The sugar rush she got from just one bite was enough to keep her going until the caffeine from her coffee with hazelnut cream kicked in.

She took her mug with the words "I'd rather be reading" etched on the front and went outside and took a seat on her top back step. She would have loved to have a deck or patio, but that type of amenity was out of her price range. Her little patch of grass and stone pathway that led to her one-car garage was all the outside space that she had. But as long as she had somewhere private to sit and enjoy the summer breeze, she was happy.

After taking a few sips of coffee and polishing off

her doughnut, Veronica closed her eyes and lifted her face to the sky, letting the bright sun warm her skin. As the sun worked its magic, she let her mind wander, touching upon a subject before flitting off to the next. It wasn't long before her mind settled on Malcolm. Her eyes flew open and she attempted to swat the unwanted thought away. It didn't work. Malcolm was firmly embedded in her brain.

It wasn't fair that after all this time, he still had the ability to make her think about him. Though she tried not to, she remembered just how good he'd looked last night. No matter how often she'd forced herself to look away, her gaze had been repeatedly drawn back to him. Though she'd seen him two years ago at the bachelor auction, she was still adjusting to the new and improved Malcolm Wilson. He'd always had a nice face, but he'd been short and scrawny in school. Girls would pass by him without giving him a second look or taking the time to get to know the person inside. She'd been the only one who'd known he was a prize. Now he was every woman's dream.

Just not hers.

Oh, if she were simply a shallow woman who didn't know him and who looked at the external and ignored the internal, she could totally fall for him. But the two of them had a past. He had let her down when she'd needed him—and so he didn't deserve to clutter up her head anymore. It was her day off and she wasn't going to entertain negative thoughts.

Veronica always did her household chores and ran errands on workdays so her days off were completely open.

It often made for some long days, but it was worth it to be totally free to do whatever struck her fancy.

Veronica was still lingering over her coffee when her phone rang. She looked at the screen and then smiled. "Hi, Mom. How are you this morning?"

"Wonderful. I was wondering if you would like to have lunch this afternoon."

"Sure."

"Great. Let's meet at Rocky's Burgers. I've been craving a burger and milkshake for days."

Veronica laughed. "It's amazing how much your diet has changed since I moved out. No more vegetables for you."

"Oh, I still eat them. I just don't feel the need to set a good example by eating them all the time in front of you now that you're grown. Your diet is your responsibility."

After they confirmed the time, Veronica hung up her phone and leaned against the doorpost for a few minutes. She tried to regain her initial serenity, but her thoughts of Malcolm had ruined that, so she went back inside. She was digging in her purse for her wallet when she pulled out the letter she'd received at the library yesterday. She'd totally forgotten about it.

There wasn't a name attached to the return address and she didn't recognize the extra loopy penmanship. "Odd," she muttered.

Veronica slid her fingernail under the lip of the envelope and pulled it open. She took out the lined paper and unfolded it. After reading the first line, she dropped the letter onto the table. It was from the half sister she had never met. The daughter her father loved. The only one he acknowledged.

Her head began to pound and Veronica pressed her fingers to her temples, massaging them in a futile attempt to banish the pain. She squeezed her eyes shut as if trying to rid herself of the words she'd read. Unfortunately they were seared into her brain.

Dear Veronica,
You don't know me, but I am your sister, Bianca.
I would like to meet you in person.

There were other words written there, but Veronica didn't read them. She didn't want to. The idea of reading even one more word was out of the question. From the time Veronica had realized that her father no longer cared about her, there had been a pain in her heart. A jagged hole that he had put there. Over time, it had scabbed over but it had never completely healed. The sloppily written words had ripped off the scab leaving a painful, gaping wound.

This girl had her nerve reaching out to Veronica. Deep down, Veronica knew that Bianca wasn't responsible for the choices Walter had made, but that didn't do anything to heal the hurt she felt over the fact that Bianca had grown up with him while Veronica had grown up fatherless. Bianca had all of his attention and love. He'd been there for her birthdays and graduations. She'd seen the pictures accompanying the article about Colorado's designer couple. The house they lived in had been huge with views of the mountains from every room. Veronica's father was a famous architect and Harley, his second wife, was an interior decorator and the daughter of

a successful builder. They'd met while Veronica's father
had been working on a project. How cliché.

Not that the size of the house or the vistas mattered.
All of that was background noise to the one fact that
had mattered. Veronica's father had abandoned her and
her mother, not caring if they sank or swam. Though
he'd stopped being a father to Veronica, he'd been fully
present for his other daughter, and even for Harley's
sons from her previous marriage. She could still recall
the ache in her heart on her birthdays and each of her
graduations when she realized that once again her father
would not be coming. Her stepfather had done his best to
fill in—escorting her to her father-and-daughter dances
and taking pictures of her at basketball tournaments—
but his presence hadn't removed the sting of her father's
absence. There were just some things a girl never got
over even when she was no longer a child.

But she wouldn't let his rejection control her. She
lived her own life—and there was no place in it anymore
for her father, or for any of the family he'd chosen over
her. For her own peace of mind, keeping her distance
seemed like the wisest, safest option.

Veronica shoved the letter back into her purse, doing
her best to put her negative thoughts in there too. She
wasn't going to let that letter steal her joy. Veronica took
a soothing shower, using her favorite lilac bodywash,
dressed in a stylish summer dress and sandals, then
drove downtown. She parked and then strolled down
Main Street. As usual, there were lots of out-of-town-
ers bustling about, carrying shopping bags embossed
with the logos of the various boutiques. Their presence
didn't disturb Veronica. Quite the opposite. The vaca-

KATHY DOUGLASS 71

tioners helped Aspen Creek flourish. Since quite a few
of Veronica's friends owned their own businesses, she
knew more people meant more customers meant more
money. And their tax dollars were what made the library sustainable.

She stopped into the Sweet as Pie bakery and joined
the long line of shoppers. Now that Leslie was also willing to admit to a sweet tooth, Veronica was thrilled to
be able to treat her mother to her favorite indulgence
on any occasion.

"How are things going?" Veronica asked when it was
her turn to step up to the counter.

"Great. If I would have known how many people
wanted home-baked goods, I would have started my
own business a long time ago," Maggie said.

"I told you that your pastries were better than anything around."

"You had to say that. You're my friend," Maggie said
with a laugh.

"That's why you should have believed me. I would
never lie about something that important. The last thing I
want is for you to take a leap and then fall on your face."

"I think I knew that," Maggie said softly. "So, what
can I get you?"

"Four large walnut brownies."

"Two for you and two for your mom?" Maggie guessed.

"I really am predictable."

"You're a good daughter. Should I wrap hers?"

Veronica nodded. "She'll know what it is, but everyone likes getting beautifully wrapped gifts."

"I couldn't agree more."

Once Veronica had paid for the brownies, she took

her bag and headed out the door and continued down the street. Leslie was approaching the restaurant from the other direction and Veronica stood outside until her mother reached her.

"Right on time," Leslie said before kissing Veronica's cheek.

"Of course. My mother raised me to respect other people's time," Veronica said with a grin.

"Smart woman."

"And this is for you," Veronica said, handing over the gaily decorated gift bag.

Leslie didn't even pretend not to know what was inside. "My favorite brownies. I don't know what I ever did to deserve such a wonderful daughter."

"There are too many things to list," Veronica said. "And if I start, the restaurant will be closed before I reach the end."

Leslie smiled and they went inside. Most of the tables were occupied, but they managed to find one near the middle of the room.

"Well, it's my two favorite customers," Natalie, their waitress, said as she handed them their menus. "What can I get for you today?"

Veronica and Leslie looked at each other, smiled, and nodded. As one, they handed their menus back.

Natalie smiled. "I take it that the two of you already know what you want. Let me guess. Mushroom burgers, seasoned fries, and vanilla milkshakes."

Veronica laughed. "You guessed right."

"There wasn't a whole lot of guessing involved. I'll be back with your orders as soon as they're ready."

"I hope we aren't becoming too predictable," Leslie said after Natalie walked away.

"Because we got our usual order?"

"I don't know. Maybe."

"What makes you say something like that?" Veronica asked. "What's going on?"

"Oh, I don't know. It's just that people like some surprises in their lives. You know, variety is the spice of life and all that."

"People? Or men? Is there something going on with you and Willie?" Veronica's heart froze as she awaited her mother's answer. She really liked Willie. When he'd first started coming around, Veronica had kept him at a distance. A small part of her had been leery, afraid that he might let her down. A larger part had feared that if her father knew about Willie, he wouldn't come back as he'd promised. But Willie had been patient and understanding. He'd never tried to force a relationship with her. Over time Veronica had grown to love him and he'd made his own special place in her life.

"No. Everything is great between us. And I want it to stay that way. I don't want to get stale."

"We could always get new hairstyles," Veronica suggested. "Or maybe dye jobs. I think you would look really sexy with a rainbow on your head."

"Not a chance. I spotted a gray hair the other day and quickly yanked it out and made an appointment at the salon. Dark brown in the only color for me."

Veronica laughed. "Well, then. I remember how when I was a kid, you used to tell me that if it wasn't broken, don't mess with it. Or words to that effect."

Leslie nodded slowly. "So you're telling me to take my own advice."

"Yes. You and Willie are already perfect together. Anyone can see that he adores you whether you have gray hair or not. When he looks at you, it's obvious that you're exciting enough just as you are."

"I know." Leslie sighed. "I don't know why I'm behaving so foolishly today."

"I do. It's coming up on that anniversary." The date when Veronica's father announced that he was leaving to be with another woman, devastating Leslie and Veronica in the process.

Leslie blew out a breath. "I can't believe that after all of these years, I still let it bother me. I have a wonderful husband who I love with my whole heart and who loves me just as much. I'm happier than I've ever been. Much happier than I ever was with Walter. You would think I would be over it by now."

"Just because you're over it doesn't mean you've forgotten. You don't have amnesia after all."

"You're right." Leslie reached over and patted Veronica's hand. "Did I mention that I have a wonderful daughter?"

"That goes without saying, but I appreciate you saying it."

The waitress brought their food and they were quiet as they doctored their burgers to suit their tastes. Veronica picked up her burger and took a bite. When the flavors hit her tongue, she groaned in pleasure. Her mother did the same and they laughed together.

"Speaking of men and relationships," Leslie said with a grin, "I heard that Malcolm is back in town."

Veronica grimaced. She didn't bother to ask how her mother knew. There was a small but thorough network of gossips in town. When something—anything—happened, everyone knew about it. Malcolm returning to town, even if just for the reunion and farewell party, was out of the ordinary and therefore newsworthy. Even so, Veronica didn't want to talk about him with anyone, even her mother. Just thinking about him made her heart race and set butterflies loose in her stomach, which threatened to ruin her enjoyment of her lunch. Still, she couldn't let her mother's comment go unremarked upon.

"Yes. He's back in town. The reunion is next weekend, remember? As a matter of fact, I ran into him last night at Grady's." Veronica congratulated herself on how normal she sounded. Clearly she could discuss Malcolm like an adult even if her emotions were behaving like a lovesick teenager. She reached for her shake and her hand trembled. Apparently speaking about Malcolm was as hard on her body as it was on her emotions.

"Did you talk?"

"Of course." They'd actually had a pleasant conversation, something she would never have predicted.

"That's good. Hopefully you can become friends again. I always hoped that the two of you would fall in love."

"Really? Why?" And why did the idea not sound as ridiculous as it should?

"I guess because he was always there for you when things were hard. For a while he was the only person who could make you smile."

Veronica had never told her mother about what happened in college, and since she didn't want to ruin Leslie's good opinion of Malcolm, she saw no need to inform her now that he hadn't always been there for her. But she *could* argue against the other point—the idea that Malcolm had had some special power over her. "That's not true. I was happy when I was with my other friends."

"Maybe. But there was always something different when you were with Malcolm. You seemed…lighter. And I always thought he was good husband material. Not to mention that he lived close by at the time. I wouldn't have had to worry about you moving away."

"You don't have to worry about that anyway. I love Aspen Creek. I'm never moving away from here."

Leslie gave Veronica a long look. "I don't know if I like the sound of that."

"Why? Didn't you just say that you wanted to keep me around? Now that I've said that I'm staying, you have an issue?"

"I don't know the right words to say." Leslie took a swallow of her shake before continuing. "I love Aspen Creek and I love having you near. But I don't want you to miss out on seeing the rest of the world because you're hiding out here."

"I'm not hiding out. I'm happy with my life. I have a great job. I love the people, and I appreciate that they've always been here for me. I don't think I could replicate that relationship in another place."

"Nothing can ever be duplicated," Leslie said, her voice gentle yet firm. "But you don't have to re-create what you have here to build something new that makes you happy."

"So you want me to leave? Is this because Malcolm lives in Chicago?" Just saying the words made her shiver.

Leslie shook her head. "Nothing of the sort. I love having you here. But I want you to have a full life. I want you to be bold."

"Speaking of bold." Veronica reached into her purse and pulled out the letter that she'd gotten from her... Bianca. She hadn't intended to show it to her mother, because Leslie didn't deserve to have painful reminders of the past. But they'd already mentioned Veronica's dad and Leslie hadn't fallen apart. Besides, Veronica wanted her mother's opinion.

"What's that?"

"A letter."

"I can see that. From whom?"

Veronica couldn't force out the words, so she handed over the envelope.

Leslie didn't say anything while she read the letter. When she was finished, she folded it and stuck the paper back into the envelope then handed it back to Veronica. "So, what are you going to do?"

"Nothing. I didn't even read the whole letter and don't plan to. I'm not sure why I even showed it to you."

"Because you wanted to see how I would react?"

Veronica shrugged. "Maybe that was part of it. But mainly I can't understand why she'd send it. I'm not part of her life, she's not part of mine—and it's better for things to stay that way."

"Honestly, I don't know what she was thinking. Who knows with teenagers?" Leslie reached across the table and took Veronica's hand, giving it a gentle squeeze. "But know this. Whatever you decide to do is okay with me. I don't have a problem with you meeting her if that's what you want to do. Like it or not she's your sister."

"*Half* sister." Even that was a stretch. The girl was a stranger.

Leslie shrugged. "Still…"

"You really are quite remarkable, Mom."

She grinned. "I do have my moments."

"I'll think about what you said. But not right now. Besides, I don't think anything can change my mind. My life is fine the way it is. I don't want any complications."

And that included from Malcolm. *Especially from Malcolm.*

Veronica and Leslie finished lunch. They said their goodbyes then went their separate ways. Veronica always felt so good after spending time with her mother and she was smiling as she walked down the street. She was nearly to her car when she heard her name being called. *Evelyn Parks.* For a moment Veronica considered pretending that she hadn't heard, but she decided against it. Her mother had raised her to be considerate and respectful of her elders. Besides, Mrs. Parks was nothing if not determined. She would track Veronica to the ends of the earth if necessary in order to have whatever conversation she wanted to have.

Pasting on a smile, Veronica turned. "Hello. How are you?"

Mrs. Parks shook her head. "So disappointed. But not surprised. And hopeful because I know you'll do the right thing."

"I have no idea what you're talking about."

"Malcolm Wilson and his horrible plan for the town. He's going to sell his family ranch to some outsider to build a factory on it."

"Where did you hear that?" Evelyn Parks was known

for jumping to conclusions. Veronica couldn't count the number of times she'd gotten people all riled up because she'd spread bad information all around town.

"I heard it from the horse's mouth. He was talking about it with that guy in the diner. I couldn't believe my ears."

Veronica couldn't believe hers so they were even. "I see. That is disappointing."

"Yes, but I have hope because of you."

"Me? If what you heard is true—"

"It is true."

"Then I don't know what you expect me to do."

"Well, change his mind. You've been friends forever. If anyone can convince him to do what is right for the town, it's you."

"I don't have any influence over him. And even if I did, it's not my place to interfere in his business."

"Ordinarily I would agree with you. But this is for the good of the town. And I know you'd never view that with indifference."

"Of course not."

"Then think about it." Evelyn checked her watch. "I need to go. We'll talk again soon."

Before Veronica could reply, Evelyn had turned on her heel and walked away. Veronica didn't want to believe what she'd heard. After all, Evelyn Parks wasn't exactly a reliable witness. But Malcolm had been with a stranger. He'd even brought him to Grady's with him. Maybe there was something to the story. But even if it was true, Veronica wasn't going to get involved. On the other hand, what about the good of the town?

* * *

Malcolm stared up at the starry night. Today had been exhilarating and exhausting. It had brought back memories of his days as a teenager working the ranch beside his father. He worked long days now, but his job was more mental than physical. It didn't involve tossing scores of heavy bales of hay and his body ached from the unfamiliar activity. Even though he worked out regularly, lifting weights and running a few miles a day, this was a different kind of tired.

He stretched and then smiled. Despite his tired muscles, he felt the same contentment he always felt when he was home. His happiness would be complete if he was sharing this beautiful night with someone special. One person immediately came to mind. *Veronica.*

It was Saturday night. No doubt she had a date or was hanging out with some of her friends. Going by the way Kristy had been trying to get her to talk to him last night, he didn't think that she had a boyfriend. Real friends didn't encourage you to cheat.

But they did try to get you to patch up a friendship. He whipped out his phone and then called Kristy. The three of them had been close before. Though he and Veronica were no longer friends, he and Kristy still kept in touch. He called her cell and after a greeting and a few minutes of small talk, he got down to the reason that he'd called her.

"Um. I was wondering if Veronica was seeing anyone."

"Why, are you thinking about starting something with her?"

"What? No." That wasn't entirely true. He had been thinking about it...and he'd decided it was a terrible idea.

"I want to get back to the way things were before, if possible. But if she's dating someone, he might not want me coming around. I don't want to cause problems for her."

To him, any man who tried to control who his girlfriend could and could not be friends with was a jerk and not worthy of any woman's love, but Veronica's opinion might be different, and he didn't want to make her life more difficult.

"Really? So it would be okay with you if she was dating someone else."

"Yes." Malcolm kept his voice calm, even though the very notion of Veronica with another man roiled his stomach.

"You're in luck. She hasn't dated anyone seriously in a while. And judging from the way things went last night, you might be on your way to becoming friends again."

Things must have looked different from where Kristy was sitting, because it hadn't looked that way to him.

They talked a few more minutes before they ended the call. He had almost four weeks before he had to go back to Chicago. That was plenty of time to win over Veronica.

He hoped.

Chapter Five

The following Thursday, Malcolm stood outside the library, staring at the three-story redbrick building where Veronica worked. He'd wanted to get in touch with her before now, but he'd been busy around the ranch. One of the ranch hands had quit and Malcolm had been filling in. Yet as busy as he'd been, he hadn't been able to get Veronica out of his head.

Malcolm hoped he didn't come across as a stalker, but he wanted the chance to talk with her in person. The library was a public place, so technically he had as much of a right to be here as anyone else. Even so, the last thing he wanted to do was make her feel uncomfortable around him.

Maybe he should wait and hope to run into her naturally. There were only a few places that people their age hung out, so there was a chance that he could run into Veronica in one of them eventually. Besides, he knew he would see her at the reunion. But waiting passively would only add to his stress level. And there were already enough concerns weighing on him as it was. He resolved that he'd go in and try to talk to her. If it turned out that Veronica didn't want to talk to him, then he would respect her wishes and leave.

Malcolm stepped inside and immediately felt at ease. The open space felt welcoming. Colorful posters advertising a family movie night hung beside a chart listing upcoming activities for children. He had no doubt that this was Veronica's doing. She'd always been so creative, finding ways to make even the most mundane task interesting. He'd always believed she could have had a successful career in marketing if she'd chosen to go that route.

There was a large circular desk a few yards away from the entrance and Malcolm approached it. He smiled as he drew nearer. Veronica was standing behind the desk, listening intently as a little boy talked about the book he held in his arms. The boy's excitement rang in his voice.

"I'm going to read it every night," the boy was saying. "It's a chapter book because I'm a good reader."

"Yes you are," Veronica replied. Her voice was significantly quieter than the boy's and Malcolm needed to step closer in order to hear it. The familiar warmth in her tone brought back happy memories of the hours they'd spent together, discussing every topic under the sun. He could stand here all day and listen to her talk, but that wouldn't get their relationship back on track.

When she finished helping the little boy check out his book, Veronica glanced in his direction, a warm smile of welcome on her beautiful face. When she realized that it was him standing there, her eyes widened and her smile faded away. She inhaled and his eyes were drawn to her perky breasts. He'd seen her several times recently and should be used to how sexy she was. Even so, his heart skipped a beat. He still couldn't believe he hadn't noticed before just how desirable she was. He must have been sleepwalking through life before now. But his reaction was totally inappropriate for someone who only wanted to be friends. He needed to find a way to stop lusting after her body before she noticed.

Veronica looked at him, holding his gaze but not speaking. He realized that he was going to have to start the conversation. "It looks like you have quite the enthusiastic customer."

"Terrence is a good reader. His mom and dad have been bringing him in a few times a week for books since he was a little guy. He finishes them very quickly, so we decided that it was time to start him on chapter books. They're hoping to decrease their visits."

"Or maybe he just has a crush on the pretty librarian."

Veronica actually blushed and Malcolm was glad to see it. In his memories, Veronica had never received the male attention that she deserved. Of course, time could have changed that. Perhaps the men of Aspen Creek now appreciated her grace and beauty. But even if that was the case, it never hurt to remind a woman that she was attractive.

"I don't think that's it. He just loves to read."

"Do you have time to show me around?" Malcolm asked, mentally crossing his fingers. She could refuse. After all, it wasn't as if he hadn't been here before.

Veronica hesitated.

"It looks different than I remember. I would love to see the changes you made."

Veronica nodded, a smile playing on the edges of her lips. "I suppose I have time."

"Thanks." He'd been right to seek her out here. The library was her happy place. She'd be more inclined to talk to him here than almost anywhere else.

She stepped from behind the desk and came to stand beside him. Dressed in a pink cotton blouse and pink-and-white-striped skirt that floated to a place above her knees, she looked absolutely stunning. Her calves were tone and, though her legs weren't long, they were gorgeous. Her low-heeled sandals didn't add much to her five foot five inches, so the top of her head only reached his shoulder.

"Is there any place in particular that you want to see?"

"Not really. If you don't have time to show me everything, then show me your favorite spots. That way when my parents mention one of your new initiatives, I'll be able to picture it and you better."

She stopped midstep, one foot in the air, and looked at him, an odd expression on her face. "You and your parents talk about me?"

"Sure. But not in a bad way, of course," he hastened to assure her. "My parents think the world of you. I just like to keep up with what you're up to."

She blinked and shook her head in the familiar manner that meant she was trying to work out something that confused her. He didn't speak, giving her time to process his words until she came up with a satisfactory answer. "Why?"

"Why what?"

"Why would you want to know how I was doing? Why would you even care?"

He sighed. "Because you were my friend, Veronica. I know that I made mistakes in the past, but I never stopped caring about you. You might not believe this, but despite my behavior in the past, I still cared. There has never been a time that I didn't want the absolute best for you. If my mom or dad would have told me that you were in trouble, I would have been on the first plane home."

Veronica blinked. "I don't know what to say to that."

"Say whatever you're thinking."

She glanced around and then frowned. Although the people sitting at nearby tables weren't listening to them, clearly she didn't want to take the risk that their conversation might be overheard.

"You know, we can table this discussion for later or skip it altogether if that's your preference. We can talk about books and library programs or whatever subject you prefer," Malcolm offered.

"That is so like you."

"That doesn't sound like a compliment."

"It isn't." She folded her arms across her chest and compressed her full lips. She was clearly annoyed but he didn't understand why. He'd been trying to be compassionate and considerate.

Well, since that had failed, he might as well keep going. "What do you mean?"

"You bring up a painful subject and then instead of discussing it, you immediately start to walk away from it. Or you try to make me the bad guy for wanting to keep talking about it."

"What?" He shook his head. That was some twisted thinking, even for her. "I'm sorry if my words came across that way. That's not at all what I intended. You seemed uncomfortable and I was just trying to make it better."

"And avoiding a tough conversation is your way of making it better?" she scoffed.

"Okay. Let's talk. But not here. We need more privacy. This is your territory, so I'll go wherever you want. Just lead the way."

Before answering, Veronica checked her watch. "It's just about lunchtime. Give me a couple of minutes and then we can go out."

That was even better than he had dared to hope. They were going to share a meal. When he'd walked in here, the best he had hoped for was a minute or two of Veronica's time. A pleasant word from her would have been a win. Of course, he still hadn't gotten that pleasant word yet.

"Sure. I'll wait right here for you." Malcolm clicked his heels together before giving Veronica a mock salute.

She shook her head, a reluctant smile on her face. "Don't get into any trouble."

Malcolm watched as she walked away, a gentle sway to her hips that he couldn't help admiring. She really was a stunning woman who'd make some man very happy someday. He just hoped he never had to hear about it.

A few minutes later, Veronica returned. She'd brushed her glorious hair and now it tumbled in large curls around her shoulders, bouncing with each step she took. She'd put on lipstick and now her lips were a shade of red that looked wonderful against her brown skin. The urge to kiss her and smear that lipstick struck him even though he knew that would be a colossal mistake. Hadn't he decided not to complicate their relationship? Especially when he was finally beginning to break through her reserves.

"Ready?" he asked unnecessarily.

"Yes." She draped her purse strap across her torso.

"Where do you want to go?" Malcolm asked as he held the door for her.

"It's really nice. Do you want to get something at the park?"

"They have food in the park? Like food trucks?"

Veronica laughed. "You really have been gone a long time. There are a few vendors selling sandwiches, hot dogs, and walking tacos. And there's an ice cream truck. I'm sure our little setup doesn't compare with Chicago."

"Maybe not in scale. But that doesn't make it lesser by any means."

She smiled and he realized that he'd said something right. Finally. "What do you have a taste for?"

"I would love to have a walking taco," she said.

"I was thinking the same thing."

They left the library and began walking down the street. The sun was shining in the clear blue sky and a gentle breeze blew. As they strolled down the paved sidewalk, he felt his heart rate slow as the pleasure of being in Veronica's presence began to affect him.

As they neared the downtown area with the shops and boutiques, the streets grew crowded with tourists. A resident winter Olympian emerged from the diner and there was an audible gasp before fans rushed over to get an autograph. Although the citizens of Aspen Creek were used to seeing their famous neighbors around town and barely reacted to their presence, the tourists weren't nearly so blasé.

They turned a corner and were walking past a restaurant when the sign drew his attention and he stopped walking. "What is this?"

"It's The World-Famous Aspen Creek Grill. It opened up about a year ago."

Malcolm looked up at the sign in front of the building and guffawed. "Is that the actual name? *The World-Famous Aspen Creek Grill.*"

Veronica nodded.

"Talk about a lack of humility."

"Believe me, the food totally lives up to the name and then some."

"I don't doubt that it's good. But world-famous? How? I've never heard of this place."

"Oh. *Talk about a lack of humility.* It's not famous unless Malcolm Wilson has heard about it."

"Oh no," Malcolm sputtered. That wasn't at all what he'd meant. He was trying to clean up his mess when he realized Veronica was laughing. It was a merry sound that warmed his heart. He'd gladly be the butt of her jokes to hear it.

She nudged his shoulder. "I'm just giving you a hard time, Malcolm."

"Good, because the minute I said it, I realized how vain I sounded."

"We can come here one day and you can let me know if you think it lives up to the name."

"I'm ready whenever you are," Malcolm said, trying to sound casual even though he was jumping with joy on the inside.

She grinned at him—and then seemed to catch herself, because the smile wiped off her face as if it had never been there. His own smile faded in return. Every time he thought they were starting to get back to being friends... But then, maybe that was the problem. They had been friends for so long that it was easy to slide back into the rhythms of laughing and teasing each other. But there was still a tangle of unresolved issues between them, and until they sorted it all out, he doubted Veronica would slip into friendliness with him for more than a minute or two at a time before pulling back again.

They started walking again and in under five minutes they reached the park. Even though Aspen Creek was a small town, it had quite a few parks. This one, in the center of town, was the largest of them all. Playground equipment filled one end and children's laughter floated over to them. "What's with the artwork?" he asked, pointing at several large and colorful sculptures spaced around the grassy area.

"It's part of the summer series. Every couple of weeks there's something new. Winter is really busy for obvious reasons. The summer events are one more way to attract vacationers. Of course, the locals like it too."

They walked to the food trucks. Veronica led the way to a purple truck advertising Mexican food. Several people were in line, and Malcolm and Veronica took their places at the back. Judging from the number of people sitting at the tables or on the benches, the food trucks were popular. The town businesses were doing well and it didn't look like they were having problems hiring people. He just wished that would translate to the ranch. Perhaps then his father wouldn't feel so pressed.

"What will you have?" a smiling teenager asked when they stepped up to his window.

Veronica gave her order and then opened her purse.

Malcolm placed his hand on hers, stopping her. "I have this."

"That's not necessary."

"I insist." Malcolm turned to the teenager, who was looking between them. "Our orders are together. I'll have the same thing." He opened his wallet, pulled out a few bills and handed them over to the teen, putting an end to the conversation.

"Thank you," Veronica said, stiffly polite.

Malcolm nodded. He took his change and they stepped away, taking a seat at a table beneath a purple-and-green-striped umbrella. When his ticket number was called, he got up and grabbed their food and drinks. He handed Veronica her bag and then sat across from her.

"Ready to pick up that conversation again?" Malcolm asked. He dug his fork into his Fritos bag, stirring the seasoned ground beef, cheese, chips and lettuce into a delicious mix.

"No." She set her bag on the table then blew out a breath. "Yes."

"It won't ruin your appetite, will it?"

"No. What about yours?"

"No." He looked into her eyes. "Why were you surprised to hear that I asked my parents about you? Why are you surprised to learn that I care about you?"

Veronica took a sip of her soda before folding her hands into her lap. When she realized she was twisting her fingers—her worst, most obvious tell that she was unsettled—she flattened her hands onto her thighs. This was ridiculous. She exhaled. "I guess because when I needed you, you turned your back on me. I can take a hint. That was a clear sign that I no longer mattered to you."

"You're talking about when we were in college."

"Yes."

"I know I should have handled things better, but at the time, I couldn't think of anything else. That was the last day of pledge week. I couldn't leave—or at least, that was how it felt to me then. Looking back now, I wish I'd made different choices. I'm sorry that I hurt and disappointed you. I can't undo what happened, but I can promise you that I've grown up a lot since then. I really want to be friends again. Tell me what I need to do to make that happen."

Veronica heard the plea in Malcolm's voice. She recognized the sincerity and something inside her shifted. The pain of that day was still in her heart, but maybe she should stop feeding it. Perhaps then it would starve and die. "Okay, thank you for apologizing. I appreciate that you're sorry, and I know that you're not the same person you were then, but…"

"But that doesn't automatically fix things, does it?" Malcolm asked with a sigh.

"No, it doesn't," she admitted. "Maybe it should, but I can't help the way I feel—and that hurt doesn't go away so easily."

"Do you think it ever will?"

"Maybe?" She felt conflicted. "I don't know why it's so hard for me to get over this. Everybody makes mistakes. I know I've made my share."

"I don't know either. Maybe because we were so close and you had such high expectations of me. Maybe that's why everything is outsized."

"That's probably it." Or maybe she was conflating the pain of her father's rejection with what she perceived was Malcolm's. It had happened at the same time.

"But we're older now and you've obviously survived whatever it was you were going through. I know you said it still hurts, but maybe we can work through that together. Is it possible to get back to where we were before? Can we pick up where we left off?"

"I don't know if I can do that."

"Oh."

His smile faded and regret churned her stomach. There was a part of her that truly wanted to just get over it, but there was something holding her back. Learning that her father had completely—and publicly—erased her existence from his life had been painful. At the time, it had felt as if Malcolm had done the same. Still, holding on to hurt was just making her miserable. And she had missed having Malcolm as a friend. Perhaps she could fake it until she could make it. That would show growth. And she was all about personal growth.

"But I'm willing to try," she announced. "I'm ready to bury the hatchet."

"As long as it's not in my head."

"No." She laughed. "Nothing like that."

"Then I'm all for it."

Veronica dug her fork into her walking taco, pleased at the tastes and textures that hit her tongue. The food really was good. She didn't eat here often but maybe she would change that. Of course, she could be enjoying the food so much because she was with Malcolm. Now that she and Malcolm had cleared the air, she could see him more clearly. Not just physically—although he was still gorgeous—but inside to the man that he had become.

Though she'd seen him when he'd participated in the bachelor auction, she'd been too angry to actually look at him. The last few times she'd seen him, she'd done everything in her power to keep from noticing anything positive about him. She'd been so determined to hold on to her anger that she'd been blind to everything else.

Now she was free to see Malcolm as he was now. She was looking forward to getting to know his personality—seeing what had changed and what had stayed the same. But the changes she couldn't ignore were to his body. Long gone was the short, skinny boy she remembered. His upper body was well-developed and each of his muscles was massive. His stomach was flat and she could only imagine that he had a perfect six-pack. He'd always possessed strong legs, and given the strength of his upper body, she had no reason to believe that had changed with time.

She allowed her eyes to travel over his body, and when her gaze reached his face, she realized that he had been aware of her inspection the entire time. One side of his lips lifted in a sexy smile and he winked. Her skin warmed and she forced herself not to look away. As she stared into his eyes, she saw no sign of mockery. Instead, there was only warmth. And...was that a hint of desire for her in return? No, that couldn't be right. Malcolm wasn't attracted to her. The idea was ludicrous. He'd never seen her as anything other than a friend and there was no reason to think that his feelings had changed.

"So, what have you been up to?" Veronica asked. Initially she'd just been trying to fill the silence, but once she'd asked the question she realized that she really wanted to know. She was curious about his life in Chicago. She'd often wondered how his life was going, but she'd never given herself the freedom to ask anyone. She knew his parents would have told her, but she also knew that they would have let Malcolm know that she'd asked about him. Her pride would never have permitted that.

"Work mostly. It's good. And I love Chicago."

"What's it like?"

"Great. There is so much to do. You can never get bored. If you like it, we have it. Whatever *it* may be. Museums, sports, lakefront, bike paths, theater. Shopping. Although I have to admit I don't do much of that."

Veronica laughed. "You never did care about clothes."

"Nope. I was happy with my jeans, boots, and shirts. A hoodie if it was cold despite my mother's nagging to put on a coat."

"Your wardrobe has taken a step up from high school days."

He brushed his hand over his shirt, drawing her attention back to his muscular chest. Ridiculously, her mouth was suddenly dry and slight tingles skipped down her spine. She really hated that her body had a mind of its own. "I may have upgraded for work or special occasions such as this, but the rest of the time I'm dressed comfortably."

Her heart skipped a beat at his reference. Did he really think eating lunch with her in the park was a special occasion? No, of course not. He was just flattering her to keep on her good side. He was definitely smoother than he'd been in high school.

Before she could think of a suitable reply, he contin-

ued, "Veronica, you, on the other hand, are too glamor-
ous for words. Of course, you always dressed nice when
we were kids."

"Maybe when we were really young. After my father
left, my clothes were secondhand. My mother made little
changes to make them look special."

"They looked good because of the person wearing
them."

Laughing, Veronica shook her head. "Are you flirting with me?"

"No. I hope not." Malcolm sounded positively ap-
palled at the notion. Clearly any attraction was one-
sided. Message received. Of course since she was of the
same mind, it shouldn't be a problem. So why did it hurt
to think that he was rejecting her?

"This is delicious, by the way," Malcolm said.

"Is it as good as the food trucks you have in Chicago?"

"Chicago has lots of good food trucks there, but this
is right up there with them. I'm impressed."

"I'll be sure to let them know."

"Have you ever considered coming to Chicago?" Malcolm asked, his tone extremely casual. "I'll take you
around and you can see for yourself."

"Oh, I don't know," she replied quickly, shooting
down the idea before it could take hold. It did carry
some unexpected appeal.

"Why not?"

"It just doesn't seem like the kind of place I would
like. It's so...crowded." That sounded lame even to her.

"Not everywhere. Believe it or not, there are places
that remind me of Aspen Creek."

"You're kidding me."

"I'm not. It's not all high-rises and concrete. There are lots of small neighborhoods that have a sense of community. There are lots of parks and the lakefront is second to none." He must have been able to tell that she was unpersuaded because he continued. "At least think about coming for a visit."

She shrugged.

"Do you ever go on vacation?"

"Not really. The only time I've ever spent away was when I went to college. It was okay. But I missed home. It turned out that everything I need is right here."

"Maybe. But there are other places that might have what you need too. They might have things you didn't even know you needed. Don't limit yourself to one small town. Not when there is an entire world to see."

She knew he didn't mean it negatively, but his words hit her the wrong way. "Are you saying that Aspen Creek is not good enough for you now?"

He raised his hands in front of him as if trying to ward off her anger. Too late. "That's not at all what I meant. I'm just saying that there is more to see in the world than what Aspen Creek holds."

"That's the difference between you and me. I'm not looking for anything more than what is in my backyard. I don't need something bigger. I'm happy with my life. I have good friends. A fulfilling job. I'm not willing to abandon what I have in search of some elusive 'better.'"

He opened his mouth as if to reply. Instead, he simply stuck in his forkful of meat and Fritos and chewed. When he spoke again, it was to ask about her mother. Veronica wasn't sure how she felt about the way he'd changed the subject. Once, they would have had a spirited discussion, disagreeing the entire time, and remained friends with no hard feelings. Now it appeared that Malcolm was walking on eggshells, being more polite than the situation warranted. On the one hand, it was good to move past that tense moment. On the other, it felt as if he had decided it wasn't worth trying to change her mind. That she wasn't worth it.

She sighed. "My mom is great. She's really happy with my stepfather."

"That's good. She deserves to be happy. Be sure to give her my best."

Veronica and Malcolm finished their lunch in silence and then dumped their trash into the can. There was a pall hanging over them that neither of them seemed to know how to remove. Perhaps even with both of them trying to move on from the past, they couldn't go back to being friends again. That thought was heartbreaking, but Veronica couldn't ignore what was staring her in the face.

They couldn't be friends again.

Chapter Six

Veronica was only slightly surprised to see the envelope on her desk at work the following day. The fact that she hadn't responded to the earlier one apparently hadn't dissuaded the teen. In the first letter, she'd included her cell phone number and said that Veronica could call her anytime. Again she emphasized the desire to meet her *big sister*. Just reading those two words made Veronica frustrated. Who was this person to try to create a familial relationship? They weren't sisters. They had never been. Nor would they ever be.

Veronica dropped the envelope into the garbage can and then turned on her computer. The missive called to her. Though she felt like five kinds of fools, she pulled it out of the trash and tore open the envelope. It would bother her all day not to know what was in the letter.

The letter started much the same way as the other one. She introduced herself as Veronica's sister and again expressed a desire to meet. Once more she described herself and mentioned her hobbies. She liked riding horses although she had only been riding a couple of times since she didn't live close to stables. She would love to work on a dude ranch. She liked sewing and knitting and often made her own clothes. Her friends really liked the clothes. Perhaps she could make something for Veronica?

Did this girl really think that she could rewrite the past and create one that fit her view of the world? Was she intending on photoshopping herself into Veronica's life as if she'd been there all along? Though it might be unfair, Veronica had no more interest in connecting with Bianca than she did with Harley or their shared father. She didn't bear the girl any ill will, but she had no desire to see her to talk with her. Even just thinking about her brought up feelings Veronica would much rather do without. In short, Bianca was not someone she ever wanted to share air with.

"Not in this lifetime," she muttered to herself.

"Did you say something?" Helen Watson asked.

Veronica looked up and smiled at her mentor. "Just talking to myself."

Helen pulled out the chair across from Veronica and sat down. "There was a time when you would talk to me. Do you need to do that now?"

"No. I suppose I should get used to not having you around." The idea was unpleasant. Helen Watson had been a godsend. A second mother.

"Arizona isn't that far. And even then, I'll only be a phone call away."

"I know. But it won't be the same around here without you. You always know the right thing to do and say."

"So do you. Veronica, look around. You've single-handedly created a children and youth program that is the envy of the state."

"You helped."

"No. I encouraged. The ideas and effort were yours. That's why you were named librarian of the year."

Veronica smiled at the praise, then sighed. "Thanks, Helen. Everyone is going to miss you and Mr. Watson."

Helen laughed. "I see you still can't bring yourself to call Barry by his first name."

"There are some rules that are unbreakable. He will always be my high school principal."

"I suppose that's an acceptable answer."

"Is he excited about the party?" Mr. Watson had been a very popular principal. He'd created an environment where every student felt loved and had the freedom to achieve their goals. To his way of thinking, the students were his children, which made them one big family.

Helen smiled. "He is. He still can't believe that all of his past students are actually holding a farewell party slash school reunion for him."

"Our library family would have held a big party for you too."

"You know I'm not much for big shindigs. That's too many people at one time for me. I was perfectly happy with our little luncheon. The bracelet was a nice touch."

Although Helen had insisted she didn't need a party, the other librarians had gotten together last week and hosted a get-together for her. They'd had the meal catered and invited current and past volunteers and employees to attend.

"We were glad to do it. It was our small way of letting you know how much you mean to us."

"Are you excited about the reunion?" Helen asked, switching the subject. As usual, she didn't like to talk about herself.

"I am." It would be good to see the classmates that she hadn't seen for years. She imagined they all had great stories to tell. Especially Shayna Givens. Shayna had become a big star their sophomore year. Originally part of a girl singing group, she'd quickly left them behind after their first hit and struck out on her own. Now she was a superstar who went by one name.

Veronica had been surprised when she'd RSVP'd *yes* to the reunion. She hadn't stepped foot in Aspen Creek since the last day of classes senior year. She'd already been a star and hadn't bothered to attend the graduation ceremony. Instead, she'd gone on a world tour not long after. Her family had sold their little house and begun to travel with her. Now her parents lived in California in the big house that Shayna had purchased for them.

"I imagine that you'll be happy to see everyone. Or *almost* everyone."

Laughter burst from Veronica's mouth. Helen had been her confidante in the tough years. Veronica hadn't wanted to burden her mother—who already had enough on her shoulders—with more problems, but there had been things Veronica hadn't been able to keep to herself. Helen had provided a nonjudgmental ear. She'd also given sage advice. Their relationship had grown closer over the years. "You can say that."

"And Malcolm is still here," Helen said softly.

"He is."

"The present will be a lot happier if you let go of the past."

"I'm doing my best to work through the pain. I'm not still holding a grudge."

"That's progress."

"I'm just not sure I can trust him again."

"You won't know unless you give him a chance to prove himself. What's the worst that could happen?"

"He breaks my heart again."

"You're not the same fragile child you were before. You've been through a lot and come out on the other side. You can handle anything." Helen gave Veronica a long look before leaving her alone to ponder those words of wisdom.

The rest of the day sped by quickly and by the time Veronica arrived home she was practically vibrating with excitement. She sang the school fight song as she showered and dressed for the party that night. The committee had requested that everyone dress in the school colors of black, gold, or red. She had purchased a red minidress and black sandals especially for tonight. She'd splurged on gold earrings and bracelets to complete the outfit. Now as she stood in front of a mirror, she smiled. She looked fantastic if she said so herself. She was going to wow Malcolm.

That thought shook her and her breath caught. She shouldn't care one bit what Malcolm thought about her appearance. They weren't in a relationship. He was just another one of the alumni attending the festivities. She reminded herself of that fact numerous times as she drove down the street, but she never quite managed to convince herself.

The party was being held in the high school gym. Although Veronica had not been on the decorating committee, she'd seen some of the renderings. Even knowing what to expect, her mouth dropped open in awe when she stepped inside. Balloons in the school colors had been used to create huge arrangements that lined the walls and formed arches over the doors. Other arches were set up around the room for alumni to take pictures. Two photographers were already at work, capturing memories. Red-and-gold centerpieces were on the round tables which were covered with black cloths.

Tonight was a plus-one event, so former students could bring their spouses or significant others. Since there was no one special in her life she'd come alone. Veronica had just signed in and was attaching her name tag to her dress when Malcolm walked in. Knowing that he was going to be here tonight, she'd steeled herself against the possibility of seeing him with another woman. She was about to step away when he called her name. Having no choice, she waited while he walked over to the table and gave his name to the current chemistry teacher, who happened to be their former classmate.

"As if I wouldn't recognize you," Hillary said, handing over his name tag. "I'm still disappointed I was outbid on you in the bachelor auction two years ago. I was hoping to bid on you again this year. Imagine my disappointment when you weren't there," she said with a chuckle.

"One time was enough for me," Malcolm said, his eyes moving from Hillary and landing on Veronica. The mirth dancing in his eyes sent a shiver down Veronica's spine.

"I don't blame you," Hillary said. "I wouldn't have been bold enough to enter even once."

"We did raise a lot of money for charity," Veronica felt compelled to point out.

"True," Hillary agreed. "You're all set, Malcolm. You two have a good time."

"No plus-one for you?" Veronica wanted to call the words back the minute they fell out of her mouth. She didn't want Malcolm to get the idea that she cared about his love life.

"No. No matter how friendly the people are, class reunions can be insular. Outsiders just won't get the inside jokes or references to past events. The stories won't resonate with them the same way they do to the people who lived them."

She nodded. "I always feel sorry for new friends who don't know our old stories. It's hard to catch up."

"Luckily that isn't the case for us. I would much rather get reacquainted with old friends with someone by my side who was there." He gave her a challenging look. He could probably tell she'd been planning to walk away after a minute of small talk. But she couldn't do that now. He would think that she was too afraid of her feelings to be around him.

"Then it looks like we are of one mind."

He held out his arm. "Ready?"

After hesitating briefly, she placed her hand on his bicep. His muscle was hard and her fingers tingled at the contact. Her eyes flew to his and her heart skipped a beat. If anyone had told her that she would have such a physical reaction to Malcolm Wilson, she'd have laughed in their faces. She'd always known he was one of a kind, but her feelings had never veered from friendship. Now that she was experiencing serious attraction, she didn't find it remotely funny. "I want to speak to Mr. Watson before it gets too crowded."

"That's a good idea."

There was a line of people waiting to speak with the guest of honor and Malcolm and Veronica joined in. They chatted with another couple who'd attended school about a decade before them, laughing at the story they told about the principal in the beginning of his career. When they finally reached the front of the line, Veronica sighed with relief. Malcolm's cologne was subtle and mixed with his natural scent was totally intoxicating. It had taken maximum effort to hold up her end of the conversation without getting distracted.

Mr. Watson smiled as he looked at the two of them. "Well, if it isn't two of my favorite students."

Malcolm laughed. "I bet you've already said that a hundred times tonight."

"Probably. But I've meant it every time." Malcolm and Mr. Watson shook hands. "How are things in Chicago, Malcolm?"

Malcolm's eyes widened in obvious surprise. "You recognize me? And you know where I live?"

"Of course. I remember all of my students and I do my best to keep up with them. I like to know how their lives turned out. I might be older than I was when you were in school, but my mind is just as sharp."

"I never doubted your mind. But you were principal for thirty-five years. That's a whole lot of students to remember. And to keep track of."

"It's all about relationships," Mr. Watson said, his gaze including both Malcolm and Veronica. "Think about it. I know something about each of you. We spoke in the hallways or at lunch at least once a week for four years. That's a lot of conversations. I know that you were best friends all throughout high school. Right?"

Veronica and Malcolm exchanged looks and then nodded. "I interacted with all of the other students the same way. When you have a real relationship, it survives the passage of time. It survives distance and disappointments. You don't suddenly forget what that person meant to you."

Those words struck Veronica in the heart, and her chest began to ache. Did those words hold a special message for her? There were scores of other people waiting to speak with Mr. Watson, so she nodded and then walked away beside Malcolm. Why did it seem as if everyone was conspiring against her? Why was everyone trying to remind her of how great things had been with Malcolm? It was as if they had a vested interest in her happiness.

"Mr. Watson really is amazing," Malcolm said, clearly unaware of her inner turmoil. "I suppose that's why people have come from all over the country for this party."

Before Veronica could reply, a hush came over the crowd followed by a loud buzz. She turned to the doors in time to see Shayna enter the gymnasium. Dressed in a black blouse and a gold skirt, she looked quite elegant. Veronica knew that Shayna said she was coming, but a part of her had doubted it. Shayna was an international superstar. She regularly rubbed elbows with A-list celebrities. Heck, she was an A-lister, so it had seemed highly unlikely that she would attend a small-town reunion.

Shayna stopped and spoke with the people that had suddenly swarmed her. Although Veronica had expected her to travel with an entourage, there wasn't one. Only

Hank Morrow, the sheriff and one of their former class-mates, was by her side. A look passed between Hank and Shayna and Veronica wondered what that was about. By the time she was in high school, Veronica's life had returned to some semblance of normalcy. Leslie had a steady, well-paying job and the two of them were living in a nice house. Even so, Veronica had never forgotten the lessons she'd learned during those hard years when they'd struggled to make ends meet. As a result, she'd been focused on her education and athletics, preparing herself to be self-sufficient. She hadn't kept up with gossip, so she really didn't know if there had been anything going on between Hank and Shayna.

She did know that Hank had been a star football player in high school and college. He'd even played in the NFL for several seasons. He and Veronica hadn't been friends in high school but he was always cordial now when they met. He parted the crowd and helped to steer Shayna into the line to meet with Mr. Watson.

Veronica was trying to think of a way to get away from Malcolm without being obvious when Kristy approached them juggling three cups of punch. She handed one each to Malcolm and Veronica then took a sip from the one she still held. "Looks like the gang's all here."

"The Three Musketeers," Malcolm said with a laugh.

Veronica couldn't help but smile as her friends reminisced about fun times they'd shared. Being with them had helped Veronica survive the rough times.

They sat at a table together and reminisced while they sipped their punch. The anger and hurt Veronica had felt at Malcolm faded and she wondered if their friendship was as recoverable as everyone suggested. Maybe for-giveness and an honest conversation really were enough to begin healing. She thought of the years they'd lost be-cause of her hurt feelings and grudge and suddenly her eyes swam with tears. The last thing she wanted to do was cry in front of her friends, so she rose.

"Excuse me. I'll be right back." She jumped up and hurried to the ladies' room before either Malcolm or Kristy could comment.

Veronica stepped into the ladies' room and blew out a big breath as she headed for the sinks. Shayna was al-ready there, staring at her reflection. She was beautiful and not a curly hair was out of place.

Shayna turned, a smile on her face. "You're looking good, Veronica."

"I was just thinking the same about you. You look like the cover of a magazine."

Shayna's lip twisted into a frown. "I guess after a while, you get used to piling on the paint. It becomes second nature, you know?"

That was an odd statement and Veronica didn't know what to say. She and Shayna hadn't been close friends although there hadn't been any animosity between them. Back then, Shayna had been traveling a lot and hadn't been in town on the weekends. She'd missed most of the football games and school dances. Veronica smiled and then touched up her lipstick. "One thing I can say, the bathrooms haven't changed."

Shayna laughed. "No. Take it from me, high school bathrooms are the same all over."

"You must have seen a lot of them back then."

"Yes." Shayna smiled wistfully. "I spent a lot of time

at other high schools performing at their dances. I would have given anything to be here for one of ours."

"Really?"

Shayna nodded. "You and Malcolm and Kristy were so close back then. You always had each other's backs. I was a little bit jealous of your group."

"You were?" Veronica couldn't keep the shock from her voice.

"Didn't you know?"

"Not really." Veronica couldn't imagine anyone being jealous of her life. "You were famous. You had a number one song. The radio station played it all the time. You were on TV. Everybody wanted to be like you."

Shayna smiled, but it looked forced. And sad. "I guess it's human nature to want what other people have. Anyway, I suppose we should get back to celebrating Mr. Watson."

"How long are you going to be in town?" Veronica asked, hoping to remove the sorrow from Shayna's eyes.

"I don't know." A shadow passed over Shayna's face and she seemed haunted. Veronica didn't read the tabloids but she did see them in the aisle at the grocery store. Shayna's face occasionally graced the cover although she seemed to shun the spotlight more than most superstars.

"Do you want to join us at our table?"

Shayna smiled—a genuine one this time. "I would love to."

Veronica led the way as they walked through the gymnasium. Several people snapped pictures or shot videos with their cell phones, but other than sighing, Shayna didn't react. Malcolm and Kristy welcomed Shayna into their group and before long the four of them were laughing as they talked about the teachers they'd had.

"Do you mind if I join you?" Hank asked, coming up to their table and standing behind the empty chair beside Shayna.

"By all means," Malcolm said, and the others nodded. "I think we could use another man. The women are outnumbering me."

"And you love it," Kristy said.

"Well, yeah," Malcolm admitted.

"Thanks," Hank said as he pulled out the chair and sat. Before long, dinner was served accompanied by speeches. Videos and photos were shown of Mr. Waston throughout his career, first as a teacher and then as a principal. After dessert was finished, Mr. Watson stood and thanked everyone for coming. Then he thanked Helen for standing by him through the years. He gave a heartfelt speech sprinkled with humorous anecdotes and sentimental recollections. He then concluded it with the words he'd said over the loudspeaker to students every day for years. "Be kind to each other. Be kind to yourselves. If you do that, you'll make the world a better place."

As one, the audience rose and applauded as he and Helen walked from the stage and out of the gymnasium one last time.

"The end of an era," Veronica said softly.

Malcolm nodded in agreement at Veronica's comment. It applied not only to Mr. Watson but to Malcolm's life too. One by one his ties to Aspen Creek were weakening and his connection was growing more tenuous with each passing day. Sitting here with his former classmates who'd once been his best friends, he realized all that he had missed out on by not coming back more often. He'd let his friendships fade away as if these people hadn't been the most important part of his life at one time. Years had passed since he'd seen most of them. If he and his parents sold the ranch, there would be no reason left for him to return to Aspen Creek ever again. *Unless he created one.*

The band began to play and he held out his hand to Veronica.

"I don't really feel like dancing. You can find another partner. I'll just sit here and talk to everyone else."

"Who else are you going to talk to?" He gestured at their empty table. At the first note, Shayna and Hank had gotten up and were dancing together. Kristy was dancing with an old classmate. "I suppose we can talk if you'd prefer."

"No. Dancing sounds like fun."

He bit back a laugh. It was clear that Veronica would rather do anything other than talk to him. Did she think he was going to bring up topics that would upset her? Surely she knew him better than that. But he wanted to dance with her, so her motivation for saying yes didn't matter.

They found a place on the dance floor and began dancing to the up-tempo song. Veronica was a gifted dancer and her moves were smooth. And sexy. That song was followed by two more fast numbers before the band began to play a ballad. Malcolm's eyes searched her face and he watched the play of emotions there. Her expression ran the gamut from dismay to delight and something he couldn't quite name.

He held out his hand and after the briefest second, she placed her soft palm against his. They stepped closer and he wrapped his arm around her slender waist. He heard her faintest sigh as she placed her head against her chest. Ridiculously, his heart began to pound as if he'd run a mile uphill. Though Veronica was his childhood friend, his thoughts were as far away from friendly as they could get.

Veronica fit so perfectly in his arms she could have been made just for him. The ridiculous thought brought him up short and he stumbled. Smiling quizzically, Veronica glanced up at him. "And you were doing so well. Don't tell me that you lost count?"

Malcolm laughed and shook his head at the memory her words brought to mind. They'd been fifteen and she'd been trying to teach him how to dance. No matter how hard he'd tried to concentrate or how loud they'd played the music, he just couldn't find the beat. At the time, he'd attributed his lack of rhythm and grace to feet that had been too big for his body. Now he wondered if the problem hadn't been something more basic. Perhaps his clumsiness had been his body's reaction to Veronica's nearness. Maybe he'd felt an attraction he hadn't been able to name.

"You may not believe this, Veronica, but I really am a good dancer."

She laughed and his stomach lurched in reply. Malcolm was never one to ignore the truth, especially when it was staring him in the face, and he wasn't going to start now. His attraction to Veronica was growing stronger and threatening to turn into something more. It was more than her physical beauty that appealed to him. It was her sweetness. The kindness she showed to everyone she met, whether they were friends or strangers. And if he didn't get himself under control he was going to be in big trouble.

"You're right. I don't believe that. You don't seem to have any more skill now than you did as a kid."

"Au contraire. I don't think I've stepped on your toes once tonight."

She laughed again. "You have quite a low standard for what constitutes good dancing."

Though she hadn't challenged him explicitly, he felt the challenge nonetheless. "My standards are just as high as ever." He then pulled her closer and began to step. Humming along to the music, he expertly danced around their small area of the dance floor, doing his best to impress her with his moves. After a moment when she'd frozen in apparent shock, she began to follow his lead. When the song ended, he looked into her deep brown eyes. They were slightly glazed and he wondered if she had been as affected by their closeness as he had.

"Well?" he asked when she didn't say anything.

She shrugged one slender shoulder. "It was all right, I suppose. A solid six."

"*All right? A six?* You have got to be kidding me."

She laughed, unable to keep up the act. "At the risk of giving you a big head, that was really fantastic. But then, you already knew that."

He grinned. "Part of the credit goes to you. It took a while, but your lessons finally took."

She ducked her head in a slight bow. "I'm glad to have been of service."

"How about another dance? You should reap the benefit of all of your lessons."

Veronica smiled and nodded and they joined in the line dance that was starting. Malcolm had enjoyed holding Veronica in his arms, and if he'd had it his way, every song would have been a ballad so he could have the pleasure of inhaling her sweet scent as he pressed her soft body against his. But seeing her eyes alight with happiness as she performed the intricate steps was a close second.

From the time they'd been kids, Malcolm had made it his business to make sure that Veronica was happy. It hadn't always been easy. There were times when he'd pulled out his funniest jokes and made himself the butt of jokes in an effort to wipe away her sorrow if only for a minute, but for a couple of years there, nothing worked for long.

He'd been thrilled beyond words when Veronica and her mother had found their way back from the brink of disaster. When Leslie had begun to date a man who treated Veronica like she was his daughter, Malcolm had all but cheered. All he'd ever wanted was for Veronica to be happy, but trying to keep her that way had been a burden too heavy for someone his age to carry. Even so, he'd do it again in an instant. Veronica's happiness would always be paramount.

After one more line dance the band announced that they were taking a short break and that the DJ would be taking over. Malcolm could have danced with Veronica all night, but he didn't want to tire her out. This was a good time to catch their breath.

"How about a drink?" he asked.

"That would be great."

They walked together to the punch bowl. Once they filled their cups, they decided to wander around the building and check out the changes. The lights were on in the hallways and the classrooms. Now that school was over for the year, the desks were empty and the lockers were standing open.

"Do you ever wish you could go back and relive those years?" Veronica asked as they stepped into the biology lab. The posters hanging on the walls were updated versions of the ones that had been here when they'd been lab partners.

"You mean do high school again?" he asked incredulously.

"Never mind. Your tone of voice was very clear. It's a no."

"If I never have to write another book report it will be too soon. And I can do without pop geometry quizzes."

"I'm with you there," she agreed.

"But I would write a report every week and take two quizzes a day if it meant you and I could be that close again."

"Malcolm…"

"You don't have to say anything. You made your position quite clear." He looked at his watch. It was 11:55. "Come on. The party's almost over. I'll walk you to your car."

Veronica looked as if she had something to say, but decided at the last minute to keep her comment to herself. Instead she nodded and walked beside him to the gymnasium. People were saying their last goodbyes, promising to get together in the future, before heading for the exit. Veronica and Malcolm waved to their friends and then walked to the parking lot.

When they reached her car, Veronica heaved out a breath. "You have got to be kidding me."

"What's wrong?"

She pointed at her front tire. "I have a flat."

"No problem. I can put on your spare. It'll take ten minutes tops."

"You could do that if I had a spare."

"Don't tell me. You're using your spare."

"Yes. I had a flat and never bought a new tire to replace it."

Malcolm smothered a smile. It looked like he was going to have more time with Veronica after all. Best of all, they'd be alone. "Hop in. I'll give you a ride home."

She actually stood there as if debating his offer. What? Was she considering walking home at midnight? Or waiting who knows how long for a tow truck? She looked around as if hoping to see a friend whose company she would prefer, but there was nothing to see but red taillights. People in Aspen Creek might love a good party, but when it was over, they wasted no time hitting the road.

"Thanks," she finally said.

Malcolm was parked nearby and they walked through the empty parking lot in silence. When they reached his car, he opened the passenger door and waited until Veronica had secured her seat belt before circling the car and getting in beside her. After starting the car, he turned to her. It occurred to him then that he had no idea where she lived. The fact that their friendship had deteriorated to the point where he didn't know that basic fact hurt. But there was no sense bemoaning the past now.

"Where do you live?"

She gave him her address and he nodded. Her house was nearby, but that could be said about any two points in Aspen Creek.

"I really appreciate this."

"What are friends for?"

She only shrugged.

They didn't speak again as he drove down the dark streets to her house on the outskirts of town and he wondered if she was counting the seconds until she could be rid of him. It was as if the fun they'd had together never happened.

"My house is on the right. Third from the corner," she said, breaking the uneasy silence.

He slowed and pulled next to the curb. "Will you need help getting your car tomorrow?"

"No. I can call Craig at the garage. Clearly I'll have to get a set of new tires. He's been on me for a while to do that."

"Okay." Apparently spending big sums of money was still difficult for her. He didn't think the issue was that she couldn't afford it—likely, it was more that she still had the mindset that she should hold on to every penny. When they'd been in high school, he'd tried to assure her that he would be there if she was in need, but that hadn't helped. It had been a while before he realized that Veronica didn't want to depend on anyone ever again. The idea of being vulnerable was anathema to her.

"You don't need to park," she said, yanking at her seat belt. In her haste to free herself, she dropped her purse onto the floor and the contents spilled out.

"Let me help," he said.

"I have it." She grabbed her belongings and shoved them into her purse before jumping out of his car.

He waited until she was safely inside her house before he pulled back into the street. Though he hated to admit it, it was clear from her behavior that she wasn't ready to be friends again.

Perhaps she never would be.

Chapter Seven

Veronica stared into her cup of coffee. She'd contacted Craig first thing this morning and he'd towed her car to his garage and put on four new tires. Then he'd picked her up and taken her back to the garage to get her car. The whole thing had taken less than ninety minutes, but it had made a dent in her savings account. Not that she didn't have substantial savings. She made a point of putting away a third of her salary each month. That wasn't what was souring her mood.

It was Malcolm.

Thoughts of the time they'd spent together last night kept replaying in her mind. She'd had more fun with him than she'd expected to. Kristy had insisted on taking several group pictures, which she'd forwarded to each of them. Veronica hadn't looked at them last night. Now, unable to resist, she grabbed her phone, and opened her texts.

She looked at the first picture, and her eyes were immediately drawn to Malcolm. He had a broad smile on his face as if he was thinking of something especially pleasant. Veronica had been standing beside him, and though her smile looked relaxed, she knew that she'd been anything but. Being that close to Malcolm had sent her imagination into overdrive. Every cell in her body had been on high alert and she'd wondered more than once how he would react if she did something outrageous like run her hands over his muscular chest. She'd been curious about whether it was as hard as it looked, but after slow dancing with him she'd gotten her answer. It was even harder. And warmer. Everything about him was more than she'd imagined.

She began to sweat and she forced herself to stop thinking about Malcolm's body. She downed her coffee in one big gulp and then changed into a pair of shorts and a T-shirt for her morning run. There were generally a few others who liked to run before the heat of the day hit, as well as a group of older women walkers.

She put on her running shoes and then headed out her back door and straight to the path. Her heart skipped a beat as she anticipated the freedom she always felt when running along the trails. Even though she had rented this house for three years, she still couldn't believe her luck in stumbling on a place this close to one of her favorite trails. The trail was five miles around with enough twists, turns, and hills to be challenging. After stretching, she greeted the two women who were sipping from covered mugs.

"Getting a late start?" Emma asked. "You should have lapped us by now."

"We were about to leave without you," Jane said with a chuckle.

"I guess you won't believe me if I say that I planned to give you ladies a head start today." Veronica stretched from side to side, and then pulled her right leg behind her. She held it for five seconds and then let it drop before doing the same with her left.

"Not for a minute. Late night with a handsome and exciting man?" Emma asked hopefully.

"No such luck," Veronica said, pushing down the image of Malcolm that suddenly appeared in her mind. He'd been both handsome and exciting last night, and she'd dreamed all night of being in his arms, but he didn't count. Not in the way that Emma and Jane meant.

"I don't know what is wrong with the young men around here," Jane said. "You're pretty and smart with a great personality. You should be beating the men off with sticks. Instead you're spending date nights alone."

"You'll meet someone soon, I'm sure," Emma said as if Veronica needed that comfort and reassurance.

Veronica smiled. There was no sense in reminding the older women that she was content with her life. She'd told them several times that she didn't need a man in order to feel complete, but it hadn't sunk in. Since she didn't expect today to be the magical time her older acquaintances got the message, she didn't bother to repeat herself. Instead, she held up both hands with fingers crossed before she began jogging down the path.

Birds chirped in the trees, filling the fresh air with happy sounds. The path wound around a small pond and geese flew across the blue sky before diving to earth and landing gracefully on the clear water, barely making a ripple. Veronica inhaled and the scent of wildflowers and grass filled her lungs. Gradually she increased her speed until she was running her fastest. Despite her speed, she couldn't outrun the images of Malcolm that once more assaulted her or the memory of how good he'd smelled last night. Nor could she stop herself from remembering how heavenly it had felt to be in his arms as they'd danced together. The warmth from his body had practically seared her skin. The strong, steady beat of his heart against her cheek had made her feel safe. No matter how close they'd gotten, she'd yearned to be closer still.

Veronica spotted a branch on the path seconds before she nearly tripped over it. Annoyed with the path her thoughts were on, she ordered herself to pay attention to her surroundings instead of daydreaming about Malcolm. When she finished her run, she jogged back to her house.

After taking a hot shower, she dressed and went to the kitchen. She didn't feel like cooking, so she cut a banana into a bowl of cold cereal and popped two pieces of bread into the toaster for a quick breakfast. The library was open from noon until four on weekends during the summer, but since she'd expected to be out late last night, she'd swapped days with a coworker.

After she finished eating, she grabbed her calculator, pencil, and paper. Now that she had spent money on new tires, she needed to tighten her belt until she'd recouped the funds. She was still working out the math when there was a knock on her door. She wasn't expecting anyone, but as she passed through her front room, she glanced at her reflection in the mirror to make sure she was presentable. She was wearing one of her favorite sundresses that showed off her suntanned legs. Her hair was in a ponytail on top of her head and several tendrils of hair floated around her face. Satisfied that she looked okay, she opened the front door. And gasped.

"Malcolm. What are you doing here?" She realized how rude that sounded but he didn't seem to notice.

"I tried to call, but I didn't get an answer. I found this in my car this morning." He held up the second letter from her father's daughter. "I thought it might be important since you were carrying it around with you. I needed to come to town anyway, so I decided to drop it off."

Why oh why hadn't she changed purses yesterday? Because her everyday black leather purse was new and had a gold clasp. School colors.

Veronica reached for the envelope and he held it over his head, out of her reach. His lips lifted in a playful smile. "Surely you aren't going to just take it and slam the door shut in my face."

"I wasn't going to *slam* it."

"Oh, that's cold."

Shaking her head, Veronica stepped aside and swept out her arm in a dramatic manner. She knew that Malcolm would leave if she really wanted him to, but she didn't want him to. Perhaps it was the memory of how much fun they'd had last night that had her wanting to spend more time with him. More than likely it was because just being around Malcolm made her smile. And who didn't like to smile? "Come on in."

"Don't mind if I do."

He stepped inside and looked around. A wide smile on his face, he walked over to the built-in bookcase that separated the cozy living room from the dining room and picked up a framed picture of the two of them with a group of friends. They'd gone skiing and someone had taken a picture of them at the foot of the mountain.

They'd been laughing and horsing around. As usual, Malcolm and Veronica had been side by side.

"You have a picture of me in your living room." He smirked and she knew that he was trying to get a rise out of her.

"With six other people. Besides, I like the way that I look in that picture."

"So do I. I wish I had a copy."

She sighed. Was he serious? She couldn't tell with him. Not these days. Once she'd known him so well she knew what he was thinking or feeling with just one look. Of course, he'd been an open book back then. He'd always been pretty easygoing and he hadn't had many moods. Or had he? Perhaps he'd always put on a happy face for her because he'd wanted to make her smile. Maybe he'd had problems he hadn't shared with her.

"Sure. I can have one made for you. I'll even get it framed."

He seemed surprised by her answer and she wondered what he must think of her. She'd run hot and cold this past week. And her cold had been frigid. Just thinking about the way she'd dashed from his car last night made her face burn with embarrassment. Of course, he had no way to know that she'd been wondering if he would try to kiss her and if she would let him. Though she didn't know the answer to the first question, the answer to the second was a definite yes—and that had rattled her so much, she'd felt like she needed to run.

"Thanks."

They stood there for a moment as if neither knew what to say next. She looked at the envelope in her hand. At one time she would have told him everything about the letters from Bianca without hesitation. A few weeks ago, she wouldn't have told him a thing. But now she wondered if she should unburden herself. Maybe he could carry part of the stress on his shoulders. Unbidden, her eyes immediately shot to his upper body. His shoulders were broad and she knew from being held in his arms just how powerful they were.

He gestured to the envelope she still held. "I hope I didn't bring bad news."

"No." She hesitated. Frowned. Inhaled and then blew out the breath. "Can you stay for a minute?"

His smile of pleasure set butterflies free in her stomach. Whatever mistakes she'd made, he wasn't holding them against her.

"Yep." He returned the picture to its place on the bookshelf and then sat on her sofa. The room wasn't particularly small—she and her three closest friends were always comfortable in here together—but he had such a large presence that suddenly the room felt half its size. "If you want to talk, I'm here to listen."

"I don't want to dump on you." It was only now that she realized just how unbalanced their relationship had been in the past.

"Unburdening yourself isn't dumping on me. My shoulders are strong. I can help carry the load."

The fact that his words echoed her earlier thoughts was the push she'd needed. She inhaled deeply and then blurted out, "This is a letter from my father's other daughter."

"Your half sister?"

She nodded. Why was it so hard to think of Bianca

that way? It wasn't as if denial was going to change the fact that they shared a father.

"I didn't know you were even in touch with her."

"I'm not. She just started sending me letters."

"Have you written her back?" Malcolm asked.

"No. I hope if I ignore her she'll get the hint and leave me alone."

"Wow." Malcolm sounded disappointed and Veronica felt ashamed.

"I didn't ask her to write. I have a right to decide who gets to be a part of my life and who doesn't."

Now he only gave her a long look. In the past, Malcolm would have spoken his mind and they would have dealt with the fallout. Apparently, he was still being reticent in an effort to keep from upsetting her.

"Say what you want to say, Malcolm. I'm not a fragile flower. I won't break if you criticize me."

"I don't doubt your fortitude. I'm more concerned about the fragility of our relationship."

She waved away his concern. "A relationship isn't much of one if you have to tiptoe around each other. Say what you want and we'll deal with it."

"Okay. Just don't throw me out if you don't like what I have to say." He looked her dead in the eyes and she held back a wince at the intensity she saw in his. "I'm disappointed that you seem so resistant to forming a relationship with a girl who has really put herself out there to try to connect with you. Why would you do that? You're not blaming an innocent teenager for something she didn't do, are you?"

Each of his words was a body blow, but she'd asked him to be honest. Even so, knowing that he was disappointed in her broke her heart. "Of course not. I don't blame her for the distance between me and my father. That was his decision. He's the one who chose to walk away from me."

He nodded. "That's true."

"But I don't want to be reminded of the fact that he abandoned me either."

"How would responding to her letter do that?"

"Because she's a constant reminder. Her mere existence is proof that he didn't love me enough to be there for me the way he is for her. He's been in her life for eighteen years though he walked out of mine before I turned ten. For over twenty-four years he chose to ignore my existence. And you expect me to be friends with the daughter he preferred?"

Her voice broke on her last words and she clamped her mouth shut. In a flash, Malcolm was beside her, pulling her onto her feet and then wrapping his arms around her. Veronica gave a token struggle before leaning her head against his strong chest. Tears that she'd bottled up long ago burst free and began streaming down her cheeks. She tried, but she couldn't stop them. Before she knew what was happening, she was sobbing. She tried to regain control of her emotions, but her shoulders still shook and the sobs kept pouring out of her.

Malcolm's hands ran up and down her back as he murmured comforting words to her. Gradually her tears slowed and finally stopped. Veronica told herself that since she no longer needed comfort she should step out of Malcolm's embrace, but she couldn't make herself move. It felt so good to have him hold her, infusing her with strength, and she wasn't ready for the moment to end.

Gradually Veronica began to become even more aware of him. He smelled so good. It was more than his musky cologne, although it was top-notch. It was him. His own personal scent appealed to her as a woman and she found herself getting aroused. That was the last thing she needed. After one more deep inhale, she forced herself to take a step back. Immediately his arms fell away and she felt a strange sense of loss.

"Sorry about that," she said, swiping at her wet face.

"Don't apologize. You don't have to hide your feelings from me."

"How can you say that? You just judged me for admitting how I felt about my father's other daughter."

"If it seemed like I was judging, I apologize. That wasn't my intent." The corner of his lips turned down. "I suppose I was jumping to conclusions. I know that your father and his wife hurt you."

"And they hurt my mother. They ripped our family apart. My father didn't care if we starved. And we would have if not for the people of Aspen Creek. You and your parents saved our lives."

"I wouldn't go that far."

"I would." She looked into his eyes. They held a hint of embarrassment. "I didn't know it at the time, but I realized years later that they invited me to the ranch so often in order to keep me fed."

He shook his head. "My mother loved your company. You were the daughter she never had."

"Mrs. Henderson started the sewing and knitting class at her store for kids my age. She and her club knitted sweaters for the three students who signed up, but

I believe it was just to make sure that I had something warm to wear."

"According to my mother, the classes have grown in popularity and lots of girls and boys have joined. And they still knit sweaters for everyone."

"They have. They're teaching valuable life skills. I'm proud to say that I can knit and sew with the best of them."

"I'm sure you can."

"But my point is, so many people with no ties to me at all stepped up to make sure I was taken care of, while my father couldn't have cared less about me. He certainly didn't care about how I felt when he disappeared from my life. Thinking about his other family reminds me of that, and then I feel hurt and abandoned all over again. Why should I be expected to try to build a relationship with someone who makes me feel like that? Is it wrong for me not to want her in my life?"

"No. But if that is the case, I don't think you should wait for her to get the hint. Teenagers are unpredictable. Who knows what she'll do?"

"I'll write her back if she continues to send me letters."

"That's a good idea." He grinned suddenly. "So, what are you doing the rest of the day?"

"I went for a run this morning and took care of my car. I have the rest of the day to myself."

"Do you want to go horseback riding?"

"I haven't ridden in years. I doubt that I still know how."

"It's not brain surgery or even rodeo. All you need to do is sit in the saddle and let the horse do the rest."

"I don't know…" She had spent countless hours on horseback when she was a teenager. She'd loved every minute of it. And she really did miss it.

"My parents would love to see you."

Veronica felt herself weakening. "You don't play fair."

"I play to win."

"Fine. Give me five minutes to change."

Veronica didn't wait for Malcolm to reply before she turned and dashed up the stairs. She unbuttoned her sundress as she ran upstairs, so when she reached her bedroom all she needed to do was pull it over her head. Tossing it on the foot of her bed to deal with later, Veronica pulled open her bottom dresser drawer and grabbed a pair of faded jeans. After she stepped into them, she grabbed a floral cotton blouse from her closet and shoved her arms into the sleeves before fastening the buttons. She glanced in the full-length mirror on the inside of her closet door as she put on her boots and frowned. She could do better. She dabbed on lipstick and mascara then freed her hair from its ponytail and ran a comb through it. This might not be a date—in fact it *definitely* wasn't one—but she still wanted to look her best. Especially since Malcolm looked good enough to be on the cover of an outdoor magazine.

She snatched her purse from the chair beside her bed and then dashed from her room. She told herself to at least try to look sedate, but it was too late for that. Malcolm had already seen her racing up the stairs in her eagerness to get changed.

Veronica stepped into the living room and Malcolm stood and turned to look at her. His eyes widened and his mouth dropped open before he snapped it shut. That one appreciative look made all of her efforts worth it.

They walked out of her house and got in his car. Once they were on their way, Veronica couldn't help the excitement that built inside her. Being with Malcolm was the best way she knew to get the bitter taste of hurt out of her mouth.

Chapter Eight

"I forgot how much fun it is to ride," Veronica said as she and Malcolm trotted along the green hills of his parents' ranch. Over the years she hadn't allowed herself to recall how many afternoons they'd spent on horseback on this particular patch of land. Now the pleasurable memories came rushing back.

"You know you're welcome to ride here anytime you want."

"Your father said the same thing. It just doesn't seem right to come out here on my own. Besides, it's not as much fun to ride alone as it is with you."

Malcolm swung around and looked at her. "Did you just compliment me?"

She grinned. "You must have misheard."

"No I didn't."

"Well, don't let it go to your head."

"I'll do my best." He flashed her a grin that made her toes tingle. This ridiculous attraction was getting out of hand. And more than that, she was starting to believe he shared her attraction. That bit of information didn't help matters.

"Riding alone might not be as fun, but it does help me to clear my head in a way nothing else does," he continued. "I don't have many opportunities to ride in Chicago. Truthfully none. There are a couple of stables that I can visit, but riding those horses isn't the same as riding on Hercules. And those riding trails don't come anywhere close to the ranch when it comes to beauty."

"It is beautiful here."

"That it is."

His voice sounded wistful—almost sad—and she wondered what that was all about. Could Evelyn Parks be right? Was Malcolm thinking about selling the ranch? She waited a few minutes for him to expound, but when he didn't she simply let the matter drop. Maybe she was reading more into his tone than was there.

By unspoken agreement they headed toward their old swimming hole. When they arrived, Malcolm swung from his horse, then reached up to help Veronica dismount. She threw her right leg over Buttercup's back and Malcolm grabbed her by the waist, slowly lowering her to the ground. Her legs were rubbery and she wobbled a little.

"I guess I haven't gotten my riding legs back as well as I thought," Veronica said with a little laugh.

"Sit down. I'll get the blanket and the food that my mother packed for us."

Cheryl had insisted on providing lunch for them. Although Veronica had not intended for this to be a long ride, after ten minutes in, she knew a short trot around the corral wouldn't satisfy her. But she wasn't used to spending this much time on horseback and she knew a good soak in the tub was in her future. But she was enjoying herself too much right now to worry about that.

Veronica sat on a fallen tree trunk while Malcolm

spread the blanket on the grass, then began opening the plastic containers of food. If Veronica didn't know better, she would think that Malcolm and his mother had been in cahoots. She wouldn't put it past him to have asked his mother to prepare a special meal for them once she'd agreed to go riding. But maybe she was jumping to conclusions. After all, Cheryl had generally packed fruit and sandwiches for them in the past.

Malcolm knelt on the blanket, held out a bottle of chilled water, and smiled at her. She took the bottle, twisted off the cap, and took a long sip before she sat down. "What did your mother pack for us?"

"Chicken salad sandwiches, chips, carrot and cucumber slices." He frowned.

"Do you still hate raw vegetables?"

"Yep." He held up a rectangular container. "And chocolate brownies with walnuts."

"My favorite."

"I know. It's amazing how Mom was careful to pack your favorite snack while packing my least favorite vegetables."

"That's because she likes me more than she likes you."

"You joke, but that wouldn't surprise me."

They dug into the containers, filling paper plates with food. Veronica gestured at Malcolm's plate. "You really aren't going to eat any of those vegetables?"

"I'll eat double tonight."

They talked companionably while they ate and Veronica felt more relaxed than she had in years. After they'd eaten their fill, Veronica lay on her back and sighed contentedly. Malcolm lay down beside her, a smile on his face. His nearness began to fill her with desire. Though a romance with Malcolm was out of the question, she was starting to enjoy the feelings he awakened in her.

The wind blew suddenly, sending the paper plates flying across the grass. While they'd been enjoying their lunch, dark clouds had gathered in the previously clear sky. The wind was soon followed by large raindrops that plopped on the blanket they'd been sharing. Before they could move, the sky opened up and the rain began to fall more steadily. They jumped to their feet and raced around. Veronica began gathering the containers while Malcolm chased after the paper plates. Then he bundled the blanket into a ball and shoved it into the saddlebags.

"I guess we won't be going skinny-dipping," Malcolm said with a wry grin as they mounted their horses.

"Was that on the agenda?" Veronica asked. "I wasn't aware of it."

"A man can hope."

"That is way beyond hope."

Malcolm laughed and Veronica glanced over at him. His brown eyes danced with mischief and a dimple flashed in his cheek. Images of him without clothes suddenly popped into her mind and her stomach lurched unexpectedly. The hard rain was drenching them and his soaked shirt clung to his muscular upper body, so she could easily make out his sculpted torso. He caught her staring and then his grin shifted from mischievous to something else entirely. Something hot. Wolfish.

His eyes began to travel down her body. Her soaked cotton blouse was now transparent and left very little to the imagination. Their eyes met and his hot gaze made her shiver.

Lightning flashed and thunder rolled as they rode into the stable. They dismounted and she reached for Buttercup's saddle.

"I can do that if you want," Malcolm said.

"No way. I love brushing horses. There's something soothing about the motion. You know that."

"As long as you're not too cold."

Cold? Was he kidding? She was practically sizzling with desire. It was a wonder that steam wasn't coming from her body. "Nah. I'm good. It's warm in here."

When they finished caring for the horses, they stood together at the stable doors, looking out. The rain had stopped and the sky was clear again.

"It must have been just a passing thundercloud," Malcolm said.

"Destiny's way of keeping us from skinny-dipping," Veronica said with a cheeky grin.

"*Today.* I look at it as a postponement."

She laughed then nudged his shoulder. "Keep hope alive."

Veronica shelved a picture book then began making her rounds. She didn't have any programs scheduled for the day, but there were a few kids around and she wanted to be sure that she spoke to each of them. Although the little kids ran up to her whenever they saw her, rattling on about their lives, their attitudes always seemed to change once they reached middle school. At that age, the children grew reluctant to approach her if she was sitting at her desk, but they would seek her out if she was walking around.

"Miss Veronica. Look," Leon, one of her most avid

library kids, called. He held up the picture book she'd reserved for him.

"I see you got your book."

"It still has that new book smell," he said, squeezing the book against his skinny chest.

"I love that smell," she said. "And you're going to be the first person to read it."

"I know," he said as, library card in hand, he walked to the self-checkout counter where his mother awaited.

Smiling to herself, Veronica walked around, pausing to engage other children in brief conversations and make book recommendations. Once she'd spent time with everyone, she walked back to her desk. A woman was standing there, her back to Veronica. There was nothing familiar about her, so Veronica surmised she was new to the library.

"How may I help you?" Veronica asked as she approached her desk. The woman turned and Veronica realized that she was only a teenager.

"Are you Veronica Kendrick?"

"Yes. And you are?"

"I'm your sister."

"What?" Veronica asked. She realized that she'd spoken more loudly than she'd intended, drawing the attention of several nearby patrons. After looking at her for a moment, they returned to what they'd been doing.

"You heard me. I'm your sister. Bianca. I wrote you a couple of letters, but when you didn't write back or call me, I figured you didn't get them. So, I decided to come and see you in person. I don't know where you live, but I know that you're the librarian. The library was easy to find. Well, with the help of a couple of people who gave me directions."

It was tempting to tell the girl that she had indeed received her letters and hadn't responded because she wasn't interested in knowing her, but something stopped her. That would have been unnecessarily cruel. Cruelty was her father's modus operandi, not hers. Besides, the girl wasn't the one who'd hurt her.

She forced herself to speak calmly. "Why are you here?"

"I wanted to meet you." Though she'd spoken in a matter-of-fact manner, the answer sounded rehearsed and Veronica's Spidey senses went on high alert. She was a children's librarian. She had a lot of exposure to teenagers and could tell when one was holding something back. And Bianca was definitely not giving Veronica the entire story. She supposed it would come out eventually.

Veronica pulled out her chair and sat down. Though she hadn't been invited, Bianca took the seat on the other side of the desk.

"Why did you want to meet me?"

"Because we're sisters." She said it as if the answer was obvious. "I know my brothers. We grew up in the same house. But I don't know you. And now that I'm eighteen I can do what I want."

The shock of the moment was wearing off and Veronica actually laughed. "That's not exactly true."

Bianca folded her arms over her chest. "Well, they can't stop me from hanging out with you."

"Did they try to?" Veronica didn't know why she asked that question. Though she hadn't been interested in meeting Bianca, it would hurt to know that her father had actively told his preferred daughter to avoid her.

Bianca picked at the hem of her shorts instead of answering. "So, what time do you get off work?"

"At four."

"Okay. I'll come back then so we can talk."

"Wait. Where are you staying?"

Bianca avoided her eyes. "I haven't really picked out a place yet. I'll look around until you're finished."

Veronica sighed. "Aspen Creek is a vacation destination. People schedule their reservations months in advance. You'll have a hard time finding somewhere to stay."

"I'll figure it out."

"Really? How?"

"Don't worry about me. I'll be back at four."

Veronica tried to focus on her work, but after that unexpected visit, she couldn't concentrate. Instead she called around to see if any of the inns or resorts had a vacancy. As expected everyone was booked up.

The time dragged on and it seemed like years before the last patron walked out the door. It was ten past four and Bianca was nowhere to be found. Veronica was wondering if Bianca had decided not to return when she came racing through the front door.

Bianca smiled and waved. "Believe it or not, I got a little bit turned around. I was hoping you wouldn't leave before I got back."

"I knew you were coming back, so I waited for you."

Bianca smiled, clearly pleased by Veronica's response.

"Did you find a place to stay?" Veronica asked even though she knew the answer.

"No. You were right. Everywhere is full. I guess this is another example of me not making a smart decision." Bianca gave a self-deprecating smile, but it didn't reach her eyes. How many times had Bianca been belittled for her decision-making? And who had been doing the criticizing? Teens needed supportive guidance as they navigated the path to adulthood. Veronica hadn't anticipated feeling protective of Bianca, but she did.

"You aren't far from home. If you leave now, you should be back in Denver before it's late."

Bianca folded her arms. "But then we won't get a chance to talk."

Veronica sighed. She should have known this wasn't going to go smoothly.

"Wait a minute," Bianca said slowly, her eyes narrowed. "How do you know where I live?"

Busted. "I actually got your letters. I read the return address."

"Then why didn't you write back or call me?" Bianca's indignation immediately turned into sadness and she stepped away from Veronica. "I get it. You didn't want to meet me. I think I will go now."

"Hold on. Let me explain a few things." Veronica reached out and grabbed Bianca's hand. "Have you eaten? The Aspen Creek diner has great burgers."

"I'm a vegetarian."

"Oh. Then let's go to the Dandelion Café. It's a tourist spot, but it's vegan so there will be lots for you to choose from. And they have delicious smoothies." Best of all, they weren't likely to run into anyone Veronica knew.

Bianca scuffed her shoe on the pavement. "I guess I can eat."

"Wonderful."

Veronica's head was spinning as she walked to the restaurant. She'd had the perfect opportunity to be rid of Bianca once and for all, but she'd passed on it because she couldn't bring herself to hurt the feelings of an innocent teenager. The outside tables were occupied with people enjoying the beautiful weather so rather than wait, they grabbed a table inside. After they ordered their salads and iced tea, Veronica took a good look at Bianca. She might not want to claim Bianca as a sister, but there was no denying they shared genes. Though Veronica bore a striking resemblance to her mother, she'd inherited a couple of traits from her father that Bianca also shared. They'd each inherited their father's dark brown eyes and the shape of their chins were similar. It wasn't much, but it was enough to mark them as family.

Veronica was not alone in her examination. Bianca was staring at her too. "You must look like your mother."

"I do."

"I wish I did. My mom is really pretty. Everybody says so. Unfortunately I took after Dad."

"You're pretty."

"You have to say that. You're my sister."

Veronica mustered up a strained smile. She wasn't as willing to make the same connection that Bianca was, but the thought of having a sister seemed to make the girl so happy that Veronica couldn't bear to burst her bubble. "Considering the fact that we've only just met, I think you can trust me to be honest with you. We don't really know each other well enough to go out of our way to lie."

Bianca nodded slowly and then smiled. "I guess that's true."

Their salads came and they each took a forkful. Veronica was still searching for words when Bianca began telling her about her life and friends. Veronica might not think of Bianca as her half sister, but she had to admit the girl was quite charming and delightful. Before she knew it, she was laughing at a ridiculous story that Bianca was telling her. Veronica didn't know if the tale was true, an exaggeration, or completely fabricated, but it was clear that Bianca had a gift for storytelling and a flair for the dramatic.

"So, why did you want to meet me?" Veronica asked when the story ended.

"I told you. You're my sister. I want to know what kind of person you are."

"I'm a lot older than you are. We might find that we don't have much in common."

Bianca frowned and put down her fork. "You really don't want me around, do you?"

Veronica took time to swallow and then dabbed at the corner of her mouth. If Bianca were anyone else, Veronica would have done her best to reassure her. It would be wrong to do anything less now, especially to her half sister.

Veronica forced herself to think about Bianca's feelings and not her own. "I'm just surprised. You caught me off guard. I'm not saying we won't get along—I'm just saying that we'll have to see how we click. But I really would like to get to know you better."

Bianca gave her a skeptical look. "Do you really mean that?"

Veronica nodded. "Yes."

Smiling broadly, Bianca picked up her fork and resumed eating. She peppered Veronica with questions as they ate. After they finished their salads they ordered caramelized bananas with vegan ice cream. Bianca wanted to see more of the town, so Veronica walked her around, showing her some of her favorite places. It was late by the time they got back to the library.

"I suppose I should get going," Bianca said, leaning against her car. She yawned and quickly covered her mouth.

"It's getting late and you're obviously sleepy. You need to stay the night."

"There isn't anywhere. Remember?"

Veronica sighed. There was one available bed in town. In Veronica's guest room. "You can stay with me."

Chapter Nine

Veronica picked up her phone and punched in Malcolm's number before she had time to think. It had been a reflex and as she listened to the phone ringing, she realized how easily she'd slipped into the pattern they had established as kids. She decided to stop fighting it. Especially when she needed his ear.

"What's up?"

"You won't believe who is in my guest room right now."

"Are you going to make me guess?"

She rolled her eyes. That was a typical Malcolm answer. "I should, but I won't. It's Bianca."

"Your…"

"Half sister. Yes."

"How did that come about?"

"You were right about teenagers being unpredictable. She showed up at the library today so we could meet. She hadn't reserved anywhere to stay and of course all of the rooms were booked. I couldn't just send her out on the road in the middle of the night."

"How do you feel? Do you want to talk about it?"

"Yes." She inhaled deeply and then blew out the

breath. "You know what bothers me the most?" she continued before he could reply. "I hate that I'm not really over it. I don't understand why something that happened more than twenty years ago still hurts."

"I'm not a therapist, but I think things that happen in our childhood haunt us until they're dealt with. Naturally your father's abandonment made an impression on you. It also colors your view of the world and your relationships. How could it not?"

"I just want to stop feeling the way that I do."

"You can't control your feelings. Nobody can. But you can keep them from determining your actions."

"That's easier said than done."

"Aren't most things? The fact that you've invited Bianca to stay with you is proof that you're in control."

She frowned and then confessed. "It was a battle. I'm still surprised that I actually told her to spend the night here when she was going to drive home."

"I'm not. You've always been a kind person. Your empathy is one of your best qualities."

"You're just saying that because I did what you would have done."

He laughed and the sound sent shivers down her spine. That darn attraction wasn't dulled by the fact that they were discussing a serious topic. Clearly nothing could diminish that. "Honestly? I don't know if I would have allowed her to stay if I were in your shoes."

"Yes you would. Remember that kid who lived in Aspen Creek for a few weeks when we were in second grade? He was staying with his grandparents. I forgot his name."

"Randy."

"Yes. He was really quiet, but you welcomed him right away. You told him to sit with us at lunch and made a point of inviting him to come out to your ranch to ride horses."

"He only came once or twice. Then he was gone."

"Yes, but while he was there, you were a friend to him. If you were in my situation, you would have welcomed her too."

"So I guess I'm rubbing off on you."

She laughed. "I wouldn't go that far."

"Does this change things between you and your father?"

"No," she replied instantly. She had no desire to speak with him. He'd walked out of her life and as far as she was concerned, he could stay out. "Enough of that. What did you do today?"

"I worked on the ranch."

His voice sounded strained. She could have pretended not to notice, but she wouldn't. Not after he'd been so kind to her.

"What aren't you saying?"

His sigh, filled with deep emotions, came over the phone. "My parents are thinking about giving up ranching."

"Really? Why?"

He hesitated and she wondered if her query came across as prying. Maybe he didn't feel comfortable confiding in her. She was on the verge of apologizing when he sighed and then answered. "Because of my father's health."

"Oh no." She couldn't keep the panic from her voice. Mr. Wilson had played an enormous role in her life.

"He's not seriously ill. He just needs to slow down."

"Are you going to take over the ranch?" The idea of him moving back permanently was exciting as well as unnerving. Now that they were becoming friends again it would be good to have him around. But her intense attraction to him would be a problem. She couldn't risk getting involved with him. If things didn't work out, she didn't see a way their friendship could survive. And now that she had it back, she wanted that friendship to last.

"That's not my first choice. I love the ranch but I can't imagine running it for the rest of my life."

"Even if your father needs your help? Or is his health so bad that he needs to give up ranching?"

"It doesn't seem quite that bad—though he might step back from ranching for reasons other than his health. My parents have a long list of places they want to visit. It could take years for them to see them all. Dad says that it's my mother's turn to do what she wants. And I agree with him. She sacrificed a lot to be a rancher's wife. Now she wants to travel."

"So if he's going to be away, and you don't intend to run the ranch yourself, will you sell it?"

"I have no idea. My father just told me about all of this a week ago. To be honest, I'm still in shock. But I suppose at this point that everything is on the table."

"Wow. I wasn't expecting that." That nosy Mrs. Parks *was* right. Not that Veronica intended to tell her anything. Another thought occurred to her. If Malcolm sold the ranch, would his parents buy a place in town? Or would they relocate to a warmer climate like Helen and Mr. Watson? If his parents moved away, there would be no reason for him to return to Aspen Creek. He only made rare visits to see his parents and she doubted anyone else in town warranted a special trip. Knowing that there could be a time when Malcolm wouldn't come back made her heart ache. She'd just gotten him back in her life. She didn't want to lose him again.

"Once we all sit down and discuss the pros and cons, we'll make a decision that works for all of us."

She hoped the decision would work for her too. Before she could say anything, she heard footsteps on the stairs. A minute later Bianca stepped into the living room.

"Do you mind if I get something to drink?"

"Of course not. Give me a second." She'd expected Bianca to step away. Instead she simply turned her back in what Veronica supposed was her attempt to give her some privacy. As if she couldn't hear Veronica if she couldn't see her. "Malcolm. I need to go. I'll talk to you later."

Veronica ended the call and then stood. "You don't have to ask for food or drink. Help yourself to whatever you want."

"Does that include alcohol?" Bianca asked, a mischievous grin on her face.

"There's none in the house, so I suppose the answer is yes."

"Figures."

Veronica laughed. There was none because she and her friends drank all of the wine the last time they'd gotten together and she hadn't replaced it yet. Of course, there was no need for her to share that information.

They stepped into the kitchen and Veronica opened the refrigerator. "What would you like?"

Bianca took a peek and then heaved a long sigh. "I suppose some lemonade will do."

"Would you like something to eat? It's been a while since we ate."

"What do you have?" Bianca asked.

"Not as many vegetarian options as you might think. Do you eat eggs and dairy?"

Bianca nodded. "I'm used to that."

"How about an omelet?"

"Sounds good. Breakfast for a midnight snack. Or rather a nine o'clock snack."

Veronica grabbed the ingredients and set them on the counter. "You're used to what?"

Bianca's brow wrinkled in confusion and then she gave a laugh that didn't hold the slightest bit of mirth. "I'm the only vegetarian in the family. My parents and brothers say that since it's not a medical reason but my personal lifestyle choice, they aren't going to go out of their way to accommodate me."

By some miracle, Veronica managed to bite back her response to that. "Oh. Okay. Well, I'm sure I have enough around here to come up with something appetizing."

"Thanks." They chopped vegetables for a moment before Bianca looked at her. "Is Malcolm your boyfriend?"

"What? No. He's...we were good friends a long time ago. He moved to Chicago after college and we fell out of touch for a while, but he's back in town for a short visit and we've reconnected. As friends."

Bianca slid the last of the mushrooms she'd been slicing into the bowl with the tomatoes, green peppers, onions, and spinach, then looked up at Veronica, a sly smile on her face. "That was a lot of words when a simple 'no' would have done. Judging from the expression on your face, I think the answer is yes."

"It's complicated."

"Do tell."

"There's not much to tell."

"I'll tell you who I like if you tell me who you like." Bianca giggled. "We're sisters. We're supposed to talk about things like this."

"Is that right?"

"Yes. So tell me about Malcolm. Is he cute? A good kisser?"

"I wouldn't describe him as cute. And I have no idea if he's a good kisser or not. Our lips have not met."

"That's sad. But looks aren't everything. Do you have a picture of him?"

Veronica thought of the pictures from the reunion on her phone as well as the one on her bookshelf. "Yes. I'll show you later. Do you want toast?"

Bianca nodded. While they'd been talking, she'd cooked an omelet. Now she slid it onto a plate and started on a second one. "I'll show you Gary's picture too."

"Is he your boyfriend?"

"No, but I want him to be."

"Does he know?"

"Of course. I told him."

"I sense a story," Veronica said as she put buttered toast on each of their plates beside their omelets.

Bianca rolled her eyes. "Not one with the ending that I want. At least not yet."

"Oh no. Now I need more than that. Who is Gary? How old is he? You're the one who said sisters talk about the boys they like. I need details."

"I'm going to tell you," Bianca said, then shoveled a forkful of omelet into her mouth. Once she'd chewed and swallowed, she looked directly at Veronica. "I just don't want you to act like I'm weird or something."

"What's weird about liking someone?"

"He's not just someone. He's *special*. He's always been really nice to me."

"I would hope so. Especially since you asked him to be your boyfriend. When did that happen, by the way."

"Five years ago. On my thirteenth birthday."

"I see." Veronica couldn't help smiling at the image that she conjured up in her mind. She pictured herself at that age and imagined what Malcolm—or any thirteen-year-old boy she'd known—would have done if she'd asked him to be her boyfriend. Probably head for the hills. "And what happened?"

"He told me no because he had a girlfriend. But they broke up a while ago and he doesn't have a new girl-friend now."

"I see. So do you plan to make a move?"

"I did. A couple of weeks ago. He turned me down again. He said he was too old for me."

Veronica set down her fork and looked at Bianca. "Just how old is he? And where did you meet him?"

Bianca sighed. "I met him at home. I've known him all of my life."

"And?" Veronica raised an eyebrow.

"He's my brother Michael's best friend. He's twenty-two. That's only four years older than me."

Veronica didn't miss the defensive tone in Bianca's voice. "I know. And ten years from now those four years won't make a difference. But right now those four years are filled with a lot of experiences that he's had that you haven't."

"So what? You're telling me to just get over him?"

Veronica held her hands in front of her. "I'm not saying anything like that. I have it on good authority that you can't control your emotions. You feel what you feel."

Bianca smiled. "I knew you would understand."

"Wait. I'm not finished yet. You might not be able to stop liking him, and I'm not saying that you should, but you don't have to act on your feelings. At least not now. Do you want to go to college?"

"Yes. I've already applied to a bunch. I'm a good student, so I got into most of them."

"Then I'd suggest you focus more on your education right now and less on Gary. Enjoy the college experience. Love will come."

"Is that what you did? Because you've been out of college for a long time and you're still single." Her eyes went wide as she seemed to realize what she'd said. "That sounded mean. I wasn't trying to be mean, I just—"

Veronica laughed. "It's fine. I'm not offended. And yes, I'm single…but it's by choice. I've dated a lot of guys. I've had a couple of serious relationships that didn't work out for one reason or another. But even when I'm not involved with anyone, my life is still good and fulfilling. I'm happy."

"You sound like my guidance counselor. I guess she thought I was going to do something ridiculous like throw myself at Gary. I may like him, but I'm not a fool. I don't want anyone who doesn't want me."

"That's good to hear."

They finished their meals and washed the dishes. When the kitchen was clean, Bianca turned back to Veronica. "So where is that picture of Malcolm? Is it in your wallet where you can take it out and look at it whenever you're missing him?"

"Is that where you keep your picture of Gary?" Veronica teased.

"I do have one there from a birthday party when I was little. The rest are on my phone."

"The one I want to show you is in the living room."

Bianca didn't wait for Veronica, but instead dashed into the front room. She looked around for a framed photo. Veronica watched as Bianca struggled with her curiosity. When it looked like she might bust, Veronica picked up the framed photo from the bookshelf. Was it only yesterday that Malcolm himself had held the frame in his strong hands?

Veronica turned on a lamp and then held out the picture. "We were kids here."

Bianca took the picture and stared at it. "Which one is him?"

Veronica pointed at Malcolm.

A slow smile crossed Bianca's face. "He was cute. I bet he's really gorgeous now."

Veronica smiled.

"He is. I knew it. Come on, Veronica. Spill. I told you everything."

"Oh. All right." What could it hurt? Bianca was only here for one night. What was the harm in satisfying her curiosity? She wasn't going to be a permanent part of Veronica's life. Besides, Bianca and Malcolm would never meet. And if they did what would it matter? Veronica sat on the sofa and Bianca dropped down beside her. If possible, her smile was even wider.

"Tell me all about him. Do you have a newer picture of him? Alone? You know, for reference."

Veronica started to shake her head no, but then she realized that she did have one. When she'd been the auctioneer at the Aspen Creek Bachelor Auction, the men had all submitted photos of themselves. She still had one or two of the catalogs and fliers advertising the auction. "Hold on. I can get one."

"I knew you were holding out on me. Is it on your bedside table?"

"Nope. It's in a drawer in my office desk."

"That's not romantic at all."

Chuckling to herself, Veronica jogged to her office and pulled out the catalog. It had been a while since she'd thought about it, much less looked at it. Once she and Bianca were sitting together on the sofa, she opened the catalog. Bianca scooted close and leaned over Veronica's shoulder.

"Which one is he? No. Don't tell me. I want to guess."

Veronica flipped the page to the page advertising the first bachelor. There were two photos and a short biography.

"I don't know who he is, but I could look at him all night."

"That's Marty Adams. He's very popular with the ladies."

"I can see why. My panties are melting just looking at him."

"What?" Veronica sputtered and then laughed. "I can't believe you said that."

"Like you weren't thinking the same thing."

"Actually I wasn't. He's the brother of one of my best friends."

"So. He's not *your* brother."

"Point to you."

Bianca turned the page and pointed. "He's cute too."

"Nathan Montgomery. He's engaged to another friend."

"Lucky her."

Bianca had a comment about every man. After she'd seen all of the bachelors, she closed the catalog and she sighed. "I think I'm living in the wrong place. All of the men here are gorgeous."

"They do grow them nice around here."

"Malcolm was the best-looking."

Veronica laughed. "You're just saying that because you think that's what I want you to say."

"Would I do that?"

"I think so. You wouldn't want to hurt my feelings."

"Okay. I might. But I'm telling the truth. He has a nice face. And since he's your boyfriend, I won't point out that he has a lot of muscles. Big muscles. He probably looks great in swim trunks."

And just like that, Veronica could picture Malcolm without a shirt. She recalled how strong and hard his chest muscles had felt under her face when they'd been dancing and she knew without a shadow of a doubt he would look more than great in a swimsuit. Perhaps they should have gone skinny-dipping. She settled for a neutral answer. "I'm sure he does."

For whatever reason, that comment made Bianca laugh. A moment later, Veronica was laughing with her.

They talked for an hour or so longer before they each began to yawn. "I think it's bedtime for me."

Bianca stood. "Me too."

They walked up the stairs together and then Veronica headed for her bedroom while Bianca opened the door across the hall, disappearing into the guest room.

Veronica dropped onto her bed. If you would have told her a week ago that she would have welcomed her half sister into her life and even provided her a bed for the night, she would have laughed in your face at the absurdity of it all. And if you would have told her that she was starting to think of Malcolm as a friend, she would have scoffed. And look at her now.

Apparently life was full of surprises.

Chapter Ten

Malcolm stared at his phone as if willing it to ring. He'd hoped that Veronica would call him back with an update, but with every passing minute that notion diminished until he had to face reality. She wasn't going to reach out. He hoped that everything was going well between her and her sister. Maybe the saying that no news was good news applied here. Well, there was no sense sitting around waiting to hear back. His parents had turned in for the night, so if he wanted human interaction, he would have to find it elsewhere.

He grabbed his keys and headed for town. He didn't have any particular destination in mind so he drove aimlessly until he ended up at Grady's. Malcolm stepped inside and looked around for a familiar face. When he spotted his friend Cole, he walked over to his table. "Are you meeting anyone?"

"Nope. Have a seat."

Malcolm pulled out the chair across from his friend. "Thanks."

"This is a surprise," Cole said. "You're about the last person I expected to run into tonight."

"I could say the same thing about you. I figured you would be on Daddy duty."

A waitress approached and Malcolm ordered a beer. When she stepped away, Cole replied.

"School is out and Crystal is spending the weekend with her best friend."

Malcolm smiled. "So you're enjoying a free night out alone? No date?"

"Date? What's that?"

"It's that bad, is it?"

Cole shook his head. "I have a daughter to raise on my own. Dealing with a teenage girl and all of her moods is hard enough. I'm not looking to add a woman to the mix. Maybe once Crystal starts college I'll give it another chance." His mouth twisted. "Or maybe not."

"Far be it from me to give you romantic advice. I'm the last person to force a relationship on anyone. I'm happy on my own." Would he continue to feel that way if Veronica told him that she was interested in him? He doubted it. But since their friendship was shaky at best, there was little chance of that happening.

Cole held up his bottle in toast. "To the single life."

Malcolm echoed that statement and took a long pull of his beer.

"Besides," Cole continued, "I've got the business to run."

"That's right. You bought the feedstore. How is that going?"

"Good. Plenty of customers."

"Do you ever miss living on a ranch?" Cole had been a hand on the Montgomery ranch until a few years ago The Montgomery spread was near Malcolm's family ranch and he and Cole had run into each other from time to time, eventually becoming friends.

"Of course. Aspen Creek isn't a big city by any stretch of the imagination, but there are a whole lot more people around than I like and a lot more noise. Every once in a while, I miss the peace and quiet of the ranch. Who knows, maybe one day I'll buy a small one of my own. But my daughter loves living in town. Naturally what she needs comes first."

Malcolm nodded. Family looked out for each other. His parents had always put his wants and needs ahead of their own. Now it was his turn to do the same for them. "You're a good dad."

"I hope so. It's been just the two of us since the day she was born so I've been figuring it out as I go."

Malcolm took another swallow of his beer and then grabbed a laminated menu from between the salt and pepper shakers. "I think I could go for a sandwich."

"Me too."

They gestured for the waitress who took their orders for two Reubens with fries and promised to be back soon. She was as good as her word and before long they were enjoying their food. The band took the stage and then began playing. Malcolm and Cole leaned back in the chairs and stopped talking as they listened.

"So how long will you be in town?" Cole asked when the band took a break.

"That's undecided. I had planned to stay another couple of weeks, but now I'm not so sure. I can pretty much work from anywhere although I do prefer going into the office. Not to mention that I have eight weeks of unused vacation." His father's health was definitely making him

reconsider the amount of time he spent at work, accu-
mulating time off that he rarely took.

"What's keeping you here?"

"My parents." He briefly described the situation with
his father's health and the conflicting emotions he felt.
"Selling the ranch feels like a betrayal to my parents
and my ancestors. They worked so hard to buy the land
and to work it all these years. They sacrificed so much
to make the ranch a success. But my father's been having a hard time finding good ranch hands who want to
stick around. I don't see how things would be any different for me."

"It's not a job for everyone. I speak from experience."

"I can't imagine not being able to ride my horse whenever I come back home. And if they travel as much as
they plan to, they won't be here for weeks at a time.
They could just as easily come to Chicago to see me. I
won't have a reason to come back to Aspen Creek at all."

"No?"

He thought of Veronica but still shook his head.

"Tough choice."

"The toughest."

"But I'm sure you'll make the right one."

"I wish I had your confidence."

"It comes from being a single dad. There's not a lot of
space for going back and forth. Once I make a decision,
I stick with it and do my best to make it work. Only after
I've given it my all and failed do I try something else."

It all sounded simple but Malcolm knew it wasn't as
easy as Cole was trying to make him believe.

They hung around for the next set before deciding
to call it a night.

"There is one major benefit to living in town," Cole said as they stood outside.

"What's that?"

"I'm only a couple of blocks from home. I'll be there in a few minutes and you'll still be on the road."

Malcolm chuckled. "Maybe. But I'll take that trade-off every day of the week."

As he drove down the highway, the pressures of the decision he needed to make returned with full force. Time was running out. If he didn't want to run the ranch, and his father wasn't able to continue working it, they were going to have to sell it. Although he hated the idea, he hated the notion of letting the property fall into disrepair even more. He was sure there was a solution he hadn't considered, but he was too close to the situation to see clearly. It was hard to be logical when his emotions were involved.

When he got home, he parked in the driveway and got out of the truck. Instead of going inside, he leaned against the truck and looked around. Though it was dark, the moon and stars provided enough illumination for him to make out the buildings and the silhouettes of several stands of trees. The wind blew and he inhaled a deep breath of fresh air. If he sold, this could be one of the last times that he could simply enjoy a quiet night on the ranch.

What would he do with Hercules? He couldn't imagine selling him. But it wouldn't be fair to bring the stallion back to Chicago and stable him there. Sure they would take good care of his horse, but being that far away from home and all that was familiar would be cruel. Hercules was used to having acres of land to roam freely.

Sighing, he crossed the yard to the house, then he sat on the back step, trying to bring order to his thoughts. He knew his parents would consider his input when deciding what to do. They'd always made major decisions that way. But he was conflicted. He didn't know what he wanted. He had no idea what was best for him much less what was best for them. It was all so much easier to make decisions when they only affected him. Now his parents' happiness was on the line. He couldn't get this wrong.

Veronica started the coffee maker and then leaned against the counter. She'd heard Bianca's voice coming through the door when she'd come into the kitchen, so she knew the teenager was awake and on the phone with someone. Though she couldn't make out the words, Veronica could tell that the conversation was not a pleasant one. But since it was none of her business, she wouldn't ask.

She rummaged through the cabinets, trying to come up with ingredients for a vegetarian breakfast. She pulled out a container of oatmeal and a loaf of bread then took the bowl of fruit from the refrigerator and set it on the table.

Veronica was just about to call Bianca when the teen stormed into the kitchen. She took one look at the girl's face and the good morning she was about to say died in her throat.

"What's wrong?"

"Mom and Dad."

Veronica didn't like thinking about her father and his second wife, much less talking about them, but Bianca was clearly upset, so Veronica was going to have to suck it up. "You're going to have to tell me more than that."

Bianca frowned and grabbed a bunch of green grapes from the bowl. "Are these clean?"

"Yes."

Veronica leaned against the counter and folded her arms across her chest, sending Bianca a silent message. *I can outlast you.*

Bianca ate her grapes and then sighed. "They're mad at me."

"Why?"

"Because they didn't know I was coming here."

"You didn't tell them?"

"No. But in my defense, I didn't expect them to find out. They were supposed to be out of town for two more days. I guess something happened and they came back home last night. They were pissed when I wasn't there and they didn't know where I was."

"I think they were probably more scared than anything."

"I doubt that was it," Bianca said with a sneer.

"Why do you think that?"

"If they were so concerned about me, they would have called. Check my phone. You won't find a single message from them there. The first time they tried to reach me was this morning."

"Maybe they thought that you spent the night with a friend."

"That's what my mom said. She said they thought that I would be home by now."

"And if they would have stuck to their schedule they never would have known that you came here to meet me."

Bianca nodded. "You didn't write me back and I wanted to get to know you. I couldn't think of any other way."

"I'm sorry for that. Now that I know you I realize that I would have been missing out if we hadn't met."

Bianca's expression brightened and she smiled. "That's what I think too."

"What did you tell them?"

Bianca made a big show of picking individual grapes from another bunch. Veronica's stomach began to churn. She could tell that Bianca was holding something back and there was only one reason for that. It would hurt Veronica's feelings. "I don't remember."

"Surely you don't expect me to believe that. You only ended the call a few minutes ago."

"It's not important."

Despite the pain in her heart at what she was sure was another rejection from her father, Veronica was determined to know what he'd said. Not because she was a glutton for punishment, but because she didn't want Bianca to have to bear the burden of a secret that would only eat at her.

Veronica crossed the room and stood in front of the teenager. She placed her hands on Bianca's shoulders. "It's okay. You can tell me. I'm sure it's nothing I haven't heard before."

"They just said that I shouldn't have come here."

"So I suppose you'll be going back home after breakfast."

Bianca nodded. "I'm glad that I got to meet you. And I'm mad at them for not telling me I had a sister all this time."

"You didn't know about me?" Veronica was proud that she'd kept the hurt and disappointment from her voice although she wasn't sure how she'd pulled it off. It hurt knowing her father had kept her a secret from his own daughter.

"No. I would have written you sooner if I had known about you."

Veronica told herself not to ask, but she couldn't hold back the question. "How did you find out?"

"Mom and Dad were arguing. I heard him say something about his other daughter Veronica in Aspen Creek. After that, it was easy to find you. We have the same last name. There were a few mentions of you online." Bianca gave her a sweet smile that took away some of the hurt of rejection. "And I really wanted to get to know you."

"Why?"

"Because we're *family*."

Those quietly spoken words were nearly Veronica's undoing. She had been so willing to reject this girl simply because she was a reminder of how hurt Veronica had been by their father's behavior. She'd come so close to making a huge mistake that would have punished someone who hadn't done anything wrong. Thankfully Malcolm's words had come to her at the right time. Otherwise she might have missed this opportunity. "Yes we are. And I'm glad that we got to know each other."

"So I can come back? I can visit you again?"

"I would like that. But I don't think it's a decision that we can make on our own. You have to let your parents know. No more sneaking around."

"I don't see why they get a vote. I'm eighteen."

"Yes. But you still live in their home."

"I'll be going to college soon and living on campus."

"Are they going to pay your tuition and living expenses?"

Bianca heaved a heavy sigh. "Yes."

"Then they get a say in your life, I'm sorry to say."

"That sounds like blackmail. Do what we say or we'll take away your education and make it harder for you to have a good future."

"Wait a second. I didn't say they would do anything like that." She honestly didn't know whether they would or not. Truth be told, she was inclined to think they were horrible people. The lowest of the low. But she knew she was biased on the matter. "Still, it would be adult of you to consider their opinion."

Bianca gave Veronica a side-eye. "You think I didn't notice the way you slid the word *adult* in there. No wonder you're such a successful librarian. You get people to do the right thing and make them believe it's their idea."

"So you think being open with your parents is the right thing?"

She inhaled deeply before nodding. "Only kids sneak around. And as you pointed out, I'm an adult."

"Agreed."

"But I don't care if they don't want me to keep in touch with you. I'm going to do it anyway. I'll tell them that too. That is if you still want to talk to me."

Veronica smiled and pulled Bianca into her embrace. "I would like nothing more. As you said, we're family."

Suddenly the idea didn't seem unbelievable at all. She and Bianca were family. More than that, they were *sisters*.

They ate breakfast and then Veronica walked Bianca

to her car, an expensive vehicle with all of the bells and whistles. "Let me know when you get home."

Bianca giggled and shook her head. "Oh no. Another person making me check in."

"Another person who cares about you."

Bianca hugged Veronica again. "I'll text you the minute I pull into the driveway."

"Thank you." Veronica watched as Bianca pulled off and drove down the street, not looking away until the car turned at the corner. A myriad of emotions swam through her and she couldn't put a name on them to save her life. Instead of shoving her feelings into a place where she could ignore them, she forced herself to stay put and feel them. After a moment, she took them out one by one and examined them.

The pain and anger she felt at her father and his wife was tempered by the happiness she felt from being on the receiving end of her sister's generous spirit. Veronica might have lost her father's love years ago, but today she'd gained the affection of her younger sister. That was a win in her book. There was also a bit of worry for how Leslie would react to the turn of events. Sure she'd said that she was okay with Veronica corresponding with her sister back when it was just a possibility, but would she feel the same way about her maintaining a relationship with her now that it was really happening? The answer came immediately. Of course Leslie would be okay with it. She wouldn't have said it if she didn't mean it. She was a loving person with a big heart. Veronica's happiness had always come first.

Breathing in a cleansing breath, Veronica went into her house. She'd taken the day off and hadn't made any plans. After wandering around her house at loose ends for fifteen minutes, she picked up her phone. She wanted to talk to Malcolm. More than that, she wanted to *see* him.

He answered the phone, a smile in his voice, and her heart skipped a beat. She was still adjusting to the fact that she was physically attracted to him. Truth be told, she liked the idea. It had been quite some time since she'd felt this giddy about a man. Part of her thought that it would be nice to date him and see where things led. Of course, given everything that was going on in her life, and the fact that his stay in town was temporary, she still believed that might not be the wisest thing to do.

"Is this a good time?"

"Any time I hear from you is a good time."

She smiled. Malcolm might only want to be friends but he had flirting down to a science. "You mentioned the other day that you like to ride out to that quiet place and think. I was wondering if you would let me do the same."

"Sure. Just name the date and time."

"How about today? In an hour or so? I understand if you're busy and can't ride out with me. I can go on my own."

"In an hour is fine. That gives me time to wrap up a couple of things. But if you would rather go on your own, you can do that too."

"Either way sounds nice. How about we play it by ear. That way if something comes up, you can deal with it without feeling as if you broke a promise to me."

Malcolm's heavy sigh came over the phone. "You're never going to forgive me for not being there for you before, are you?"

Veronica blinked and for a second she didn't know what Malcolm was talking about. When it hit her, she shook her head. She hadn't been thinking about that time in college. Apparently she was truly over it.

"Malcolm…"

"It's okay. I understand. Just come on out to the ranch. We can work out the details when you get here."

Veronica wanted to clear up the misunderstanding now, but before she could say a word, Malcolm had ended the call.

She was already dressed in jeans, so all she needed to do was put on her boots and she was ready to go. While she drove, she thought about everything that had happened over the past couple of days. Her days were usually predictable and this spurt of excitement was new to her. It took a moment for her to recognize that she was actually exhilarated. Perhaps her life had become just a bit too safe and routine. Maybe it was time for her to stop being the librarian who encouraged other people to follow their dreams and time to begin to chase after her own.

As she drove, she was struck as always by the beauty of the countryside. The trees were filled with big green leaves and red and yellow wildflowers grew in random bunches along the side of the highway. Birds chirped as they flew across the blue sky. The snowcapped mountains in the distance provided a perfect vista. This was definitely among the most scenic spots in Colorado if not the entire country.

As much as she loved Aspen Creek, she loved the ranches even more. They were so serene. She loved coming upon a family of deer or foxes drinking from the babbling brooks. She would never tire of looking at the acres and acres of green grass, the stands of trees, and the hills. Although she had never told anyone, she'd always felt a little bit envious of her friends who lived on ranches. Even when she'd been living in the big house with her parents, a part of her had longed to live on a ranch. Though she no longer envied her friends' lifestyles, a part of her still yearned for the freedom and peace of mind that came with the wide-open spaces. Of course, given her financial reality, living on a ranch of her own was a pipe dream.

She drove a few more miles to Malcolm's ranch and turned onto the driveway, continuing until she reached the outbuildings. She was getting out of her car when Malcolm ambled over. He smiled when he saw her and she couldn't help but smile in return.

"How was the drive?" he asked.

"Fine. It's always been a nice ride." He nodded and she touched his arm. "I need to say something."

He stiffened but his smile remained the same. "Sure."

"I hadn't been thinking about college when we talked earlier. I know that I can rely on you."

"Since when?"

She shrugged. "I think since forever. I just forgot about it for a while. But now that we're together again, I remember."

Chapter Eleven

Malcolm's heart stopped and then began to race as the full impact of Veronica's words hit him. Though he'd longed to hear her say that she no longer held a grudge and truly meant it, now that it had happened, he had no idea how to respond. Had Veronica actually put their past behind them for real this time? He was too happy with the possibility to press his luck by furthering the discussion. That might lead to disaster.

"Okay. I have your horse saddled and ready to go."

"You aren't going to say anything?" Veronica asked, her brow wrinkled in obvious confusion. "You're just going to act as if I didn't say anything important?"

He blew out a breath. So much for avoiding land mines. "That was the plan. I don't want to jinx anything by getting into a long, drawn-out discussion and possibly saying the wrong thing. You said the past is behind us and I'm willing to go from there."

She gave a look that said she didn't believe him, but when she didn't push the matter, he realized that she was as worried about shattering the fragile peace as he was.

"Now," he continued, "do you want to ride alone or would you like company?"

"I would love your company as long as I'm not keeping you from doing anything important."

"I was just going to ride fences. We're moving the cattle to another grazing field in a couple of days and I want to make sure that everything is secure. I can just as easily do that tomorrow as today."

Her eyes lit up and his stomach lurched in response. She was truly beautiful. "Can we do that together? I can help."

"Really? Do you still know how to repair fence?"

She gave him a long look. "Of course I do. We worked together for years. All I need is a pair of gloves."

"Come with me and I'll get you a pair."

They went into the stable and straight to the equipment locker. He pulled out a clean pair of gloves that belonged to his mother. Cheryl had confessed that a lot of time had passed since she'd used them. Malcolm had always believed that his mother enjoyed ranching. Now he wasn't so sure. But it was clear that Veronica was looking forward to a few hours of work. He had to admit that her presence was going to make the task much more enjoyable.

She took the gloves and he grabbed the wire and tools he would need. Once they were on horseback, she smiled up at him. "I'll follow your lead."

"I'd rather that you rode beside me."

"Okay."

He signaled for Hercules to move and Veronica did the same with Buttercup. As they rode, a gentle breeze blew, sending Veronica's hair flying over her shoulders. Even when they'd been kids, she'd never worn a cowboy hat, preferring to wear sunglasses to keep the sun out of her eyes. No matter how many times he'd tried to get her to put on one, she'd shaken her head, saying she didn't want to have hat-head. Back then, she'd worn her hair straight with the ends turning under in the middle of her back. Now it was almost as long but she wore it curlier.

She brushed a few stray strands of hair out of her eyes.

"You know, you can use my hat if you want," he offered. "That'll keep the wind from blowing hair into your face."

As expected, Veronica shot him a dirty look that spoke volumes. "You already know my feelings on that."

He laughed. "I don't understand this hat phobia of yours."

"It's not a phobia. I'm not afraid of Stetsons. I simply don't want to walk around with smushed hair. I spend too much time getting my hair to look good to ruin it like that."

"But windblown is acceptable?"

Though he was taller than she was and sat higher in the saddle, she somehow managed to look down her nose at him. "Exactly."

"Well, as beautiful as you are, you would be as attractive with hat hair as you are with your windblown hair. Nothing can ever take away from your looks."

Her mouth popped open and she stared at him with wide, surprised eyes. His stomach twisted and he felt a moment of panic. Had he gone too far? Sure, he believed that Veronica was stunning. That was an undisputable fact. But never in a million years had he planned on saying those words out loud. Especially not to her. That opinion was supposed to stay in the vault.

"Thank you," she said finally. "And might I say the same about you."

Whew. That was close. He breathed an internal sigh of relief. He needed to keep the moment light so she wouldn't sense his desire. "You think that I'm beautiful even with hat hair? Thank you."

She laughed and shook her head. "You are just as goofy and funny as I remember."

"You remember me as goofy and funny? That's not at all how I recall myself as a teenager."

"No?" She pressed a hand against her chest. "Do tell."

He forced his eyes away from her perfect breasts. "I always saw myself as suave and debonair. A ladies' man."

Her grin grew broader as she looked him up and down, her eyes pausing as she took in his chest and shoulders. He'd spent years working on the ranch as a kid, but his muscles had never grown. He'd measured them every month, disappointed each time his chest was not any broader and his scrawny biceps were no bigger than they'd been before. Then as if by magic, when he went away to college, his body began to develop. Of course Veronica had not been around to see his metamorphosis.

He felt his skin grow tight and hot at her slow perusal. By the time her eyes reached his face, his skin was burning. Fortunately for him, his hat shaded his eyes, protecting his hidden emotions from her view. He might be coming to accept that his feelings for her were romantic, but he didn't want her to know.

No good could come from that. He would be leaving town soon to go back home to Chicago. If his parents sold the ranch he wouldn't be coming back to Aspen Creek. Veronica was quite attached to this town. She always had been. He couldn't imagine her leaving. Since there was so much stacked against them, it made no sense to start something they would never be able to finish.

"Your memory might be a bit hazy there. But you are definitely suave and debonair now. And that, my friend, is just your base. You know, when you're dressed in faded jeans and dirty boots. Once you get all cleaned up, you're the most suave and most debonair of men. You look scrumptious in a suit and tie."

"Food is scrumptious."

"Yes, and you looked like a big old piece of chocolate cake with two scoops of vanilla ice cream on the side." She leered and he laughed.

Truthfully, it didn't bother him that she'd compared him to her favorite dessert. He actually found it slightly flattering and amusing. But now it was time to change the subject.

"How did things go with your sister?"

"It turns out it wasn't as difficult as I'd feared it would be. She's a very nice girl. Quite funny and intelligent."

"I'm glad you took the time to get to know her."

He spotted a hole in the fence, so he headed over there then swung down from his horse. Veronica followed and dismounted as gracefully as if she'd been riding horses every day of her life. She put on her gloves and then stood beside him. Her soft scent floated on the breeze and teased his senses. He inhaled deeply allowing himself to enjoy the moment.

"It's all coming back to me now," she said. "I know how to repair this."

Malcolm pulled out the extra wire and tighteners and knelt down. "Good. It'll go faster if we work together as a team. Teamwork makes the dream work."

Veronica raised an eyebrow and gave him a skeptical look. "You could probably do this a lot more quickly on your own."

"But it wouldn't be as much fun." He glanced over his shoulder and looked at her. She was smiling brightly at the compliment and his heart skipped a beat. He held out the wire cutters. She took them and together they worked to repair the fence. She was right. He could have finished it more quickly on his own, but speed wasn't everything. Her company was worth the extra time.

After they'd repaired the hole, he returned the tools to his saddlebag and they continued their ride. The temperature was perfect and there were a few puffy white clouds floating across the wide blue sky. Even so, he kept an eye on the sky, just in case the weather turned stormy again today. He didn't know if he could control his reactions if he saw her with a wet shirt plastered against her body again.

"You were talking about your sister," Malcolm said, returning to the previous conversation. Being on horseback amid vast quiet acres made it easier to discuss topics that were close to the heart.

"Yes. She wants to keep in touch."

"How do you feel about that?"

"I'm surprised to be honest."

"You are? Did you really think that she would come all this way just to take a look at you and then walk away?"

"Yeah. Maybe. I don't know. There was a time when I was curious about my father's new family. I wanted to know what they looked like. What they sounded like. What kinds of hobbies they had. I needed to know what it was about them that made my father love them more than he loved me."

He didn't know if there was an appropriate answer to that, but he couldn't think of one that didn't include cursing her father, so he simply nodded.

"I never sought them out, but I did snoop around. And then I saw that interview where my father referred to Bianca and his stepsons as his children. He never mentioned me once." Her voice cracked and she blinked rapidly as if swishing away tears before they could fall.

The echoes of remembered pain in Veronica's voice enraged Malcolm. There was no way her father didn't know how badly he'd hurt her. He simply hadn't cared. Malcolm wasn't a violent man, but he would make an exception in Walter Kendrick's case.

"He's a jerk," Malcolm said finally.

"Agreed. But that wasn't my point. After that, I decided my curiosity was satisfied, and there was no need for a personal interaction."

"And you expected Bianca to feel the same."

"Yes. She only recently learned about me, but it turns out that she wanted to do more than satisfy her curiosity. Instead she wanted to talk about boys. She wants us to go to movies together."

"She wants to be real sisters."

Veronica inhaled and then blew out the breath. "Yes."

"And you don't?"

"I'm not sure how I feel. At first I thought the idea

was ludicrous. But she's so sweet and earnest. I couldn't tell her no without hurting her feelings. Besides, I like her a lot. But the thing is…her parents."

"You don't like them."

"Not even a little bit. And I told her that if we were going to be in contact, she had to let them know. I refuse to be treated as if I am some dirty little secret. They're going to have to acknowledge my existence."

"Good for you."

"Thank you. I'm quite proud of myself."

"Did she agree?"

"Reluctantly. Not that she wants me to be a dirty secret…but I think she's worried her parents will forbid her to talk to me. She seems determined not to let that happen."

"So you'll keep in touch."

"Maybe. She might be eighteen, but she is still financially dependent on her parents. And since our father and her mother made it a point to excise me from their lives, I don't think they'll agree."

"So in other words, the two of you might not have a relationship until she's able to support herself."

"That about sums it up."

"I'm sorry to hear that."

"Why? It isn't as if my life will be any different than it was before yesterday."

"Think not? Before she was just a name with no face. A stranger who you never thought of. Now she's a living, breathing person. She's changed you and you've changed her. Every person who enters our life has an impact on it."

"I know you aren't waxing philosophical on me."

"No. But it's the truth. You're changed just from knowing her. In the most basic sense, you no longer have to wonder what she looks like or the kind of person she is. In a broader sense, you know that your heart is big enough to welcome her into your life despite everything."

"You make me sound better than I am. I didn't want to meet her. She just showed up and pushed herself into my life. I wanted to tell her to go away. That's proof that I'm not as good as you think."

"It's proof that you're human. Anyone in your shoes would have those thoughts. Some people would have acted on them. Just so you know, I wouldn't have thought less of you if you had. You need to protect your peace."

"At what cost? Hers? Besides, it turned out okay."

"Only because you made it so. You are one special woman, Veronica Kendrick. Don't you ever forget that."

Veronica's heart filled at the warmth in Malcolm's voice. He'd always had a way of making her feel good about herself, but this felt different. As children, it had been so easy to share their feelings. They'd been too innocent to know that you were supposed to keep your thoughts and deepest emotions to yourself. For him to be so direct now, given their past, was enough to make her want to return the compliment.

But life had taught her over and over again not to make herself vulnerable. She was all too aware that people took advantage when they knew you loved them. Her father hadn't been the only man to break her heart—only the first. She knew that a father's betrayal affected the way a woman looked at love and romance, so she'd done her best not to let him overshadow her relationships. But though the three men she'd gotten serious with hadn't been unfaithful, they'd been bad in other ways. Or perhaps they had just been wrong for her. Whatever. She didn't exclude men from her life. She still dated and had several men that she counted among her friends. But love and romance never worked out for her.

So why was she suddenly consumed by the notion of having a more intimate type of relationship with Malcolm? Perhaps it was because she was indulging the pleasant memories of the past. Or maybe it was physical attraction run amok. Or maybe…maybe it was neither of those things. Perhaps her attraction and romantic feelings for Malcolm were real. But what did it matter if they were? He didn't want anything other than friendship with her.

Malcolm pointed to another hole in the fence, thank goodness, putting all of her thoughts on hold.

"I'm not familiar with this part of the ranch," she said. "Is this new?"

"No. My father bought it when we were kids. You and I never rode out this way because it's not as pretty as the rest of the ranch. Not only that, the cattle graze out here and Dad didn't want us getting into trouble. After a while, the swimming hole became our place."

"I like it out here. The mountains and sky are close enough to touch."

"That may be your imagination."

"Maybe. But I like the feeling."

As they worked, they put the hard conversations behind them. She'd wanted Malcolm's perspective, but discussing serious matters was draining. Now she just wanted to enjoy the rest of the afternoon with him.

Malcolm must have felt the same way because he turned the conversation to their famous classmate.

"It was something, seeing a celebrity here in Aspen Creek," Malcolm said. "Apart from the usual Olympians who live here."

"Lots of celebrities vacation here these days," Veronica said. "I've seen a few of them walking around downtown. There's even a rumor that a movie or two will be shot around here this winter."

"Really? Real snow definitely would look better than that fake stuff they use in a lot of those movies." Malcolm flashed her a look, a mischievous grin on his face. "This could be your big break. You could get discovered and become a movie star yourself."

Veronica scoffed. "Totally not interested."

"Why? Don't tell me you still have stage fright?"

Laughter burst from Veronica. She'd nearly forgotten about her one and only foray into show business. She'd been cast as one of Santa's elves in their second grade Christmas play. Veronica had known her lines and performed them quite well in rehearsal. But on the night of the actual performance, she'd taken one look at the crowded gymnasium and then frozen. Every line of her speech fled her mind and she could only stand there mutely. That was the beginning and end of her acting career. "I don't know. Nor do I intend to find out."

"Maybe you could be an extra. They don't have lines. All you would have to do is be there. You could be in a crowd scene. Surely you could do that."

"I think I'll pass. But you could always play the part

of the good-looking rancher. Or maybe the successful businessman visiting his hometown."

"That's a possibility. After all, in that Christmas play, I did remember all of my lines."

"You only had two lines. 'Look. See all of the toys we made, Santa.'"

"And I delivered them with the skill of a Shakespearean actor."

"Did anyone ever tell you that modesty is appealing in a man?" Veronica asked, turning to look at him.

"No. But I've heard that confidence is attractive."

"You say that as if the two are mutually exclusive."

"You never know." He winked at her and her stomach fluttered.

She knew Malcolm's flirting didn't mean anything, but she couldn't control the way her body reacted. Truthfully, she didn't want to. She was enjoying their playful banter. It was so different from the way their interactions had gone when he'd first come back to town. Their time together on this visit might not last long, but she was up for the game as long as it lasted.

"Well, that is it for today. All of the fence line is secure, so the cattle will be safe to graze here."

They turned their horses and started back toward the house. Now that they weren't studying the fence for holes they were able to ride more quickly. They spurred their horses to increase their speed and in an instant they were galloping across the field. Veronica let out a whoop of pleasure as she encouraged her mount to go even faster.

Malcolm glanced over as he passed her. The race was on. Malcolm was a master horseman and Veronica didn't expect to win. But she was going to make him earn his victory. Leaning over, she encouraged Buttercup to pick up the pace. Though her horse's legs ate up the ground, the distance between Veronica and Malcolm steadily increased. She had to give him credit for treating her as an equal by not taking it easy on her.

By the time she reached the stable, Malcolm had already removed the saddle and blanket from his horse's back and was checking Hercules's hooves.

"That was close," Veronica said with a laugh as she stopped her horse beside him.

"Did the definition of *close* change in my absence?" Malcolm asked.

"No need to rub it in," Veronica said, dismounting. She rubbed Buttercup's nose. "Your horse was faster than mine."

"True. And I'm a better rider."

Though Veronica had just thought the same thing, there was no way she was going to admit that to him when he had such a smug smile on his face. Instead she focused on removing the saddle and blanket and inspecting Buttercup's hooves for rocks and other debris.

Malcolm handed Veronica a brush and she began to groom Buttercup. The motion was soothing and Veronica felt her mind drifting away to a happy place where her worries no longer existed. They didn't talk as they worked, but the quiet wasn't unpleasant. She liked being comfortable enough to not feel the need to fill the silence. Once the horses were cared for, Malcolm and Veronica led them to their stalls. Malcolm checked the levels of feed and water and then closed the inside gates. The outer gates were open to the large fenced corral so the horses could go outside if they chose to.

Veronica turned to Malcolm. She wasn't ready to go home but she couldn't think of an excuse to hang around him for a while longer. Suddenly he smiled at her, his thumbs hooked in his belt loops. "How about a game of darts?"

"Do you still play?"

"I haven't played in years. Not since college. But I should still be good enough to beat you."

"I don't remember you being quite this cocky before."

"I don't remember you taking so long to answer a challenge before either. Are you scared?"

"Them's fighting words. Where is the dartboard?"

"The same place it's always been."

Veronica started toward the covered porch at the back of the ranch house, determination in her stride. She had no doubt that she would lose. She hadn't played darts since high school and even then she hadn't been good. But she'd always loved playing anyway. Back then Malcolm's parents had often joined them and being included in their happy family had always felt so warm and comfortable that losing hadn't bothered her.

Malcolm hustled to catch up with her, grabbing her hand when he did. Her skin burned at the unexpected contact and tingles raced down her spine. He folded his fingers around hers as if it were the most natural thing in the world. Though the contact didn't appear to affect him, Veronica couldn't have uttered a word if her life depended on it.

When they were on the porch, Malcolm grabbed the darts from the case and handed her red darts, keeping the blue for himself. They each took a bad-handed shot which she won. Then the game began in earnest.

Veronica took her turn and as expected her darts landed on the board willy-nilly. Malcolm took his turn and his darts landed more firmly. Even so, his score wasn't much better than hers.

"Oh. So you're going to beat me easily, huh?" she asked with a teasing smile. "Maybe you're not as good as you think."

He smirked. "I was just going easy on you. I didn't want to make you cry."

"When have I ever cried because I lost?"

"Never. But there's always a first time."

"It won't be today." Veronica took her next throw, determined to do better this round and make him eat his words. The dart bounced off the board and landed on the floor.

"Pitiful," Malcolm said, grinning. "Let me help you."

Before she could reply, he had moved and was standing close behind her. The heat from his body wrapped around her and her knees weakened. He placed an arm around her waist and leaned closer. She was tempted to relax against his strong chest, but she forced herself to remain upright. But she couldn't stop herself from inhaling his masculine scent. It made her head swim, and her eyes drifted shut.

"I think I see the problem." His voice sounded hoarse and held a hint of playfulness.

"What is it?" she murmured.

"Your eyes are closed. You can't hit what you can't see."

Veronica forced her eyes open and then stared at the board. How could she be expected to focus on the game with Malcolm standing so near? Just being close to him was making her imagination run wild. She took a step away from him and then glanced over her shoulder and caught his eye. "I can do this."

He waved a hand. "Go ahead."

Breathing deeply, Veronica took aim and threw the rest of the darts. By some miracle, they all hit the board. Whew. She dropped onto the couch while Malcolm took his turn, hoping to have a few moments to cool off. Her eyes were drawn to his perfect body and she took the opportunity to study him, taking in every inch of toned muscles. There would never come a time when she tired of looking at him. Before she could catch her breath, Malcolm sat down beside her. Their arms brushed, and sexual tension arced between them.

Veronica felt herself being drawn to him and she was powerless to resist. Their eyes met and held. She lifted her head as he lowered his and their lips met in a tentative kiss.

Her lips were still tingling at the contact when he pulled back and looked at her, a question in his eyes. *Do you want this?* She reached out and pulled his head back down to hers, wordlessly answering. This time when their lips met, the kiss was filled with heat and fire. Desire.

Filled with need, she opened her mouth to him and his tongue swept inside, dancing with hers. Fireworks flashed beneath her closed eyes as shivers raced up and down her spine, reaching from the tips of her toes to the crown of her head. She longed to touch him everywhere and before she knew it, her hands were roaming over his chest and shoulders. The heat coursing through her turned into a raging fire as she tried to get even closer to him.

She felt him moving away and she protested, trying desperately to maintain contact. She felt the laughter on his lips as he pulled away and then leaned his forehead against hers. His chest rose and fell as he labored to catch his breath and she realized she was doing the same. When the fog of desire cleared, she realized that she was sitting on his lap. How had that happened? And when?

"We need to slow things down a bit," Malcolm said.

"Why?" She didn't try to keep her unhappiness with his comment to herself.

He chuckled and brushed her hair away from her face. "Because there are so many things we need to work out. We've just gotten our friendship back. I don't want to mess that up. Do you?"

"No. I like having you back in my life. Before, it always felt like something was missing."

"Same here. But life has changed us. We need to take time to get to know each other as adults before we cross that line."

"How long will that take? Because I want you to know that I'm ready to cross that line. Heck, I'm ready to erase it."

Chapter Twelve

"Well?" Evelyn Parks asked, coming up to Veronica the instant the library opened.

"Well, what?"

"What is Malcolm up to? Is he going to sell the ranch to that venture capitalist?"

Veronica tilted her head and gave her a look that spoke of her irritation, even if she had to swallow back any sharp words. She was at work and needed to remain professional, but there was a whole lot she *wanted* to say. She was feeling very protective of Malcolm these days.

"Why do you care so much about what he plans to do with the ranch? It's his family's property."

"I care because I live here. Who knows what that person would build? It could be a warehouse. Or a factory. Either of those two would be a disaster for the town. Vacationers won't choose to come here if they're inhaling smog or having to deal with trucks on the road. We wouldn't like that either. You need to use your influence to make sure it doesn't happen."

"I don't think you understand the situation. I told you before that I don't have any type of influence on Malcolm. He's going to do whatever he chooses to do. And that's his right." Veronica could let Evelyn know that she had no intention of even broaching the subject with Malcolm, but she didn't. As long as Evelyn thought Veronica was on her side, she wouldn't try anything else—like going straight to the source. Malcolm didn't need to deal with her right now.

"That's what I was afraid of."

"Why?"

"Because he's changed from the kind young man he was when he lived here. Certainly you have noticed the difference."

Vernoica nodded slowly. She'd noticed plenty of differences. He was much more muscular and gorgeous than he'd been. He wore cologne that gave her a glimpse of heaven. And his kisses. Whew. She'd never kissed him before, but she couldn't imagine any high school boy knew how to kiss like that. And he was much more confident than he'd been before. Much more self-assured. But she knew that wasn't what Evelyn was talking about. She was talking about Malcolm's character. It had changed. How could it not? Life and experiences had matured him. Evelyn might not think that Malcolm was reliable anymore as a result, but Veronica couldn't fault her for that. She'd made the same mistake herself. But now she was starting to believe that Malcolm was someone she could count on. Someone she could trust.

"Why are you talking about Malcolm and not his parents? After all, they're the ones who actually own the property."

"Everyone knows that Roy isn't going to run the ranch much longer. The writing is on the wall. Cheryl has always wanted to see the world. They've already started to travel. It's up to Malcolm to decide what to do next."

"Well, I have nothing for you."

"But you want what's best for the community, don't you? So keep your eyes and ears open for an opportunity to convince him to do what's right."

Before Veronica could reply, Evelyn walked away, leaving her feeling unexpectedly conflicted. Naturally she felt a sense of loyalty to the town. She would do whatever was necessary to help the people of Aspen Creek. But she didn't buy into the idea that letting Malcolm make his own decisions about the ranch would put the town at risk. And anyway, she could never try to trick him into doing something he didn't want to do. Even for the people of Aspen Creek. As far as she was concerned, the decision was his and only his.

Veronica gave herself a mental shake and ordered herself to get her head in the game. The preschool playgroup was about to begin and several parents and children were beginning to stream into the building. She'd set out toys and books for the children to play with until it was time for her to read to them.

She stepped into the room, pleased to see that a good number of her regulars were there. Although she loved summer, it was always a bit disappointing to watch attendance at her programs plummet. It was a nice day, so she decided to shake things up.

Approaching the group of moms who were talking quietly, she smiled. "How would you feel about taking this outside today? There are picnic tables out back and a few blankets we can use. We could let the kids run around for a bit and then read the story."

"That sounds good to me," Marla, one of the newer moms, said. "We should totally take advantage of the nice weather."

They gathered the kids and toys and went out into the small, fenced lawn. The kids were delighted and immediately began running around. Perhaps if the group met outside on a regular basis, she would have better attendance during the non-school months. Veronica decided to put together a poll and email the parents later.

The combination of the sunny day and the enthusiastic children worked wonders on her spirits. She felt her shoulders relax as the tension slipped from her body. The wind blew, carrying her cares away and replacing them with a lightness of spirit and thoughts of Malcolm.

She smiled as she remembered the feel of his lips on hers. Just the memory of the way he'd kissed her and run his hands over her body in sensual caresses made her warm all over again.

"Are you all right?" Marla asked. "You look a bit flushed."

Veronica blinked, clearing away the lustful memories. She'd never been this distracted at work before. Of course, she had never been this attracted to anyone before. "I'm fine. I suppose I'm so used to the air conditioner that the warmth out here is a little bit much."

"But it's nice. And the kids are enjoying it."

"Yep. But it's time for me to gather them for the story."

Once everyone was settled, Veronica began reading the book. Although she enjoyed everything about being a children's librarian, reading to the little ones was one of her favorite tasks. She knew the youngest weren't able to follow all the details of the story, but that wasn't the point. She was making readers out of them. Holding the book open so the children could see the colorful pictures, Veronica began to read the familiar story. She exaggerated her emotions as she went, drawing oohs and aahs from her young audience. Their eyes were wide as she reached the climax. When she read the last words, the kids applauded and Veronica smiled.

She placed the book on the blanket and then distributed juice boxes and cookies. The adults chatted while the kids ate their snacks and Veronica forced herself not to fantasize about Malcolm. She'd managed to convince the others before that it was the change in temperature that had made her sweat. She didn't think they would accept that explanation a second time.

After the parents gathered their children and left, Veronica packed up the toys, books, and blankets and headed back inside. The rest of the day went fairly quickly, but as she worked, she couldn't keep from thinking about Malcolm and wondering when she would see him again.

Malcolm sent off the last of the emails and then closed his computer. He might be on vacation, but he liked being kept abreast of what was going on in the office. Business was a funny thing. Everything could be going well one minute but in the blink of an eye, that could change. He had seen it occur more than once, though it hadn't happened to him. He was working hard to be sure that it didn't.

He picked up his empty coffee cup and headed for the kitchen. His mother was sitting at the table, a crossword puzzle in front of her. She wasn't looking at the paper in front of her but was staring off into the distance.

"Where's Dad?"

His mother jumped as if startled before giving him a smile. Her eyes looked sad. "Sleeping in."

Those two words struck fear in Malcolm's heart. In his entire life, Malcolm had never known a time when his father hadn't been up with the birds. "How is he, really? I'm grown so don't try to protect me. I can take it."

"He's fine for a man of sixty-two. If he had a desk job he would be able to continue to perform it without any trouble. But ranch work is too physical for him to keep up the pace he used to."

"Why didn't you tell me before? Why all the secrecy?" He managed to control his anger and disappointment. His mother was stressed enough. She didn't need him jumping down her throat and making the situation worse. But he did feel like she owed him an explanation.

"Because we didn't want to influence your decision. If you want to keep the ranch we're with you. If not, we're okay with that too."

"I know you already said you want to travel. Is that true, or something that you said to make me feel better?"

"We have enjoyed our travel. And I admit there are places that I want to go to and things that I want to see."

"But…"

"I know your father is happiest here on the ranch. Even though he has enjoyed our vacations," she added quickly.

"But vacation isn't home."

"No it isn't."

"If you gave up the ranch, would you want to move to a house in Aspen Creek?"

Cheryl shook her head. "Your father couldn't live that close to the ranch and not own it. That would break his heart."

"And living somewhere farther away would be better?"

"For his mental state?" She looked up and Malcolm nodded. "Absolutely. We might move to Chicago. Do you think he could be happy in a big city?"

Malcolm shrugged. He doubted it. Roy was a rancher to the bone. "Don't worry, Mom. We'll work it all out."

"Don't you worry either. We're the parents. It's our job to take care of you, not the other way around."

Malcolm walked over to his mother and kissed the top of her head. "We're family. We take care of each other."

She nodded and Malcolm wondered if his mother agreed or if she simply didn't have the energy or the will to argue. Not that it mattered. One way or the other he was going to solve this problem in a way that worked for everyone. He just wished he knew what that was.

He walked outside and immediately headed for the barns. It was time for routine maintenance on the vehicles. In the old days he and his father had done this task together. As a teenager, Malcolm had complained the entire time. Now, as he worked alone, he missed his father's presence; missed his instruction on the right way to do things and the words of wisdom he often imparted. Malcolm could keep the ranch, but it wouldn't be the same without his father. It would be easy for Malcolm to simply run it—well, not easy since it would require him to give up a career and a lifestyle he loved—but he would do it if necessary. Would keeping the ranch in the family be better or worse for his father? How in the world was he supposed to know?

Asking his father straight-out wouldn't help. Roy was only going to tell Malcolm what he wanted him to know. He believed it was his job to protect his son. At one time, that had been true. But Malcolm was an adult and fully capable of looking out for his own needs. It would be easier to make a decision if his parents would be honest and open with him.

"I thought I would find you in here."

Malcolm turned at the sound of his father's voice. It was strong and filled with confidence. Not the voice of a man who was being forced to change his way of life because his body was betraying him. "You know how much I like tinkering with the motors."

"Yeah," Roy said, approaching Malcolm and nudging him out of the way. "Not at all, as I recall."

Malcolm grinned. "Looking back, it wasn't all bad. I learned a few skills that have come in handy over the years."

"I know you don't expect me to believe that you change the oil in your car."

"No. But I know how to should the situation ever arise."

Roy chuckled. "If things ever get that dire I imagine changing oil will be the last thing you're worrying about."

Malcolm placed a hand on his chest and gave a dramatic sigh. "You wound me."

"I guess the truth hurts."

"Especially when delivered in such a brutal fashion."

"When have you ever known me to sugarcoat any-thing?"

"Never."

"Exactly. And I won't start now." Roy loosened a screw and oil began to drain into the pan below. "And I don't think you should either."

"What?"

Roy wiped off his hands and then leaned on the open hood of the tractor. "You have something you want to say, so get to it."

"I need to know the truth about you and the ranch. What do you really want to do? I understand traveling and going on vacations to make Mom happy. I know she enjoyed that."

"I did too. It was good to see more of the world."

"But I also know that the ranch is important to you. You've always said that it's the dirt of this land that runs through your veins and not blood. So forgive me if I find it hard to believe you want to spend the rest of your life going from cruise ship to African safari to traipsing through Europe and back again."

Roy lifted a corner of his mouth in a half-grin. "Your mother would love it."

Malcolm shook his head. "I don't think she would. Vacations are great because they're a break from real life. Not a permanent state of affairs. You both enjoy having purpose. Are you really trying to convince me that a vagabond existence is what you want?"

"Why are you pushing this so hard?"

"Because I know there has to be a way to make ev-erything work that will satisfy your desire to travel and your wishes to hold on to the ranch."

Roy folded his arms across his chest. "If you know, then please, share this brilliant plan of yours with me."

"I'm working on it."

Instead of responding, Roy pushed away from the tractor and started to stoop down to pull out the now full pan of old oil.

"I got it," Malcolm said, squatting beside his father.

"I can do it," Roy said, nudging Malcolm aside. "I'm not the decrepit old man that you think I am."

"Nobody said you were decrepit or old. I'm just trying to pay my way around here," Malcolm said, keeping his voice deliberately calm.

"Well, don't."

"Right." Malcolm stood and stepped out of his father's way.

Roy sighed. "Sorry. I don't mean to be so gruff."

"Apology accepted."

"So, are you still going to that wedding this weekend?"

"Yes." Malcolm ignored the abrupt change in subject. He understood that his father was probably tired of talking about his health and the future of the ranch. And since he really didn't have a brilliant plan yet that would resolve everything, the discussions never lead to a conclusion or even moved the topic forward, so Malcolm understood why Roy would want to be done with them.

"Are you taking anyone?"

"No. When I RSVP'd, I was seeing someone casually. Now I'm not. I'll just have to go without a plus-one."

"Really? This is the first I heard of a girlfriend."

"She wasn't a girlfriend. Not that it matters. We stopped seeing each other a while ago. I don't mind going alone." It turned out that Tori had been a corporate spy, using him to get ahead in her career. She'd made a fool of him, but he'd caught on before she could do any damage. His heart was unbroken but his ego had taken a hit. But since she was out of his life, there'd been no need to mention her.

"You could always take Veronica. To hear your mother tell it, the two of you are starting a serious relationship."

"That's just Mom's all too vivid imagination. It's those movies she watches. They put love on her brain. To her any woman I spend more than five minutes with could be the one."

Dad chuckled. "Well, you are getting a little long in the tooth."

"I'm still in my thirties."

"*Mid*thirties. How many of your friends are married or getting married?"

"More than a few. But I still have a few single friends too."

"Like Veronica?"

Malcolm sighed. "Are you sure Mom is the one pushing this whole relationship thing and not you?"

"I'm just pointing out that she's not married. From what I hear, she hasn't had a serious relationship in quite some time. And if anyone needs to get out of this town, it's her."

"What makes you say something like that?" Malcolm's heart stuttered to a stop. Was there something going on with Veronica that he didn't know about?

Roy started to stand and Malcolm held out a hand in a silent offer of help. Sighing, Roy took the hand and stood. "Don't get me wrong. Aspen Creek is the best place on earth with a lot of wonderful people. But I always had the sense that Veronica is too attached to this place. If I hadn't known her since the time she was a child, I'd think she's hiding from the authorities or some such thing."

"Lots of people stay in their hometowns."

"Maybe. So, are you going to ask her?"

Malcolm thought about it and nodded slowly. "I think so. It would be a nice weekend getaway for her."

"Well, then, call her and ask. You don't want her to make other plans before you get a chance. And she'll need plenty of time to go shopping for a new outfit."

"I don't think all of that will be necessary. After all, she's not the bride."

"No wonder you're still single. You don't have the slightest idea about what is important to women."

"Really? And you do?"

"I know what it takes to keep a woman happy. I can share some of that knowledge with you if you're so inclined."

Malcolm stretched out his arms expansively. "By all means. Educate me."

"You already know the basics. Be respectful. Open the car door. Walk on the outside of the sidewalk."

"Women like to open their own doors these days, Dad."

Roy tsked and shook his head. "They want to be treated as equals, but a little gallantry goes a long way."

Malcolm only stared at his father.

Roy pointed at his chest. "Married for thirty-eight years." Then he pointed at Malcolm. "Single with no prospects."

"I wouldn't say that."

"Of course not. Nobody wants to admit that they're a resident on the Island of Misfit Toys."

Malcolm laughed. "Harsh. Just continue. It is your duty as my father to teach me the ways of romance."

"It appears that I failed if you don't even know the basics."

"Just jump to the upper-level lessons."

"Who's teaching, me or you?"

"It sounds more like insults to me."

"Okay. You already know to compliment her—and not just her appearance. Show that you appreciate everything about her. But really, I suppose the most important lesson of all is this. If she's important to you, make sure she knows it. No woman wants to come in second place."

"I never date more than one woman at a time. You know that."

"That's not what I meant. There are other and worse ways to make a woman believe that she's not first in your life. She won't want to come behind your job. Or your ranch. And don't leave her in any doubt about how you feel. It's not enough that you know she's first. You have to make sure that she knows it."

"I know." Malcolm thought about the past. He vividly recalled when Veronica had come to see him at school. She'd been his best friend and had mattered more to him than anything in the world. The way he'd acted had convinced her that his fraternity meant more to him than her. It wasn't true—but he'd let her believe it anyway. He'd blown it big-time back then.

"So, if you're going to invite her to accompany you to this wedding, you should call and ask her now. So she won't think that she's an afterthought."

"You're right." He hadn't thought about it that way before.

Malcolm hadn't minded going to the wedding alone before. But now that the idea of going with Veronica had taken hold, he couldn't shake it. He wanted her to see where and how he lived. He wanted her to see the man he'd become. Maybe she would really like that man and want to become a permanent part of his life.

Chapter Thirteen

Veronica looked at the phone in her hand before she slowly placed in on the table. She couldn't believe that Malcolm had invited her to accompany him to a wedding at the last minute. Although it sounded like fun, she couldn't help believing she was a last-minute substitute for the woman he'd intended to take. A fill-in.

Just thinking that there could be another woman in his life made Veronica's heart ache. She had kissed him. She'd practically thrown herself at him, all but begging him to make love to her. All he had to do was name the time and the place. But if there was another woman in his life then she was thankful he hadn't taken her up on it. After the way her father had cheated on her mother, Veronica would hate knowing that she had caused another woman that type of pain even unintentionally.

She looked at her watch and then hurried from the library. She and her friends were meeting up to go shopping this evening. Veronica wasn't looking for anything in particular, but trying on clothes always put her in a good mood.

The others were standing outside the boutique when she walked up. "Sorry I'm late."

"No worries. We just got here," Marissa said.

"What's wrong?" Alexandra asked. She had the uncanny ability to read minds.

"It's Malcolm."

Her friends exchanged glances and then smiled. "We want to know everything."

"It's nothing like that. Well, maybe there was some of that, but that's not the problem. He asked me to go to a wedding with him on Saturday."

"And why is that a problem?"

"Because. That means that someone else canceled and now he wants me to fill in." They stared at her blankly. "Do I need to spell it out? Obviously he has a girlfriend."

"That's a pretty big leap," Kristy said.

"What other conclusion is there?"

"Maybe he was planning to go alone and now that you're friends again, he thought it would be more fun with you," Kristy suggested.

"Definitely not." She shook her head firmly. "He knows better than to RSVP for one and then show up with a date. It would be an incredibly rude thing to do to the couple getting married."

"For a fancy wedding, sure, but for a more casual one, would it really matter?"

"He said it's formal."

"Well, maybe he was dating someone when he sent in the RSVP but they've broken up since then," Alexandra suggested.

Veronica frowned. She supposed it was a possibility... but she still felt sure that that wasn't what had happened.

"Maybe he planned to take you all along, and he only

asked now because he finally thought you might say yes," Marissa added.

"No. I'm sure that's not it. We hadn't spoken in years. At least not civilly."

Marissa waved a dismissive hand. "Judging by how close the two of you seem lately, I think that's all water under the bridge."

"Maybe. But that doesn't mean that he doesn't have a girlfriend back home."

"No way," Kristy said. "I've known Malcolm as long as you have. I know his character. And I've seen him since he's been back. That man is honest and has integrity. Not to mention that he has the hots for you. I don't know if there was another woman before, but you are the one and only woman in his life right now."

Veronica's heart leaped with hope that she instantly tamped down. "Enough of this foolishness. Let's shop. That should help clear my head."

"And I want to know what you meant before. You said it was *like that*. What has been going on between the two of you?" Alexandra said.

Veronica should have known that carelessly spoken statement wouldn't go unnoticed. "We've spent time together. We went horseback riding the other day. And I went with him to help him repair fences."

"Oh. You're reminding him of why he likes being on the ranch." Alexandra nodded approvingly. "Good strategy."

"Why would you say that?" Veronica asked, guilt pricking at her. Did they know that Evelyn Parks had asked her to try to convince him not to sell his ranch?

"No reason. If he likes it here then he'll come back

more often. And the two of you can take your relationship to the next level."

"Ignore her," Kristy said. "She's only got one thing on her mind and that's marriage."

"Only a few short weeks and you will be dancing at my reception. Who would have thought that Nathan and I would be getting married?"

As one, the women raised their hands. Marissa said, "We always knew. You're the only one who tried to deny your feelings."

"That was because I was so afraid of getting hurt."

"Love is always worth taking a chance," Kristy said.

"Don't try to distract me," Alexandra said. "What happened when you were with Malcolm? Was there kissing involved?"

Veronica looked away. Sometimes Alexandra was like a dog with a bone. But since she wanted to get another perspective, she nodded. "Yes."

"I knew it."

"How was it?"

"The best kiss I have ever had. I swear I could have melted into a puddle. Or else spontaneously combusted."

"Ooh." The others crowded around, their eyes wide with curiosity.

"Tell us everything." Kristy had been holding a skirt in her hand. Now she shoved it on the rack and practically dragged Veronica to a quiet corner while the others followed eagerly behind.

"There is nothing else to tell. We kissed. It was… awesome. And then it was over."

"Now I know you're leaving something out."

Veronica looked down at her fingers. "I was all ready

to go to the next level when he put a stop to it. Perhaps because he remembered that he had a girlfriend."

"Or perhaps because he wanted to go slowly to make sure that your relationship is on solid ground," Kristy said. "He's cautious and doesn't want you to think that he's trying to push you into doing something that you'll regret later. After all, you were pretty upset with him not that long ago."

"If he had a girlfriend, he wouldn't have asked you to go to the wedding with him where you would be certain to meet his friends and their girlfriends. He would have to know that one of them would tell his alleged girlfriend about you," Kristy said logically.

The others nodded their agreement.

Veronica stopped to really think about it, rather than letting her fears dictate to her. She had to admit, they made a good case. "I suppose you're right."

"I know I'm right," Kristy said.

"So are you going to go?"

Veronica sighed. "I already told him no."

"So call him and tell him that you changed your mind," Alexandra said.

"But I haven't."

"At least think about it."

Veronica nodded. "Enough about me and Malcolm and our non-relationship. Let's shop."

"You said the wedding is formal?"

"Yes. But since I'm not going…"

"There's no reason we can't get a just-in-case dress."

Veronica didn't argue with them. She was outnumbered and there was no way she would win. Besides, she liked having clothes for every occasion. Since there was a sale going on, this was the perfect time to buy.

Everyone turned their focus to the formal wear, pulling out their favorites. Their tastes were diverse and Veronica had a variety of dresses in her arms. Once they'd grabbed all of the dresses they found worth trying on for her, they picked up items for themselves. Before long, they each held a pile of clothes to try on.

In addition to the numerous formal dresses, Veronica also had a selection of casual clothes in her arms. Perhaps it was a leftover from the years when she didn't have new clothes and often felt embarrassed and self-conscious, but now she made sure to have several outfits to choose from no matter the occasion.

Veronica changed into one of the formal dresses and stepped into the aisle between the rows of rooms. Her friends soon joined her and they took turns modeling their clothes for each other. Gales of laughter filled the room as they critiqued each other's outfits. By the time they decided on what to take with them and what to leave behind, thirty minutes had passed.

"Give Malcolm's invitation a second thought," Kristy said.

"It would be a shame to let that gorgeous blue dress go to waste," Alexandra added, pointing to the one Veronica had decided to purchase.

Shaking her head at her friends' determination, Veronica hopped in her car and headed home. She lowered the windows and let the cool breeze inside. As she drove, she tried to clear her mind of all thoughts of Malcolm, but she couldn't quite pull it off. She knew that her friends had her best interests at heart, but given everything and the way she was starting to feel for Malcolm, and how easy it would be to fall in love with him, it was best that she didn't go to the wedding.

When Malcolm pulled away from her the other day, he had been trying to give them time to make sure that they knew what they were getting into. Space to make a wise decision. That was probably for the best. She didn't see how accompanying him to a wedding would be in line with that. In fact, it seemed to be the complete opposite.

She parked her car and had just grabbed the shopping bags from the trunk when she noticed a luxury sedan parked across the street from her house. The vehicle was unfamiliar so she doubted they'd come to see her. She unlocked her front door and was stepping inside when she heard her name being called. She froze.

It couldn't be. Though it had been years since she'd heard him speak, she would recognize her father's voice anywhere. Her hands began to tremble. The bags slipped from her suddenly numb fingers and onto the floor, sending her newly purchased earrings sliding across the porch. Her knees wobbled and she leaned against the doorpost for support.

What was he doing here?

Veronica urged herself to move—to step inside the house where she would be safe—but her body refused to cooperate. The thud of his footsteps on the stairs behind her motivated her to move. She shook off her stupor and steeled her spine. She wasn't a nine-year-old begging her father to come home and promising to be good. No. She was a grown woman. She refused to cower in her own home.

Veronica spun around and did her best to control the expression on her face. She might have been able to keep her mouth from falling open if her father had been the only one approaching. But he wasn't alone. His wife, Harley, was trailing behind him, her shorter strides no match for his longer ones. Anger replaced shock and she stood and waited.

"We need to talk," her father said, skipping the pleasantries.

"Actually, *we* don't."

"I have something to say."

"Then get to it," Veronica said, injecting ice into her voice, feigning cool indifference. She refused to let him know how just seeing him shook her to her core. When she'd been a girl, he'd been her hero. In her mind, he'd been the strongest and tallest man on the planet. Now she looked at him without the haze of adoration and he was no longer that godlike person. Now he looked exactly like what he was—a man of average height, looks and a middle-aged paunch who was pushing sixty.

He sniffed and lifted his nose into the air. "I don't care to air my grievances in public where everyone can hear."

Veronica leaned against her front door and crossed her arms over her chest. She hoped she looked more at ease than she felt. Inhaling deeply and then blowing out the breath, she reminded herself that this was her home. Her sanctuary. She decided who was welcomed inside. And who wasn't. "I don't know what grievances you can possibly have with someone whose existence you ignored for twenty-plus years. In any event, if you want to talk, you'll do it here. And now. I don't have a lot of time for you."

"That's no way to talk to your father," Harley said, coming to stand beside Walter.

Veronica turned, making no attempt to disguise her fury. "You don't get to talk to me. Ever. You're lucky my mother raised me to be polite and gracious. I suggest you stand there quietly. If you can't manage that, then you should get back into your car and wait for Walter. He won't be here long."

Harley gasped and then looked at Walter as if hoping he would step in and say something. Instead, he stood there silently. Fuming.

Veronica tapped her wristwatch in a silent signal that spoke loudly. When it finally dawned on Walter that he couldn't intimidate Veronica, he spoke. "I want to talk about Bianca."

"So talk." Veronica had expected all of the hurt and disappointment to come rushing back as proof that Bianca was the only daughter he cared about, but it didn't. She'd always wanted to ask her father how he could have left her. Why had he turned his back on her? Now, looking at him, none of that mattered anymore. She couldn't care less who this pathetic excuse for a man did or didn't value. He no longer had the power to hurt her. There was nothing that he could say that would change the fact that he'd been a deadbeat dad. The time when she had wanted him to be a part of her life—needed him to be there for her—had come and gone. Now he was simply an unwanted nuisance wasting her time.

Although he had come up to the house with a full head of steam, now he seemed deflated. Like a balloon after the air had seeped out. The image tickled her funny bone and she could barely suppress her laughter. She couldn't keep from smiling though.

"Why did you contact her?"

"Is that what she told you?" Veronica asked, surprised. She wouldn't have thought that Bianca would lie.

"She wouldn't say a word about you. That's not like her at all. I don't know what you intended, but leave her alone."

There were so many things Veronica could say, but she bit back the nastiest. She also could make it clear that Bianca had been the one to reach out, but she wouldn't betray her sister that way. If she'd wanted her parents to know the truth, she would have told them. "I don't *intend* anything where she is concerned. But know this… Bianca is my sister. I won't turn my back on her. Walking away from family is not in my DNA. I guess I'm like my mother in that way."

Walter actually flinched. "You only have one side of the story. Your mother has poisoned you against me."

"Actually, my mother never said a bad word against you. But then, she didn't need to. Your actions spoke for you."

"Your point of view is skewed since you were a child when it all happened."

"Really?" She was enraged but she kept a rein on it because she couldn't help but notice the calmer she appeared, the more upset he became. He had actually come here believing that he would be in charge of the situation. She looked him in his eyes. "I remember quite clearly how you walked out the door with your suitcase because you had found happiness with another woman. I recall you saying that you would come to get me and that we would spend time together. And yet somehow you never showed up. My mother was not privy to those conversations. She wasn't a ventriloquist. She didn't make the words come out of your mouth. That was all you."

"She wouldn't let me see you." His voice held a desperation Veronica never expected to hear.

"Really?" Veronica held up a finger in the universal *wait a minute sign* and then grabbed her phone from her purse. "Let's call and ask her. I'm sure her memory is more in line with mine. But then Mom and I were the ones forced to move out of the house after you stopped paying the mortgage. We were the ones barely managing financially. Scraping by with the help of friends and neighbors after you abandoned us."

"This isn't about the past." He waved a hand as if he could erase the past twenty-five years from her memory. "We all made mistakes."

"I didn't."

That answer clearly shook him and he took an involuntary step back. Then he rallied, squaring his shoulders. "Anyway, I want to talk about the present. Where we go from here."

"*We* don't go anywhere. I've lived the past twenty-five years of my life without you. I see no reason why I can't live the next twenty-five that way and the next twenty-five after that."

"Bianca…"

"Is an adult. If she wants to have a relationship with me I won't reject her. Period." Veronica narrowed her eyes. "But that's not what's bothering you, is it? You're worried that I'll tell her about the way you treated me and Mom. You're afraid I'll tell her about your affair and that she'll see you both for the people you are. Well, I'm not going to volunteer anything."

He looked relieved and Veronica heard Harley's sigh. "But I'm not going to lie either. If she asks, I'm going to give it to her straight. I won't sugarcoat it or shade it so you'll look better. So what you need to do is figure out what works best for you. Do you hope she never asks? Or do you come clean on your own and admit that you were a trash father to me and an even worse husband to my mother? Do you tell her all about your affair? I don't know. Nor do I care. That's a *you* problem."

"You're just like your mother," he gritted out.

"Flattery won't work on me, so save it."

Walter sputtered and Veronica smiled. Perhaps it was finally dawning on him that he no longer mattered to her. It was a new concept to her also, so she wasn't surprised that he was only now getting it. "Now, if there's nothing else, you both need to go."

"Take some time and think on things," Walter urged. He reached out as if to touch her and she quickly moved out of his reach.

"Just what things am I supposed to think on? You haven't said anything today that makes me believe you're sorry. *You're* the one who needs to think on things. Think about this bed you made and how now you need to lie in it. But do it far away from me."

Walter stared at her as if trying to silently bend her will to his. When it became clear that she was not going to submit and do as he wanted, he sneered at her. "Don't ever ask me for anything."

"You're the one who came here looking for a favor. Now leave."

He opened his mouth and she held up a hand, stopping him. "You aren't going to get the last word here, Walter. I've asked you to leave. Don't make me call the sheriff to remove you. He's a friend of mine. You don't have any of those in this town."

Walter looked around and noticed for the first time the number of her neighbors who had found a reason to come outside. They were all glaring at him. He sniffed, turned, and then stomped down the stairs, leaving Harley behind.

Veronica laughed. "I think that's your cue. I suggest you hurry and get in the car before he leaves you behind. He has a bad habit of doing that. But then, you already know that."

Harley spun around so fast she nearly fell over. Veronica had only been taunting the other woman, but apparently the idea of being left behind wasn't farfetched to her.

"Is everything okay?" Diana Lowrey, one of Veronica's neighbors, called.

"Yes." Veronica realized that she actually was fine.

"He has his nerve showing his face around here after all this time. I brought my cane just in case you needed me to knock him upside the head."

Veronica laughed. There was no doubt in her mind that the older woman would have done it too. Diane had been known to be cantankerous on occasion. "I'm okay. You don't need to worry about me."

"Well, to be on the safe side, I called for backup the minute I saw his car drive up. I didn't like the way he was sitting there waiting to pounce on you the minute you got home. I knew he was up to no good."

Veronica imagined that Diana had reached out to the other seniors in town. They were a tight-knit group who were as likely to knit booties and caps for newborns as they were to cause all kinds of ruckus at the bowling alley. They might be unpredictable, but she could always count on them to be there if she ever needed help.

"You can call your crew and let them know I'm fine."

"It's too late now." Diane pointed her cane at the street. Veronica turned in time to see Malcolm's truck careening into the spot her father's car had recently vacated. "Your hero is here to the rescue."

Chapter Fourteen

"Are you okay?" Malcolm asked as he hurried over to Veronica. He placed his hands on her shoulders and searched her face, looking for dried tears or other signs of distress. He didn't see any. To his surprise, she laughed.

"I'm fine, Malcolm. You didn't need to come rushing over here."

He released her, but not before noticing how good her body felt. A sudden and inappropriate fire ignited inside him and he ordered the lust to go away. This wasn't the time or place.

"I see that. When Mrs. Lowrey said that your father was hanging around your house, I thought the worst."

"And came to rescue me."

Suddenly he felt foolish and started to back away. He should have known she could handle it. Veronica smiled. "Do you have time to come inside?"

"I have all the time in the world."

Veronica unlocked the door, picked up her earrings, grabbed her bags, and stepped inside. He followed and the feeling of being at home grabbed a hold of him. As cozy as it was, he knew that it wasn't this little room that made him feel so comfortable. It was Veronica. Being with her *felt* right because it *was* right. A few weeks ago, he would have been content with her friendship. Heck, he would have been happy to just have her acknowledge him. Now he wanted more. He was falling in love with her. He wanted her to be a part of his life as far more than just a friend.

That was one of the reasons he'd invited her to go to the wedding with him. He wanted to show her another side of him. The man that he was in his element. He wanted her to see that she could be a part of that life.

"Good. I was going to warm up some leftovers, but I'm not really in the mood for them now."

"Don't tell me that your father stole your appetite."

"No. I just want something else."

"Do you want to go out or would you rather order in?"

A sweet smile crept over her face. "You know, I could really go for a pizza."

"As long as you don't get pineapple on it."

"What do you have against pineapple?"

"Not a thing. As long as it's not on my pizza. That's a sacrilege."

"I'll get it on my half."

"I suppose that will be okay."

"The usual for you?"

He nodded. "Sausage and pepperoni."

"Some things never change." Veronica grabbed her phone. While she placed the order for their pizza, he took a moment to study her. Dressed in a simple yellow dress that was belted at the waist and stopped at her knees, she looked as elegant as any woman he'd seen on the streets of Chicago.

"What did you buy?" he asked, gesturing to the bags that she'd leaned against the couch.

"Clothes."

"No." He feigned shock.

She giggled. "I suppose the bags gave me away. I bought two dresses and a pair of shorts. And some earrings."

"I have no doubt that you'll look gorgeous in everything." He hoped he would have the opportunity to see her wearing some of her new clothes.

"That's one of the benefits of shopping with girlfriends. We never let each other buy anything that doesn't look good on us."

"Isn't that the saleswoman's job?"

"No. Her job is to make a sale. They aren't going to risk offending a customer by suggesting she get a bigger size or that the color she chose clashes with her complexion or hair color."

"The customer is always right."

"In matters of taste."

"I usually shop alone. I always have a plan. I decide in advance what I want. I grab whatever it is in my size and then leave. In and out in twenty minutes. Maybe I should take you with me next time I need a suit."

Up until this point they had been looking at each other. Now Veronica glanced at her hands and picked at the cuticle of one of her perfectly manicured nails. "Or you could ask your girlfriend."

"What girlfriend would that be?"

"The one that you were going to take to the wedding and reception with you. You know, your original plus-one."

He laughed and her head swung to him, fury on her face. Laughing had been a mistake—she must have thought he was mocking her. Wiping the smile from his face, he reached out to her. She folded her arms and he sighed. "I don't have a girlfriend. I would not have kissed you if I had. Surely you know that about me."

The corners of her mouth turned down and he knew she was pondering his words.

"After everything you and your mother went through with your father, do you actually think I would do something like that to you? Or anyone? I wouldn't."

"I suppose I knew that."

"I was dating someone when I RSVP'd, but that relationship didn't work out, and it ended more than a month ago. Including a plus-one was more of a hope than anything else."

"So you don't have a plus-one?"

"She turned me down flat."

"Oh."

"I mean you. You're the only one I wanted to go with."

"Oh. Well, I suppose that's okay, then." She smiled and met his eyes. Hers were shining and he began to hope. "If the offer still stands I would like to change my answer."

"You want to go with me?"

She nodded.

"Great. The wedding is going to be so much more… tolerable…with you."

"This isn't a business function, is it? Isn't one of your friends getting married?"

"Yes. The groom."

She smiled.

"I'm glad that we got that cleared up. Thank you, Mrs. Lowery, for telling me to hightail it over here."

Veronica looked at him as if seeing him for the first time, taking in his damp hair and shirt. "What were you doing when she called?"

"I'd just gotten out of the shower. I put on the first thing I could get my hands on and got here as fast as I could."

"That would explain the lack of socks."

"I didn't have time to waste. I know how badly your father hurt you in the past. I didn't want him to hurt you again."

"It turns out that he doesn't have that ability any longer. He thought he was going to come here and bully me into doing what he wanted, but he was wrong."

"What did he want?"

"He wanted me to promise not to tell Bianca how he and her mother treated me and my mother. I told him I wasn't going to lie for them."

Rage surged through Malcolm and he fisted his hands. He inhaled deeply and told himself to calm down. Veronica was fine. More than fine. Her father no longer had the power to hurt her. "Good for you. He shouldn't have done the dirt if he didn't want it to come to light."

"I'm not going to volunteer the information. That wouldn't do Bianca any good. But she must be asking questions. He hadn't even told her about me. She had to find out on her own."

"Bastard." The word slipped out but he had no desire to call it back.

"Exactly." She shook her head. "I can't believe how long I let his rejection hurt me. I actually believed there was something wrong with me that made him leave. Now I see the problem was him all along."

"You deserved a much better father than him."

"Agreed. I might not have had him around, but I had lots of surrogate fathers. Yours included. And Willie turned out to be a good stepfather."

"I'm so glad to hear that. I would hate it if I had to start disliking a man that I previously admired."

"Right," Veronica said, a smirk on her face.

"You think I'm kidding?"

"I…" Her smile faded and her eyes widened. "You're serious?"

"I am. I suppose I deserve your doubt."

"No you don't. Not anymore." She shook her head and looked at him. Her smile was warm. "I held on to that grudge for far too long. Looking back, I realize you being busy set me off in a way that was totally out of proportion. I was conflating the pain from my father's rejection with what you said, but that wasn't fair. I know now what you were doing was important to you."

He nodded. They'd driven over this ground before and he didn't know what else he could say at this point. Fortunately the past seemed to be behind them for real this time.

"Will you be able to leave Friday morning for the wedding?"

Veronica nibbled her lip, a sign that she was uncertain. "Yes. I have plenty of vacation time saved up. Plus there are fewer programs in the summer since the kids aren't in the library as often."

"Good. We are going to have a great time."

"I bought a new dress."

"Really?"

She gave him a bashful look. "The girls insisted that I get one, just in case. And yours isn't the only formal wedding I'll be attending, so I needed one anyway."

"It isn't my wedding."

"You know what I mean."

"I do. Can I see your dress?"

"Before the wedding?"

"Why not? It's not as if you and I are getting married." Saying that made his stomach feel a bit jumpy all of a sudden. It wasn't as if he wanted to get married anytime in the near future, but closing the door on marrying Veronica didn't feel right. In fact, she was the only person he could think of marrying.

"That's true." She rummaged through one of the bags and then paused. "I could hold it up to you or I could put it on."

"I would get the full impact if you try it on. But the decision is yours." He flashed her a wolfish smile, leaving her with no doubt which option he preferred.

"I'll be right back." She grabbed her shopping bags and then stood. Before she could take more than one step, the doorbell rang. "That must be the pizza."

"You're probably right."

She set the bags back on the floor and then headed for the door. Malcolm grabbed a few bills from his wallet and pressed them into Veronica's hand. "Don't argue."

"I wouldn't dream of it."

Veronica opened the door, took the pizza, and then paid the delivery person. "Keep the change."

Malcolm took the pizza box from her. "Let me."

"Thanks." She headed for the kitchen. "Come on."

He set the box on the kitchen table while she grabbed plates from the cabinet and then set them beside the pizza. She opened the refrigerator. "I have water, lemonade, and pop."

"Pop. Definitely."

In a minute they were sitting across from each other at her table. Her kitchen was small but rather than feel cramped, it felt cozy. It wasn't the size of the place that made a home. It was the people who lived there. The love they shared. Even though Veronica lived alone, her house was infused with love. The fact that she'd welcomed a previously unknown half sister into her home—into her life—proved just how kind and loving she was. Any man would be lucky to have her in his life.

"So what's going on with the ranch?"

"What do you mean?" Her voice had sounded casual, but he had a feeling that the question hadn't come out of nowhere.

"There are lots of rumors circulating that you're going to sell to someone who'll build warehouses or some such on the land."

He shook his head. He didn't want to talk about the ranch right now. Knowing that his father was struggling hurt him in a way that nothing else ever had. Thinking about not being able to ride Hercules across the range broke his heart. But keeping the ranch didn't seem like a feasible option either. Basically, he had no idea what he was going to do. But if he and Veronica were going to be true friends again—or more—they had to trust each other with the hard things as well as the good times. It couldn't have been easy for her to confide in him about her sister and her father, but she had. He would do the same.

"To be honest, I'm not sure what I'm going to do. My father's health and age make it impossible for him to run the ranch alone. I live in Chicago and I can't be much help from there. We can't just let the land sit there empty or leave the house vacant."

"You could hire a ranch manager."

"Would that I could. My father has told me how hard it has been for him to keep hands for more than a season or two. They come and go just as fast as he trains them. A ranch manager—if Dad could actually find a good one—would no doubt have an even harder time hiring and keeping people. After all, he would only be a hired employee himself. All the work might end up falling on him alone, and I doubt anyone without a deep connection to the land would put up with that for long. The frustration alone might be enough to make him quit. Then we would be in a worse position than we are now."

"How do you figure that?"

Malcolm smiled. Veronica had lived in Aspen Creek her entire life and yet she had spent very little time on ranches. When she'd visited him, they'd had fun but she hadn't been exposed to the nuts and bolts and millions of details that took to keeping a ranch operational and profitable. "Because there wouldn't be anyone there to helm the operations. Someone to keep up with the feeding schedule, the vaccinations, coordinating work schedules, breeding, getting the cattle to market and on and on."

"I guess there's more to ranching that I thought. Still, can you really sell your family ranch? I know it's not the same thing, but I really hated moving from our house. My family hadn't lived there for generations like yours either."

"We haven't made a decision. But everything is trending in the direction of selling. I really don't see another way, but I haven't given up hope yet. I can't bear the thought of letting something that my family has sweated to make a success just fall apart. It would make all of their sacrifice and hard work a waste. Wouldn't it make more sense to actually get something out of it?"

"Like money?" She spit out the words as if they were distasteful.

"You need money to survive in this world," he said quietly.

"Don't I know it? I never want to be in the position where I don't have enough to survive again."

"You don't have to worry about that. If I have, then you have."

"That's nice of you to say, but I like making my own money. I need to know that I can take care of myself."

"Given your past, I understand that. I respect your strength. But you don't always have to be strong. It's okay to lean on me and others who love you."

"I know. But back to the ranch. Have you considered trying to sell it as a going concern? You know, if you and your parents don't want to keep it, maybe one of your neighbors will want more land."

"You're awfully concerned about the ranch. Why?"

She shrugged. "I spent so much time there growing up. I suppose a part of me can't bear the idea of it no longer being a ranch. It's like another part of my childhood vanishing in front of my eyes."

"Then you understand how I feel." Even so, his parents' well-being needed to come first. Everything else—including his feelings—came in a distant second.

Veronica either sensed that he didn't want to discuss the ranch any further or maybe she thought she'd made her point, because she changed the subject. Thank goodness because the conversation had begun to feel like an interrogation. They finished their pizza and then, after firming up the time for him to pick her up for the wedding, he left.

It was only when he was driving back to the ranch that he realized he hadn't seen her in the dress.

Veronica stared out of her front window, looking for Malcolm's truck. Her heart began to race when she thought about going away with him for the weekend. She couldn't believe that she had actually said no the first time he'd asked her to accompany him to this wedding. Thank goodness she'd come to her senses. In retrospect, she'd been wrong to suspect him of using her as a fill-in or cheating on his supposed girlfriend. Now she realized she shouldn't have entertained those notions for even a minute. Malcolm was the honorable and decent person she had always believed him to be.

She was looking forward to this weekend and couldn't wait for it to start. She had never been to Chicago, and Malcolm had promised to show her as many of the sights as they could fit around the wedding events. She was eager to meet his friends and curious about the kinds of people he hung out with now.

His truck pulled into her driveway and she grabbed her bag and headed for the front door, stepping outside before he had climbed the steps.

"Well, someone is ready to go," he said with a smile that gave her butterflies.

"I don't want to make us miss our plane."

"We won't. We're leaving in plenty of time. And might I say you look pretty."

"Thanks." Though most people flew in jeans and gym shoes, she'd put on navy slacks and a white-and-navy-striped blouse. Navy pumps completed her outfit. He was wearing jeans and gym shoes and now she wondered if she should have done the same. "I hope I'm not overdressed."

"No. You could never be *over* anything." Before she knew what he intended, he leaned over and kissed her cheek. His lips were gentle and warm and her knees weakened. She couldn't believe she hadn't considered Malcolm boyfriend material before. What would their relationship be like now if she had? Would they have done something ridiculous like get married right out of school? Would they still be together or would their romance have fizzled out in the same way that so many of their friends' relationships had?

"Flattery will get you everywhere."

Malcolm laughed as he took her bag from her. "Now she tells me when there's no time to do anything about it."

"What were you planning to do?"

He flashed her a wicked smile that made her stomach tumble. "Use your imagination."

Her imagination, which had always been overactive to say the least, had increased by a factor of ten over the past days. Ever since their first kiss, Veronica had pictured them in all sorts of romantic situations. In each scenario, she got the physical satisfaction that she'd thus far been denied in reality. Now she let her gaze travel over his magnificent body. "I have. Several times."

His eyes widened and she laughed at the surprised expression on his face. She was not going to hold back and wonder *what if.* Not this time. She was going to shoot her shot and let the chips fall where they may.

This weekend was going to be so much fun. From the moment she'd decided to stop holding on to the old grudge, she felt so much lighter. Freer. The burden of anger had been lifted from her shoulders and now she could soar to the sky.

Veronica walked beside him to his truck. She was reaching for the car handle when he dropped her bag on the ground and then nudged her aside. "Let me get that for you."

"Okay."

Once she was settled inside, he closed the door and then stored her luggage behind the seat. She didn't know what had suddenly made him decide to open the door for her, but she was all for it. That little bit of gallantry made her feel special.

He hopped in beside her and then drove to the highway. As each mile passed and they got closer to the airport, her anticipation grew.

"Excited?" Malcolm asked as if he had the ability to read her mind.

"I've never been to Chicago." Truthfully, she'd never been anywhere. Sure she'd gone to school in Denver, but that was still in Colorado. She was looking forward to expanding her horizons. Perhaps she might even begin to travel in the future.

"You're going to love it. Especially this time of year."

They parked in the overnight lot and then took the courtesy van to the terminal. Check-in went fairly smoothly and before long they were on the plane. As they began their ascent, she peered out the window and watched as all that was familiar became smaller. The flight was nearly two and a half hours, but she and Malcolm talked the entire time, so the time passed quickly. Before she knew it, the flight attendant was telling the passengers to secure their tray tables and put their seats in their upright positions.

Knowing just how quickly they could go from Chicago to Aspen Creek made Veronica wonder why Malcolm didn't come home more often. But then, his parents had been traveling a lot last year. Besides, she didn't know for sure that he hadn't come back. She'd made a point of not talking about him, and excusing herself from the conversation when anyone else did. He could have made numerous visits that she'd known nothing about. She wasn't sure whether that idea made her happy or sad. Why were her feelings about Malcolm so complicated? Couldn't she simply feel one thing or the other like most people did?

The plane began to descend and Veronica felt her body being pushed into the back of the seat. Landing was the worst part of flying. It was just so nerve-racking. She squeezed her eyes shut and tried to calm down.

She felt Malcolm's hand covering hers a second before he whispered into her ear. "Don't be afraid. You're perfectly safe with me."

She opened her eyes. He was so close the heat from his body warmed hers. She gave a self-conscious laugh. "You must think I'm foolish for being nervous."

"Not at all. Besides, it gave me an excuse to hold your hand."

"You don't need an excuse."

He lifted her hand to his lips and kissed her palm and her skin tingled at the gentle touch. He closed her hand as if sealing the kiss inside it. "That's good to know."

The plane bumped onto the landing strip and her heart jolted. Of course, that could have been her reaction to Malcolm's touch.

Disembarking was slightly chaotic, but before long she and Malcolm were on their way out of the airport.

"We can get a cab here," Malcolm said as they stepped outside. There was a queue in front of the line of yellow taxis and they joined it. The line moved quickly and in a minute they were inside the car.

Once they were on the highway and headed to Malcolm's house, Veronica turned to look at him. "I'm really looking forward to getting this weekend started."

"Don't worry, we won't waste time. We can drop our bags at my house and then go get something to eat. Since I knew I would be gone a while, the cupboards are bare."

"Do you actually live in a house or do you live in a condo?"

"A house. When I moved here I bought a condo near downtown. I liked being where the action was. Plus I could walk to work. But after a year or so, I started to feel closed in."

"Was your place small?"

"No. I had plenty of room. That wasn't the problem. I needed outdoor space. I was close to parks and the beach, but it didn't feel the same. I need my own backyard. Now, don't get me wrong, I don't have a lot of land even now. But that patch of grass is mine. I'm still relatively close to a beach although I don't go very often. Oh, and I have my own pool."

"You're talking to someone who lives in a shoebox with a postage stamp as a backyard, so I'm sure what you have is great."

"But that shoebox as you call it is near hiking trails."

She grinned. "That's why I got it."

While they'd been talking, the taxi had gotten off the highway and was now traveling on local streets. He was driving so fast that everything passed by in a blur. He turned from a street lined with businesses onto a shady street with leafy trees. There was a large park on one side and children played on swings and chased each other across the grassy expanse. Their laughter mingled with the sound of birds chirping in the trees and music from someone's radio. If she closed her eyes she would think she was back home.

The driver turned again and then slowed as he drove down a wide street with huge houses on either side. He pulled in front of the largest house and then stopped. Malcolm paid the driver, who then opened the trunk and removed her bag.

Veronica and Malcolm walked up the path to the front door. While waiting for Malcolm to unlock the door, Veronica turned and looked back at the large front lawn. A mature tree was in the middle of the freshly mowed lawn. Neat rosebushes were on either side of the wide porch. Three chairs grouped around a table were on one side of the porch and a wooden swing hung from the ceiling on the other.

"This is so nice. And I love the flowers."

Malcolm grinned as he opened one of the double doors. "I can't take any credit for it. The landscaping was in place when I bought the house. A lawn care service keeps it up for me."

They stepped inside and Veronica looked around. She felt Malcolm's eyes on her and wondered if he was waiting for her reaction. Luckily she liked what she saw, so she didn't have to be diplomatic. "This place is huge. And gorgeous. How long have you lived here?"

"Four years. It was in decent shape when I bought it, but I spent a lot of time renovating it to make it what you see now."

"Did you do all of the work yourself?"

"Most of it. I had professionals update the electrical and the plumbing. I'm not trying to electrocute or drown myself."

"Wise decision."

"Come on, I'll show you around. We can start upstairs so we can drop your bags in the guest room."

She nodded at the answer to her unspoken question. It seemed he'd decided that the two of them wouldn't be sharing his bed. Despite telling herself that he was simply being a gracious host and not making assumptions, she couldn't help but be disappointed.

They climbed the gleaming, dark hardwood stairs and then started down a hall. He paused at the first door and they stepped inside. Sunlight streamed through two windows on either side of a full bed. A cream-and-brown-striped comforter matched a chair sitting beside a cherry armoire. An old-fashioned mirror was in one corner of the room.

"Is this okay?" Malcolm asked, his voice tentative.

"It's perfect." There was a familiar and comfortable feel to the room. It wasn't decorated in the sleek and modern style she would have expected from Malcolm. Instead it was in keeping with the age of the house. It was something she would have chosen.

"Then let's see the rest of the house." They stepped back into the hall. "The bathroom isn't attached, but it's only a few steps away."

He opened a door and she peeked into a small bathroom. The white pedestal sink gleamed. Malcolm entered and opened the frosted window, letting in a sweet breeze.

Malcolm showed her two more rooms, each of which had minimal furniture, and then his office before he opened the door to his bedroom. It was larger than the others. "I tore down a wall separating two rooms to give myself more space."

The furniture in here was more modern and a California king bed dominated the space. It was all too easy to picture herself lying in that bed, wrapped in Malcolm's arms, the sheets tangled around their legs, so she looked away. The windows overlooked the backyard and she moved aside a navy curtain and looked outside. "Your pool is inground."

He nodded. "The previous owner's son swam competitively in high school. It's not heated so I doubt he practiced much in the winter."

"A swimming pool was always a sign of wealth to me. So I guess that means that you've made it."

He laughed as they left the room. Once they were back downstairs, he showed her his living room, complete with a baby grand piano, dining room, and a surprisingly small kitchen that opened up to a huge family room. The back wall of the family room was made completely of foldable glass doors that showcased the gorgeous backyard. Tables and chairs were scattered around the brick patio, creating comfortable seating areas around the inground pool. The lawn beyond the pool appeared to go on forever.

"How big is your lot?"

"Two acres. It's not as big as the ranch, but I feel at home here."

"I understand why. You've created your own sanctuary in the city. All that's missing is the view of the Rockies."

"Nobody gets to have it all."

"You've come pretty close." He'd created an oasis in the middle of Chicago. No wonder he loved being here. He had the best of both worlds—the excitement and limitless entertainment of a big city and a home that mimicked the tranquility of the ranch.

"There's an apartment over the garage," he said, pointing at a red building near a fence separating his property from his neighbors. "One of my frat brothers stayed there for a while when he and his wife were on the outs. It's fairly small, which was incentive enough for him to get his act together and go back home. Thank goodness."

"I would have thought you'd enjoy having one of your friends around."

"There's nothing worse than a depressed-as-hell grown man hanging around to make me appreciate the distance from the garage to the house. I even started parking in the driveway just to avoid him. He tried to keep up a good front, but it was clear he missed Cheyenne something fierce. I was about to beg her to take him back if he hadn't finally done it."

Veronica laughed as they walked back to the house and anticipation built inside her. She was about to have the time of her life.

Chapter Fifteen

"That had to be the best show I've ever seen in my life," Veronica said as they left the neighborhood theater. They'd started the afternoon with lunch at a local soul food restaurant before they'd toured the neighborhood. Malcolm had driven past the local branch of the library, a mid-century building with huge windows across the front. When he'd told her that every time he passed by he thought about her, her heart had filled with joy.

They'd driven around the city and he pointed out many sights although they didn't stop at most of them. When he'd passed a theater, they'd impulsively gotten tickets to the production. It was an original work by one of Chicago's up-and-coming dance companies and she'd spent the past ninety minutes impressed by the glorious costumes and innovative choreography accompanied by live music.

"I'm glad you're enjoying yourself," Malcolm said. "If we had more time, we could see more of the highlights."

"How much time would that take?"

"I've lived here for years and there are still things I haven't seen or done. I haven't had the time."

"That's totally different from Aspen Creek. I don't

think there is an event that I haven't attended at least once or twice." She couldn't believe those words had come out of her mouth. She'd compared Aspen Creek to other places in the past, but her hometown had always come out on top in every comparison. That hadn't happened here. What in the world was happening to her?

"Don't sell Aspen Creek short," Malcolm said, surprising her. "Every place has its own charms. I like knowing that every December there will be candlelight skiing at the Aspen Creek Resort. I like knowing the menu at the diner is the same as it was twenty years ago. There is something special about going to Grady's and listening to Downhill From Here perform on Friday nights. The good thing about visiting a lot of places is knowing that I can appreciate them all for what they have to offer. I just wish we had more time so I could show you more of Chicago. There's only one thing to do. You'll have to come back again."

"I just got here and now you're kicking me out," Veronica joked.

"No way." Malcolm stopped walking and then turned to face her. He placed his hands on her shoulders and gave them a gentle caress. "I just want you to consider coming back to spend more time here. With me."

Veronica looked into his eyes and her breath stalled at the warmth she saw there. The sincerity. Without taking time to think, she reached up and caressed his cheek with her fingertips. Then she rose on her tiptoes and pulled his head down to hers. She might not know the right words to say, but talking could be overrated at times. This was one of those times.

She brushed her lips against his, aroused by the electricity the contact created. Her lips tingled and every part of her body yearned for more. She started to deepen the kiss, but Malcolm pulled back. Surprised and disappointed, she sought his gaze. There was a slightly amused smile on his face. "We're in the middle of a busy street. Not exactly the best place to make out."

Shaking her head, she stepped back. "You're right. I don't know what came over me."

"Hopefully the same thing that came over me. Let's just hope you feel the same way when we get back to my house."

Still burning with desire, Veronica gave what she hoped was a mysterious smile. Malcolm held out a hand and she took it, intertwining their fingers.

They practically ran the short distance to his truck. Once they were inside, he turned the radio to a local station and soft music floated around them. It was nearly ten and the moon and stars were shining in the sky. They weren't as bright as they were back home, but they were still beautiful. The wind blew and the leaves rustled. An owl hooted in the distance and Veronica smiled as she relaxed in her seat. How could she possibly feel so at home in a place that was nothing like home? The answer came immediately. It was Malcolm. Being around him felt good no matter where they were. He felt like home.

Malcolm shifted in his seat as he tried to regain control of his body. Just being this close to Veronica was awakening strong desires in him. Her sweet scent wafted over to him and beads of sweat popped out on his forehead. He pressed the button, lowering his window, hoping the cool night air would tamp down his lust.

He glanced at Veronica. Her eyes were closed and a smile played at the corner of her full lips, signaling her contentment. A contentment he shared. He couldn't remember the last time that he'd had this much fun with a woman. Though he dated and often spent pleasurable nights with women, those occasions paled in comparison to being with Veronica. The more time he spent with her, the more time he wanted to spend with her. So what was he going to do about it?

She'd been very clear that she was open to making love with him. All he needed to do was give her the green light. If she were anyone else, he'd jump at the opportunity. So why was he still hesitating? He sighed. The answer was clear. He didn't know if she was offering a fling or if she actually wanted a relationship. If she just wanted a fling…he didn't know if he could handle that. He cared too much about her to exclude his emotions. In fact, he didn't know if it was even possible. Not only that, he didn't want to make a wrong step. After living without her for all these years, he didn't want to do anything that might cause her to cut contact again.

But she might do that anyway if she believed that he was rejecting her. How would he feel if she walked away because he'd let fear keep him from trying to take their relationship to the next level? He had enough regrets in his life without adding another. If she was still willing when they got back to his house, he was going to take her up on that offer. Several times.

Malcolm pulled into the driveway, parked in the garage, and then got out of the vehicle. His father's words about treating a woman special returned to him and he quickly circled the truck. He was reaching for the passenger door, but Veronica opened it before he could.

"I was going to get that for you."

"I know. I appreciate the thought. But I'm perfectly capable."

"I was just trying to show you how much you mean to me."

"That's nice, but you show me what I mean to you all the time. It took a while for me to recognize it, but now I have."

The smile on her face and the warmth of her voice were his undoing. Unable to control himself, he pulled her into his arms. She lifted her head at the same time that he lowered his. Their earlier kiss had been tentative. Searching. A two or three on the heat scale. This one was scorching. A ten that promised to erupt into a twenty at any moment.

As if reading his mind, she opened her mouth to him and he swept his tongue inside. She tasted sweet and spicy and the fire inside him began to roar. Her tongue began to tangle with his and he wrapped her more tightly in his arms, needing to feel her soft body pressed against his. After a moment, he felt her easing away and he reluctantly released her.

"Wow." She leaned her head against his chest and wrapped her fingers in the belt loops of his jeans.

"Ditto." He tried to sound cool even though as close as they were, she had to know how aroused he was.

"I hate being the one putting a pause on...the festivities...but I would be more comfortable inside."

Unable to keep from touching her, he caressed her

soft cheek then dragged his thumb across her bottom lip. "Then by all means, let's head upstairs."

"Are you sure?" Veronica asked, nipping at his finger. She placed a hand on his chest. His heart was pounding so hard she had to feel it. "I don't want you to get me all wound up and then change your mind at the last minute again."

"I didn't want to do that before," he said, "but I didn't want to rush things between us. When we make love, I want it to be the first step in taking our relationship to the next level. Not just scratching an itch. I want you— and me—both of us to be sure it's what we want. I don't want you to have regrets. Not only that, I want it to mean the same thing to both of us. I wasn't sure of that before because we hadn't discussed it. Come to think of it, we still haven't talked about what we want yet."

Though the fiery lust burning inside him was demanding to be set free, Malcolm led Veronica to one of the chaises beside the pool. He sat down and then pulled her beside him.

"You want to talk now?" Her voice, filled with disbelief, grew louder with each word.

"Yes." He inhaled deeply. "What do you want from this relationship? Is this the beginning of something special, or is this simply going to be a night of pleasure?"

"Can't it be both?"

"I don't see how."

She looked uncertain, almost shy. "I don't want to give the wrong answer."

"There is no wrong answer. Don't try to figure out what I want to hear. Say what's in your heart. Just tell me what you want. I'll deal with it."

She nodded and then took a deep breath, like she was bracing herself. "I'm confused. I want to make love. That should be obvious. I would love for tonight to be the beginning of something more, but I don't see how it could work. You live here and I live in Aspen Creek. That said, I'm perfectly happy with having this weekend be the beginning and the end of our physical relationship. After this, we can go back to being friends again."

He didn't know what he'd wanted to hear, but he was sure this wasn't it. But he'd wanted the truth. He didn't want either of them to make promises unless they could keep them. So if a weekend affair was all that she could offer him, then this weekend would have to do. When it was over, they would be friends. It wasn't what he wanted, but it was better than what he'd had before. "I can do that."

Desire built inside him as they walked across the patio. Now that they'd decided they were going to make love, there wasn't a reason to wait. With each step they took, they picked up pace and they were practically running by the time they reached the back steps. He quickly unlocked the door, slammed it closed behind them, and then pressed Veronica against the wall and kissed her with all the passion inside him.

His hands roamed over her sexy body, caressing every soft curve. He was vaguely aware that Veronica's hands were tugging on his shirt. He broke the kiss long enough to yank the fabric over his head and tossed the shirt onto the floor.

Though he worked hard to stay fit, Malcolm wasn't vain about his body. Seeing the impressed expression on Veronica's face as she stared at his chest and abs filled him with satisfaction. She touched his stomach and his muscles quivered. Malcolm swooped Veronica into his arms and carried her up the stairs. She nibbled at his neck, laughing as she teased him into an even more frantic state.

When they reached his bedroom, he nudged open the door and stepped inside. Not bothering with the lights, he crossed the room and with Veronica still in his arms, fell onto the bed. She immediately knelt beside him and began to pull off her clothes. Instead of removing his jeans, he helped her remove her blouse. His fingers trembled as he struggled to unfasten the buttons without ripping them off. Inhaling deeply, he told himself to calm down. This wasn't the first time he'd been with a woman, even if he could never remember wanting anyone so much.

He slid the silky fabric from her shoulders and then brushed little kisses across her smooth skin. It was even softer than the fabric. Moonlight filtered through the windows, illuminating her body. Very gently, he slipped the straps of her bra down and then eased his hands around her back and unhooked it. He took one look at her full breasts and his mouth fell open. She was even more beautiful than he'd imagined.

Of their own volition, his hands reached out and cupped her breasts. She gasped at his touch and that reaction was all that he needed to stop playing around and get serious. His intent must have been evident because when he began to tear off the rest of his clothes, she did the same. In the blink of an eye, they were both naked and wrapped in each other's arms. As they touched and caressed, he felt himself losing control. When he reached his climax he was acutely aware of Veronica's cry of pleasure mingling with his.

Though he had agreed that this weekend would be the beginning and ending of their physical relationship, Malcolm was sure that he wouldn't be able to live up to that agreement.

Nor did he want to.

Veronica smiled as she looked over at Malcolm as he slept. His eyes were closed and his breathing was slow and even. The sun was streaming through the open windows, providing sufficient illumination for her to get a good look at his body. His brown skin was smooth and covered his well-sculpted muscles. Just looking at them made her recall how hard they'd felt beneath her hands and she inhaled a ragged breath.

Last night had been nothing short of magical. She'd spent nights with men before but nothing had come close to what she'd experienced with Malcolm. From the second their lips met, she'd been more excited than she'd imagined was possible. This might have been their first night together, but there had been no nerves or tension. Perhaps because they'd known each other for so long. Their friendship might have waned for a while, but the understanding they'd always shared was still there. Time hadn't destroyed their connection, and that made it easier for her to be uninhibited—to lose herself to the pleasure of being with him.

Finding it too hard to resist, she drew her fingers over his bicep, marveling at the strength. She moved her hand from his arms to his chest, letting her fingertips creep lower over his abs.

"You're going to get into trouble if you keep that up."

Veronica looked up into Malcolm's face. One corner of his mouth was lifted in a sexy smile and his eyes were dark with desire. Veronica paused her movement although she didn't remove her hand. "Some trouble can be good trouble."

"I agree." Malcolm captured her hand and brought it up to his lips where he brushed a gentle kiss against her fingers. Her skin tingled and she shivered. Longing built inside her and she yearned to give in to it. Before she could make a move, the alarm clock went off.

They groaned in unison. Veronica sighed. "I guess I'll have to take a rain check."

"Sadly. But we have to stick to today's schedule, which starts with brunch. My fraternity brothers will be there. I can't wait for you to meet everyone."

That statement made her stomach clench nervously. She didn't know any of his friends and wondered what they would think of her. "Will the bridal party be there?"

"Some of my frat brothers are in the wedding party, so they'll be there. A lot of them live out of town, so we thought the wedding would be a good opportunity for us to get together."

"And they won't mind you bringing me with you? If it's a guys-only get-together, I'm perfectly willing to stay here until it's time for the wedding."

"That's not necessary. They'll be bringing their wives and girlfriends too."

"Okay. Then I suppose we'll have to continue this later," Veronica said, unable to keep the anticipation from her voice.

They showered, dressed, and then headed for the restaurant. Malcolm and his friends had reserved a party room. The gathering was in full swing when they arrived. Three rectangular tables covered with white cloths were arranged in a U shape. Lovely floral arrangements were spaced between thick candles. Soft music played from unseen speakers. Malcolm quickly introduced Veronica to his friends and their significant others. They were all friendly and welcomed Veronica with open arms. The other women reminded her of her own friends and she immediately felt at ease with them. As she listened to the stories Malcolm and his friends told of the college days, Veronica laughed longer than she had in quite some time.

After a delicious meal, everyone scattered, returning to their homes or hotel rooms to get ready for the wedding that evening. Malcolm took a scenic route back and once more Veronica was impressed by what she saw. Instead of being one big city filled with anonymous strangers as she had expected, Chicago was made of numerous friendly communities, each with their own personalities.

Once they were inside the house, Malcolm pulled Veronica into his arms and gave her a deep kiss that made her knees wobble. When he broke the kiss, she looked at the antique clock on the table in the entry.

"How long will it take us to get to the wedding site?"

"Forty minutes or so, I guess. Why?" He nibbled at her neck.

"You know why. Think we have time for a quickie?"

"I never say no to a good time."

Laughing, they began tearing off their clothes as they raced up the stairs to his bedroom. By the time they reached his bed, they had shed everything. Last night, they'd made love slowly, taking time to learn what pleased the other. Now they had some familiarity with the other's body and moved in time to a simultaneous climax that left them each sated and breathless.

Veronica couldn't deny that she was feeling more than a physical attraction. Her emotions were growing stronger with each passing minute. If she wasn't careful, she could fall deeply in love with him. So she would be careful.

She could have lain in Malcolm's arms for hours, but there wasn't time. After a few more minutes in bed, they got up and headed for their separate bathrooms to shower. Veronica returned to the guest room where she smoothed on scented lotion and then carefully applied her makeup. She wanted to look her best tonight. Once she was certain that her makeup was impeccable, she styled her hair, spritzed on perfume, and slid into her dress. She took a glance at herself in the full-size mirror and nodded in satisfaction. The blue satin fabric clung to her curves, emphasizing her best attributes.

She grabbed her silver clutch, and then stepped into the hallway. Veronica heard Malcolm walking around on the main floor so she descended the stairs. When she reached the bottom, she looked around. "Where are you?"

"In here," Malcolm called from the living room. A moment later he stepped into the hallway. He took one look at her and paused. "Wow. You look great."

Smiling, she ran a hand over her dress, then turned in a slow circle, giving him a view from every angle. "Thanks. You look pretty good yourself."

He tossed his navy jacket over his shoulder and struck

a pose. The pristine white shirt contrasted nicely against his gorgeous rich brown skin was. Everything about him screamed sex appeal and for a second, Veronica's mind was filled with images of the two of them in each other's arms. But that would have to wait.

Malcolm took a step in her direction but stopped. "I'd better not touch you or we'll miss the wedding."

Smiling mischievously, Veronica closed the distance between them and brushed a kiss against his cheek. A smear of lipstick remained and she wiped it off with her thumb. His freshly shaved skin was warm beneath her fingers. The idea that she could possibly want to make love again so soon was astonishing. But since they needed to squeeze a lifetime of pleasure into this weekend, maybe it wasn't so remarkable after all.

"I still can't believe they're getting married at the Art Institute," Veronica said as they drove down the road. The bike path was filled with people pedaling along while others jogged or ran. It was just one more similarity between Chicago and Aspen Creek.

"Is that something you would like to do?"

She shook her head. "No. I've always pictured a small church wedding."

"And the reception? Something big and splashy? Magazine worthy? A four-course meal and a string quintet?"

"Not even close. I want it to be fun. A party. I want good food, of course, but I want people to be at ease. I want a good DJ. On my tenth anniversary, I want to sit with my husband and recall how much fun we had with all of our friends and family."

"That sounds nice."

"Oh. And I want a gigantic ice sculpture."

"A what?" He glanced over at her, his eyebrows raised.

"Don't judge me."

"I wouldn't dream of it. It just sounds out of place for a casual reception."

"My tastes are varied."

"Clearly."

"What about you? What kind of wedding do you want?"

"I never gave it a thought."

"Why are men like that?"

"Actually, if you think about it, you'll realize that it's for the best. Can you imagine the chaos that would result if men cared about the details as much as women? Just think about it. The bride always dreamed of a peach-and-cream color scheme, but the groom had his heart set on black and silver. The bride wants a spring wedding but the groom had always envisioned a fall wedding with a football theme."

Veronica laughed. "You started out making a good point, but now you're just being ridiculous."

"Maybe a little. But you have to admit things are easier when the bride gets her way and the groom is happy just to go along with the program."

"Is that the kind of groom you're going to be?"

"Who said I want to get married?"

The answer caused a pang in her heart, which was ridiculous. It wasn't as if he was rejecting her. She was the one who had made it plain that she wasn't looking for a relationship. The one who'd put a time limit on their little fling. He'd seemed like he might be open to more, but she'd said no. If anything, she had rejected him. Her reaction was further proof of how confusing a romantic relationship with him would be. It was so much simpler when they were merely friends and kept the physical part out of things.

Of course, it was too late to go back now. But after the pleasure she'd experienced, she didn't want to.

The Art Institute was even more impressive than Veronica had imagined. As she and Malcolm walked side by side to the room where the ceremony would be held, they passed through several galleries. Her heart caught in her throat as she took in the exquisite artwork hanging on the walls. But despite the beauty all around her, Veronica was distracted by the handsome man beside her. She tried not to fantasize, but she wondered how she would feel if she and Malcolm were the ones getting married today. The ones promising to love each other until death parted them. She had to admit that she wasn't entirely opposed to the idea.

After about five minutes, they reached the room where the ceremony would take place. A three-story wall of windows provided a view to the glorious gardens outside. Enormous glass vases filled with colorful flowers were spaced throughout the venue. The chairs were separated by a wide aisle and they took their seats on the groom's side beside some of Malcolm's friends. Veronica smiled at Cheyenne, the wife of Malcolm's frat brother who'd stayed in his garage apartment. It was clear from watching Cheyenne and Trevor together at the brunch that they'd put their problems behind them.

"Isn't this just dreamy?" Cheyenne said.

"Like a fairy tale," Veronica agreed.

"Are you changing your mind about a small church wedding?" Malcolm asked, a grin on his face.

"I'm definitely considering alternatives."

"Are you two engaged?" Cheyenne asked, her eyes dancing with excitement.

"No," Veronica and Malcolm answered in unison.

"I told you earlier that we're just friends," Veronica said. "We grew up together."

"So you're the Veronica from Aspen Creek," Trevor said.

"Malcolm talked about me?" Veronica asked, looking from Trevor to Malcolm.

"Occasionally. He didn't say anything bad, by the way," Trevor added.

Veronica sensed that silent communication had taken place between Trevor and Malcolm, but before she could ask about it, the string quartet began to play. A hush came over the guests as the groom and the minister walked to the front of the room, standing under an awning draped with countless yards of sheer white fabric. Then the wedding march began to play as the bridesmaids, wearing lilac dresses, processed down the aisle on the arm of tuxedoed groomsmen. Once they were in place, the bride entered, wearing the most gorgeous dress Veronica had ever seen. As she walked to the groom on her father's arm, Veronica sighed.

The entire wedding was like a beautiful fantasy and Veronica felt herself being swept away by the romance of it all. At some point during the ceremony, she and Malcolm joined hands although she didn't remember when. The bride and groom had written their own vows, and their voices were filled with love as they recited the sweet words of devotion. Veronica was still awestruck when the minister pronounced them husband and wife and gave them permission to kiss. The entire ceremony far exceeded the most romantic movie she had ever seen.

The bride and groom hopped over the broom and the audience applauded. As the happy couple walked down the aisle together, Veronica realized that she had witnessed something special.

"Don't tell me, you're starting to think about love and romance," Malcolm whispered in her ear. His breath raised goose bumps on her bare shoulder, bringing to mind the pleasure they'd shared not too long ago, and she trembled.

She turned her head and their lips nearly brushed. Veronica wondered how he would react if she kissed him right now in front of his friends. Instead of acting on that impulse, she nodded. "Don't you tell me you aren't feeling the same way."

He shrugged and her eyes were drawn to his shoulders. His suit jacket couldn't camouflage his strength. "I neither confirm nor deny that statement."

"That answer just gave you away."

"It's not like I was trying to hide anything. I believe in love and romance. I just don't know if marriage is for me. There's too much going on in my life right now to even think about it."

Chapter Sixteen

Malcolm's words stayed with Veronica throughout the reception, popping into her mind when she least expected them. As she danced the night away with Malcolm and his fraternity brothers, she couldn't help but wonder what he would do when his life settled down. Would he decide he was ready for marriage when he had time to breathe? Especially since his friends were settling down. If he decided to take a wife, would he choose a woman who lived here in Chicago? There was no shortage of potential mates for him here.

The same couldn't be said for her in Aspen Creek. Sure, new men moved to town all of the time, and there were any number of tourists who passed through, but not one had appealed to her. And she was not remotely interested in any of the men she'd grown up with.

Except Malcolm.

That thought came out of nowhere, but she had to admit that it was the truth. Despite her best efforts, she'd fallen for Malcolm. Once she'd gotten rid of her grudge, she'd begun to see him with clear eyes. He was better than good. She'd started to care for him. To like him again. And her attraction to him was off the charts. Now she was afraid that she'd fallen in love with him.

She shouldn't have made love with him. That had been a delicious mistake. She should have known that her feelings would grow and deepen once they became intimate. Somehow or another, she had to regain control of her feelings before she began to expect things from Malcolm he wasn't willing or able to deliver. He wasn't interested in marriage or commitment right now. If she'd harbored a secret hope that he'd want a future with her, he'd just disabused her of that notion. Since it was in line with what she'd told him last night, she should be relieved. She had no choice but to think of him as a friend once more.

Veronica and Cheyenne were sipping champagne and chatting when the DJ announced the last dance.

"I need to find that husband of mine," Cheyenne said, setting her flute on the table and then crossing the room.

Veronica's eyes immediately searched for Malcolm, who was on his way over to her. He held out his hand and she immediately took it. They stepped onto the dance floor and she automatically went into his arms.

"Tell me again why we have such an early flight?" Veronica asked, leaning her head against Malcolm's chest and swaying to the music.

"Because you need to get back to work and I need to get back to the ranch."

"Oh yeah. That."

Malcolm spun her around and sang along to the romantic song. She knew he was only reciting the lyrics, but a part of her wished that he truly was vowing to love her for all eternity. *Oh no.* Reality hit her. She wasn't falling in love with Malcolm. She was in love with him. She wanted to have a future with him. The leap from friendship to romance hadn't been as big as she would have expected. Once the trust had returned, love hadn't been far behind. At least for her.

Stunned by the revelation, she struggled to keep the beat. Malcolm gave her a look, but otherwise offered no indication that he could tell anything was amiss. Veronica ordered herself to get control, and by sheer force of will, she managed to smile as she and Malcolm said their goodbyes.

Neither she nor Malcolm talked much as they drove back to his house. By unspoken agreement, they shared his bed again. Unlike before, they didn't make love. Instead, she lay with her head on his chest, listening to the steady beat of his heart as they shared the last bits of this magical weekend.

In the morning, they ate a quick breakfast, cleaned the kitchen, and then waited outside for their Uber. They held hands as they rode to the airport and all the way on the flight home. Veronica knew that she should start separating from Malcolm, but she couldn't make herself. She wanted to enjoy their time together before reality set in.

By some miracle, she managed to uphold her end of the conversation as they drove back to Aspen Creek. When they reached her house, Malcolm parked and then carried her luggage to her front door.

"I had a good time. Thanks again for inviting me."

"Thank you for being my plus-one."

They stared at each other, suddenly at a loss for conversation. Finally he spoke. "I should get going."

"Of course." She stood on her tiptoes and kissed his cheek, determined not to let her emotions get the better of her. "See you around."

"You bet."

Veronica watched as Malcolm ambled down the stairs and hopped into his truck, waiting until he drove away before going inside. After two days of being with Malcolm she suddenly felt lonely.

She dug her phone out of her purse and texted her friends. I'm back. Can you guys come over here? It's an emergency.

The yes replies came instantly.

Veronica was putting a pitcher of lemonade on the table when the doorbell rang. Kristy, Marissa, and Alexandra were standing on her porch, take-out bags in their arms.

"What's going on?" Kristy asked as they went into the kitchen.

"Does it have anything to do with Malcolm?" Marissa asked.

"Are you glowing?" Alexandra asked. She'd been putting a container onto the table. Now she paused and gave Veronica a long look. Then she began to smile slowly. Knowingly.

"Hold that thought," Kristy said. "Food first."

They filled their plates with tacos, rice, beans, and chips, then poured glasses of lemonade. Once they were all seated, they turned to Veronica.

"Well?" Alexandra asked. "We all know something happened. Don't keep us in suspense. Tell us everything."

"Was the weekend romantic?" Marissa asked, sighing loudly.

"But first, cut to the chase. Did you sleep together?" Kristy asked.

Veronica chewed her taco before answering.

"I'll take that as a yes," Alexandra said. "How was it?"

"Was it hot and sweaty or slow and passionate?" Kristy asked.

"Kristy!" Marissa said.

"What? It's a legitimate question. We said we wanted details."

Laughing, Veronica told them about the weekend and the nights she spent in Malcolm's arms. "I have never felt this way before."

"That's wonderful. So, I take it that another wedding could be in the future?" Kristy said with a grin.

"I wouldn't go that far," Veronica said. "Especially not with the secret that I've been keeping."

"What secret would that be?"

Veronica sucked in a bracing breath. "Evelyn Parks approached me and asked me to convince Malcolm not to sell the ranch."

"Malcolm wants to sell the ranch?" Kristy said, sounding shocked.

"I don't know. I don't think he and his parents have made up their minds yet. And anyway that's not the point."

"What did you say?" Marissa asked.

"Well, at the time I was still a little bit angry at Malcolm. The feelings didn't last long, but I felt it."

"Please tell me that you didn't do anything you regret like feed information to that woman," Kristy said.

"No. I couldn't betray Malcolm that way. But I didn't give Evelyn a firm no either. She thinks I'm on her side.

I thought it would be better for Malcolm that way. It would keep her from hatching another plot or bothering him directly."

"So what do you plan to do?"

"I'm going to tell Evelyn that I'm not going to help her."

"That's good."

"And I'm also going to tell Malcolm everything. He deserves to know the truth and I'd rather he hear it from me."

"When?"

"Tomorrow. We're meeting for lunch. That gives me an opportunity to rehearse my speech. I just hope he understands."

"After the weekend you described, he'll understand," Alexandra assured her.

That handled, the conversation turned back to the weekend and they practically swooned as Veronica recounted the moments she and Malcolm shared. By the time she had told them everything at least twice, the lack of sleep caught up with her and she yawned.

"That's our sign," Kristy said, hopping to her feet, grabbing their paper plates and tossing them in the trash.

Alexandra and Marissa scooped the leftovers into storage bowls and placed them in the refrigerator. In the blink of an eye, the kitchen was restored to order.

"Good luck tomorrow," Kristy said, hugging Veronica before she followed Alexandra and Marissa out the door.

"Thanks. I think I'm going to need it."

The next morning Veronica dressed with more care than normal, wanting to use every arrow in her quiver. She knew that Malcolm was attracted to her and she was counting on that tilting things in her favor. Hopefully he would be open-minded. It was a beautiful day and luckily only one child came to the library and that was to pick up a book she had on hold so Veronica didn't have to be fully focused on work.

She was on her way to meet Malcolm when she ran straight into Evelyn Parks.

"I hear that you spent the weekend with Malcolm," Evelyn said, with a wide grin. "Smart. So what can you tell me about his plans for the ranch?"

"About that," Veronica said. Before she could continue, she heard a sound and looked over her shoulder… and straight into Malcolm's eyes. They were cold and hard, a contrast to the beautiful bouquet he held in one hand.

"Yeah. About that." There was a harshness to Malcolm's voice that she had never heard before. Even when she had been angry at him, saying unbelievably cruel things that she regretted, he had never responded in kind. The fury had been one-sided. From her to him. That was no longer the case. Darts of fire were shooting from his eyes. "Have you been lying to me all this time?"

"Let me explain."

"Why? I think I can piece it together on my own. Evelyn wants to know what's going on with the ranch even though it is none of her business. And you're supposed to pump me for information and report back. Am I right?"

"Malcolm, please," she implored. "If you would just let me explain."

"Or does your little plan go even further than that?" he said, ignoring her plea. "Are you supposed to try to sway me one way or the other? You were good this week-end, honey, but you weren't *that* good."

She gasped at his coarse statement. There was no way that he could possibly believe that she would stoop so low as to sleep with him in order to get information from him. And for what? Just to share his plans with Evelyn? She hadn't thought he'd be pleased about her talking about him behind his back, but she hadn't ex-pected this strong of a reaction.

"Perhaps I should leave the two of you alone to talk," Evelyn said, backing away so as not to get caught in the cross fire.

Why oh why hadn't she told Evelyn no the first time she'd asked? If she would have done that, Malcolm wouldn't be looking at her like she was something he scraped off the bottom of his shoe.

"Don't leave on my account," Malcolm said. "I know you two have important business to discuss."

Evelyn didn't stop walking, in fact she began to walk even faster, and in a minute Veronica was alone looking into Malcolm's infuriated face. She didn't know what to say, but she knew the words had better come quick. If not, she would lose the only opportunity she had to straighten out this mess.

"I suppose this is the part of the program where you tell me that I have it all wrong. That I misunderstood what I heard. Who am I going to believe, you or my lying eyes?"

Veronica shook her head. "No. You saw and heard just what you thought. But if you let me explain I will."

"Well, I have to give it to you. That's the second time in five minutes that you have surprised me. And I can guarantee you that it will be the last. Whatever this was between you and me is over."

Malcolm threw the flowers on the ground and then turned. Veronica knew that if she let him walk away, she wouldn't get another chance to explain things. "You and I weren't friends yet when she asked me. I was still hurt from before. A part of me—a small part—wanted to hurt you back."

"Congratulations. You succeeded."

"But I changed my mind. I wasn't lying when I said that I wanted to put the past behind us and start over."

"Yet somehow we were supposed to start over while you were still deceiving me. I don't think so."

"But I wasn't. I had already made up my mind that I was not going to tell her anything. Nor was I going to try to influence you."

"Yet somehow you forgot to tell that to Evelyn." Malcolm shook his head. "It doesn't matter. I'm not interested in hearing whatever you want to say. We're done."

"Malcolm…" She was pleading but she didn't care. "I love you."

He stopped walking away and then looked at her, his gaze icy. "That's your problem."

Malcolm managed to hold on to his anger until he pulled onto the ranch road. Then he saw the horses galloping around the corral. Just looking at them reminded him of the fun he'd had riding with Veronica, and the pain that he'd been trying to suppress forced its way to the surface. Sucking in a strained breath, Malcolm struggled to gain control of his emotions before he encountered anyone. The last thing he wanted was for his parents to know how badly he had misjudged Veronica.

What a fool he'd been. Again. The situation wasn't exactly the same as with Tori, but it still hurt. He'd been thinking of taking their relationship to the next level. Maybe trying to make a long-distance relationship work. And Veronica had been... He frowned. Even if she'd been telling him the truth today, it wasn't enough to erase what she'd done. The idea that she had even briefly considered betraying him hurt him to his core. He didn't see how he could ever get over that.

"You're back fast," his mother said, walking across the path, her brow wrinkled in concern.

"Things didn't work out," he said, deciding to cut to the chase. "It turns out that Veronica was only with me because she wanted to know my plans for the ranch."

"What makes you say that?"

He explained what he'd overheard, the pain just as intense as before. When he was finished, he expected his mother to say that she understood his anger. Instead, she just smiled sadly. "Things were so hard for Veronica when you were gone. Everyone could tell she was hurt when she came home from college one summer, but she never said what had gone wrong. I guess she was hurt more deeply than anyone knew."

"What? Surely you aren't trying to make excuses for her. Just because I messed up in the past, that doesn't give her the right to go behind my back or use me."

"No. I'm just trying to get you to see the whole picture. If you decide that you can't forgive her for deceiving you, I'll understand. It's hard enough to make a relationship work without the baggage of the past. Betrayal is hard for anyone to forgive."

Again, his mother surprised him. "What are you trying to say?"

"That nobody is perfect. Whatever you decide to do is fine with me. I'll love you either way. I just want you to be happy. But don't make a decision out of anger. That will only hurt you."

He hesitated, then shook his head. "I don't think I can ever forgive her for this. But if I don't, I know I won't be able to find happiness."

"You'll figure it out." Cheryl kissed his cheek and then walked away.

Malcolm needed to think, so he got on Hercules and headed for his quiet spot to be alone. When he arrived, he dismounted and sat on a downed log, stretching his legs out in front of him. Rabbits darted across the field, vanishing in the high grass. The meadow was peaceful as always, but instead of getting away from his thoughts, everything reminded him of the time he'd brought Veronica here. He pictured her delight as she glanced around. He couldn't forget how good it had felt to be here with her. They had begun to connect in a way he'd only hoped for. That only made the demise of their relationship more painful.

After a while he gave up trying to find the peace that eluded him, so he mounted his horse and returned home. He took care of Hercules and then went inside the house. When he stepped inside the front room, he was surprised to see Evelyn sitting in a chair across from his parents.

"What are you doing here?" Malcolm's rage flared

to life as he looked at the woman drinking coffee with his parents as if they were old friends.

"I was just explaining to your parents about everything that happened with me and Veronica."

"Why? Do you think that will win you some points?"

"Because I think it would be best if I come clean and do what I should have done in the first place. Come to the source. I was so worried that you wouldn't be honest with me."

"Why?"

"Because there is a lot of money to be made by selling the ranch. Not that I begrudge you any of it. Just know that whatever you decide will affect the town and everyone in it. But I shouldn't have manipulated Veronica the way that I did."

"She didn't say anything about that." He huffed out a breath. "I guess I didn't give her a chance to say much."

A shadow crossed Evelyn's face. "That's probably because she didn't realize I had done it. I just reminded her of how much this town means to her, and how the wrong kind of business would hurt the town and the people who have done so much for her. After that, there was no way she could say no to me."

"You should be ashamed of yourself."

"I am. Had I known that you and Veronica were in love, I would never have played on her emotions the way that I did."

"It's too late for that now."

"I know. But I just wanted to apologize to you and your parents."

"Have you apologized to Veronica yet?"

"I went back by the library, but she had left early. I

drove by her house, but she wasn't there. I'll apologize when I see her." Evelyn, stood, said goodbye and then left.

Despite his anger, Malcolm began to worry about Veronica. He knew she was upset. She had to be really hurt in order to miss work for even one minute.

"Does that change the way you feel about Veronica?" his father asked. Of course his mother had told him everything. The two of them never kept secrets from each other. Unlike Veronica did with him.

"No. I understand how she felt and I might even forgive her, but the relationship is over."

Veronica ran on the path, pushing past the exhaustion and the burning in her lungs. For the past week she had hoped to hear from Malcolm, but she'd been disappointed. She'd left him more messages than she could count and he hadn't returned a single one. She'd even emailed him. Of course she hadn't heard back. She was finally accepting the fact that his silence was an unmistakable message to her. They were through.

No matter how sorry she was, they wouldn't be getting back together. There would be no happy ending for her. Though there had never been a future for the two of them as a couple, she'd hoped that they could be friends again.

Now she knew that would never happen.

When she couldn't take another step, she sat down on the grass, out of the way of the other runners. The sweat on her face mingled with her tears. She swiped at them, but they didn't stop. She'd heard through the grapevine that Malcolm had gone back to Chicago. She'd thought that knowing she wouldn't run into him in town would make her feel better, but it hadn't.

"Some things are unforgivable," she muttered to herself. And she had no one to blame but herself. She couldn't even fault Evelyn Parks, who had begged for her forgiveness days ago.

"Yes. But other things just take time to get over."

Veronica's head spun around. "Malcolm. I thought you left."

"I did. But I came back."

"How did you know I was here?"

"This is where you go when you're upset. You run until you're too exhausted to think."

"Are you going to give me a chance to apologize this time? Because I'm sorry for even thinking about betraying you."

"I'm the one who needs to apologize to you. I should never have accused you of using sex to manipulate me. I know you much better than to even think something like that. I just needed some time alone to get my head on straight. The people of Aspen Creek are like family to you. You could never turn your back on them if you thought they needed your help."

"But I should have told Evelyn no the first time she asked me."

"Agreed. But I'm a grown man. I should have given you a chance to explain."

"And I'm a grown woman. I should have known better."

"Yes. But until we straightened out things between us, there was still a hurt teenager living inside of you. She's the one who agreed to work with Evelyn."

"You're letting me off the hook too easily."

"Maybe. But I jumped to conclusions too fast." He heaved out a sigh. "The woman who was my original plus one to the wedding had actually been a corporate spy. I caught on before she could do any damage, but I painted you with the same brush. That was wrong."

"Kind of like I did with you and my father."

"Exactly."

"Why are you being so nice to me?"

"Because I believe you when you said that you love me."

She nodded. "I do. I didn't expect to fall in love with you, but I did."

He smiled. "I didn't expect to fall in love with you either. But I did. No matter how angry I was at you, that feeling wouldn't go away."

"So what happens now? Between us, I mean."

He shrugged. "I have no idea. I haven't thought that far ahead. The only thing I know is that I needed to see you."

"Are you going back to Chicago or are you going to move back to the ranch?" She held up a hand. "I'm not asking because I'm trying to influence your decision. Whatever you choose to do is your business. I just want to know where things stand so that we can figure out what makes sense for the two of us."

"It's not a secret. I've decided to hold on to the ranch. I think I found a way to make it work even given my father's limitations."

"Really? What is your plan?"

"A dude ranch. It occurred to me that a lot of my friends, coworkers, and clients tell me how they fantasize about being a cowboy. Not forever, mind you. They just want a taste of the life. A week or two at the most. So we can give them that. They can do a lot of work—and pay for the privilege—and my father can do less. It's a win-win. Oh, and it will bring more tourists to town so it's a win-win-*win*."

"But what about having to hire ranch hands? Even if the guests are pitching in on the labor, won't you need some hands to guide the guests and show them what to do?"

"That might be a problem, but it won't be insurmountable. The hands won't live a lonely life. There'll be lots of guests staying at the ranch a couple of weeks a month. Plus we'll have regular entertainment. We might even open up some events to the town and other tourists. Hopefully that will provide the social interaction the hands need."

"And if it doesn't?"

"Then I'll think of something else. The main thing is my parents are excited about the idea. They'll still be traveling sometimes but I know my father will be happier knowing the ranch his ancestors sacrificed to build is still in the family. And if the reality of owning a dude ranch doesn't meet my parents' expectations, we can shut it down."

"Wow. I really hope it works."

"It's still in the early planning stage, but I have hope. I'll have to be a lot more hands-on in the beginning."

"Does that mean you'll be coming back to Aspen Creek more often?"

"Yes. But I was going to do that anyway. The woman that I love lives here. Hopefully you'll be willing to spend more time in Chicago with me too."

Veronica smiled, relief and joy flooding her body. She looked at Malcolm and whispered, "I thought I ruined it all."

"Really? Surely some part of you must have known I would be back."

"I hoped."

He brushed a gentle kiss across her lips, lingering for a moment before pulling away. "We belong together, Veronica. We always have. And we always will."

Veronica nodded. "We're going to be okay."

"We're going to be more than okay. We're going to be together. And there's nothing better than that."

* * * * *

*Look for the previous installments in the
Aspen Creek Bachelors miniseries
by Kathy Douglass*

Valentines for the Rancher
The Rancher's Baby
Wrangling a Family

*Available now, wherever Harlequin Special Edition
books and ebooks are sold. And look for Cole's story.
Coming soon!*